Praise for *Her Body and Other Parties*

"The stories in *Her Body and Other Parties* vibrate with originality, queerness, sensuality and the strange. Her voracious imagination and extraordinary voice beautifully bind these stories about fading women and the end of the world and men who want more when they've been given everything and bodies, so many human bodies taking up space and straining the seams of skin in impossible, imperfect, unforgettable ways" Roxane Gay

"Brilliantly inventive and blazingly smart, these stories have the life-and-death stakes of nightmares and fairy tales; they're full of urgent, almost unbearable reality. Carmen Machado is an extraordinary writer, an essential voice" Garth Greenwell

"*Her Body and Other Parties* is a love letter to an obstinate genre that won't be gentrified. It's a wild thing, this book, covered in sequins and scales, blazing with the influence of fabulists from Angela Carter to Kelly Link and Helen Oyeyemi, and borrowing from science fiction, queer theory and horror ... Not since Karen Russell [...] has a debut collection of short stories from a relatively unknown author garnered such attention, or deserved it more" *The New York Times*

"*Her Body and Other Parties* will delight you, hurt you, and astonish you as only the smartest literature can. In this collection Machado blends horror, fairy tale, pop culture and myth in mesmerizing ways that feel utterly new. These stories are peerless and brilliant" Alissa Nutting

"An intimate, unrelenting style that grabs you by the throat and sinks its perfectly polished nails in" *Harper's Bazaar*

"A blistering exploration of female desire and the insidious entitlement that society claims over the female body ... Machado writes with furious grace" *Kirkus Reviews*

"Carmen Maria Machado has a vital, visceral, umbilical connection to the places deep within the soul from where stories emanate. With a tenderness that is both touching and terrifying, *Her Body and Other Parties* gives insight into a cluster of worlds linked by their depth of feeling and penetrating strangeness" Alexandra Kleeman

"Fearlessly inventive, socially astute, sometimes pointed, sometimes elliptical, and never quite what you're expecting ... there is at once the breath of the new about these stories and the breath of the timeless" Kevin Brockmeier

"What Carmen Maria Machado has done with this collection is nothing less than stunning. Just when you think you've figured her out, she unveils another layer of story, so unexpected, so profound, it leaves you gasping" Lesley Arimah

"A gorgeously warped reflection of the world in which we actually live. It's recognisable as our own, but everything is a little more lurid, a little more queer, a little more violent, a little more magical than what we're used to" *Nylon Magazine*

HER BODY &
OTHER PARTIES

CARMEN MARIA MACHADO

First published in Great Britain in 2018 by Serpent's Tail,
an imprint of Profile Books Ltd
3 Holford Yard
Bevin Way
London
WC1X 9HD
www.serpentstail.com

First published in the USA in 2017 by Graywolf Press

Book design by Connie Kuhnz

1 3 5 7 9 10 8 6 4 2

Printed and bound in Great Britain by Clays, St Ives plc

A CIP record for this book can
be obtained from the British Library

ISBN 978 1 78125 952 8
eISBN 978 1 78283 404 5

My body is a haunted
house that I am lost in.
There are no doors but there are knives
and a hundred windows.

—JACQUI GERMAIN

god should have made girls lethal
when he made monsters of men.

—ELISABETH HEWER

CONTENTS

THE HUSBAND STITCH

(If you read this story out loud, please use the following voices:
ME: as a child, high-pitched, forgettable; as a woman, the same.
THE BOY WHO WILL GROW INTO A MAN, AND BE MY SPOUSE: robust
with serendipity.
MY FATHER: kind, booming; like your father, or the man you wish
was your father.
MY SON: as a small child, gentle, sounding with the faintest of lisps; as
a man, like my husband.
ALL OTHER WOMEN: interchangeable with my own.)

In the beginning, I know I want him before he does. This isn't how
things are done, but this is how I am going to do them. I am at a neighbor's party with my parents, and I am seventeen. I drink half a glass
of white wine in the kitchen with the neighbor's teenage daughter.
My father doesn't notice. Everything is soft, like a fresh oil painting.

The boy is not facing me. I see the muscles of his neck and upper
back, how he fairly strains out of his button-down shirts, like a day
laborer dressed up for a dance, and I run slick. And it isn't that I
don't have choices. I am beautiful. I have a pretty mouth. I have
breasts that heave out of my dresses in a way that seems innocent and
perverse at the same time. I am a good girl, from a good family. But
he is a little craggy, in that way men sometimes are, and I want. He
seems like he could want the same thing.

3

I once heard a story about a girl who requested something so vile from her paramour that he told her family and they had her hauled off to a sanatorium. I don't know what deviant pleasure she asked for, though I desperately wish I did. What magical thing could you want so badly they take you away from the known world for wanting it?

The boy notices me. He seems sweet, flustered. He says hello. He asks my name.

I have always wanted to choose my moment, and this is the moment I choose.

On the deck, I kiss him. He kisses me back, gently at first, but then harder, and even pushes open my mouth a little with his tongue, which surprises me and, I think, perhaps him as well. I have imagined a lot of things in the dark, in my bed, beneath the weight of that old quilt, but never this, and I moan. When he pulls away, he seems startled. His eyes dart around for a moment before settling on my throat.

"What's that?" he asks.

"Oh, this?" I touch the ribbon at the back of my neck. "It's just my ribbon." I run my fingers halfway around its green and glossy length, and bring them to rest on the tight bow that sits in the front. He reaches out his hand, and I seize it and press it away.

"You shouldn't touch it," I say. "You can't touch it."

Before we go inside, he asks if he can see me again. I tell him that I would like that. That night, before I sleep, I imagine him again, his tongue pushing open my mouth, and my fingers slide over myself and I imagine him there, all muscle and desire to please, and I know that we are going to marry.

.   .   .

We do. I mean, we will. But first, he takes me in his car, in the dark, to a lake with a marshy edge that is hard to get close to. He kisses me and clasps his hand around my breast, my nipple knotting beneath his fingers.

I am not truly sure what he is going to do before he does it. He is hard and hot and dry and smells like bread, and when he breaks me I scream and cling to him like I am lost at sea. His body locks onto mine and he is pushing, pushing, and before the end he pulls himself out and finishes with my blood slicking him down. I am fascinated and aroused by the rhythm, the concrete sense of his need, the clarity of his release. Afterward, he slumps in the seat, and I can hear the sounds of the pond: loons and crickets, and something that sounds like a banjo being plucked. The wind picks up off the water and cools my body down.

I don't know what to do now. I can feel my heart beating between my legs. It hurts, but I imagine it could feel good. I run my hand over myself and feel strains of pleasure from somewhere far off. His breathing becomes quieter and I realize that he is watching me. My skin is glowing beneath the moonlight coming through the window. When I see him looking, I know I can seize that pleasure like my fingertips tickling the very end of a balloon's string that has almost drifted out of reach. I pull and moan and ride out the crest of sensation slowly and evenly, biting my tongue all the while.

"I need more," he says, but he does not rise to do anything. He looks out the window, and so do I. *Anything could move out there in the darkness*, I think. A hook-handed man. A ghostly hitchhiker forever repeating the same journey. An old woman summoned from the repose of her mirror by the chants of children. Everyone knows these stories—that is, everyone tells them, even if they don't know them—but no one ever believes them.

His eyes drift over the water and then return to me.

"Tell me about your ribbon," he says.

"There's nothing to tell. It's my ribbon."

"May I touch it?"

"No."

"I want to touch it," he says. His fingers twitch a little, and I close my legs and sit up straighter.

"No."

Something in the lake muscles and writhes out of the water, and then lands with a splash. He turns at the sound.

"A fish," he says.

"Sometime," I tell him, "I will tell you the stories about this lake and her creatures."

He smiles at me, and rubs his jaw. A little of my blood smears across his skin, but he doesn't notice, and I don't say anything.

"I would like that very much," he says.

"Take me home," I tell him. And like a gentleman, he does.

That night, I wash myself. The silky suds between my legs are the color and scent of rust, but I am newer than I have ever been.

My parents are very fond of him. He is a nice boy, they say. He will be a good man. They ask him about his occupation, his hobbies, his family. He shakes my father's hand firmly, and tells my mother flatteries that make her squeal and blush like a girl. He comes around twice a week, sometimes thrice. My mother invites him in for supper, and while we eat I dig my nails into the meat of his leg. After the ice cream puddles in the bowl, I tell my parents that I am going to walk with him down the lane. We strike off through the night, holding hands sweetly until we are out of sight of the house. I pull him through the trees, and when we find a patch of clear ground I shimmy off my pantyhose, and on my hands and knees offer myself up to him.

I have heard all of the stories about girls like me, and I am unafraid to make more of them. I hear the metallic buckle of his pants and the shush as they fall to the ground, and I feel his half hardness against me. I beg him—"No teasing"—and he obliges. I moan and push back, and we rut in that clearing, groans of my pleasure and groans of his good fortune mingling and dissipating into the night. We are learning, he and I.

There are two rules: he cannot finish inside of me, and he cannot touch my green ribbon. He spends into the dirt, *pat-pat-patt*ing like the beginning of rain. I go to touch myself, but my fingers, which had been curling in the dirt beneath me, are filthy. I pull up my underwear and stockings. He makes a sound and points, and I realize that beneath the nylon, my knees are also caked in dirt. I pull my stockings down and brush, and then up again. I smooth my skirt and repin my hair. A single lock has escaped his slicked-back curls in his exertion, and I tuck it up with the others. We walk down to the stream and I run my hands in the current until they are clean again.

We stroll back to the house, arms linked chastely. Inside, my mother has made coffee, and we all sit around while my father asks him about business.

(If you read this story out loud, the sounds of the clearing can be best reproduced by taking a deep breath and holding it for a long moment. Then release the air all at once, permitting your chest to collapse like a block tower knocked to the ground. Do this again, and again, shortening the time between the held breath and the release.)

· · ·

I have always been a teller of stories. When I was a young girl, my mother carried me out of a grocery store as I screamed about toes in the produce aisle. Concerned women turned and watched as I kicked the air and pounded my mother's slender back.

"Potatoes!" she corrected when we got back to the house. "Not toes!" She told me to sit in my chair—a child-sized thing, built for me—until my father returned. But no, I had seen the toes, pale and bloody stumps, mixed in among those russet tubers. One of them, the one that I had poked with the tip of my index finger, was cold as ice, and yielded beneath my touch the way a blister did. When I repeated this detail to my mother, something behind the liquid of her eyes shifted quick as a startled cat.

"You stay right there," she said.

My father returned from work that evening, and listened to my story, each detail.

"You've met Mr. Barns, have you not?" he asked me, referring to the elderly man who ran this particular market.

I had met him once, and I said so. He had hair white as a sky before snow, and a wife who drew the signs for the store windows.

"Why would Mr. Barns sell toes?" my father asked. "Where would he get them?"

Being young, and having no understanding of graveyards or mortuaries, I could not answer.

"And even if he got them somewhere," my father continued, "what would he have to gain by selling them amongst the potatoes?"

They had been there. I had seen them with my own eyes. But beneath the sunbeam of my father's logic, I felt my doubt unfurl.

"Most importantly," my father said, arriving triumphantly at his final piece of evidence, "why did no one notice the toes except for you?"

As a grown woman, I would have said to my father that there are true things in this world observed only by a single set of eyes. As a girl, I consented to his account of the story, and laughed when he scooped me from the chair to kiss me and send me on my way.

It is not normal that a girl teaches her boy, but I am only showing him what I want, what plays on the insides of my eyelids as I fall asleep. He comes to know the flicker of my expression as a desire passes through me, and I hold nothing back from him. When he tells me that he wants my mouth, the length of my throat, I teach myself not to gag and take all of him into me, moaning around the saltiness. When he asks me my worst secret, I tell him about the teacher who hid me in the closet until the others were gone and made me hold him there, and how afterward I went home and scrubbed my hands with a steel wool pad until they bled, even though the memory strikes such a chord of anger and shame that after I share this I have nightmares for a month. And when he asks me to marry him, days shy of my eighteenth birthday, I say yes, yes, please, and then on that park bench I sit on his lap and fan my skirt around us so that a passerby would not realize what was happening beneath it.

"I feel like I know so many parts of you," he says to me, knuckle-deep and trying not to pant. "And now, I will know all of them."

There is a story they tell, about a girl dared by her peers to venture to a local graveyard after dark. This was her folly: when they told her that standing on someone's grave at night would cause the inhabitant to reach up and pull her under, she scoffed. Scoffing is the first mistake a woman can make.

"Life is too short to be afraid of nothing," she said, "and I will show you."

Pride is the second mistake.

She could do it, she insisted, because no such fate would befall her. So they gave her a knife to stick into the frosty earth, as a way of proving her presence and her theory.

She went to that graveyard. Some storytellers say that she picked the grave at random. I believe she selected a very old one, her choice tinged by self-doubt and the latent belief that if she were wrong, the intact muscle and flesh of a newly dead corpse would be more dangerous than one centuries gone.

She knelt on the grave and plunged the blade deep. As she stood to run—for there was no one to see her fear—she found she couldn't escape. Something was clutching at her clothes. She cried out and fell to the ground.

When morning came, her friends arrived at the cemetery. They found her dead on the grave, the blade pinning the sturdy wool of her skirt to the earth. Dead of fright or exposure, would it matter when the parents arrived? She was not wrong, but it didn't matter anymore. Afterward, everyone believed that she had wished to die, even though she had died proving that she wanted to live.

As it turns out, being right was the third, and worst, mistake.

My parents are pleased about the marriage. My mother says that even though girls nowadays are starting to marry late, she married my father when she was nineteen, and was glad that she did.

When I select my wedding gown, I am reminded of the story of the young woman who wished to go to a dance with her lover, but could not afford a dress. She purchased a lovely white frock from a secondhand shop, and then later fell ill and passed from this earth. A doctor who examined her in her final days discovered that she had died from exposure to embalming fluid. It turned out that an unscrupulous undertaker's assistant had stolen the dress from the corpse of a bride.

The moral of that story, I think, is that being poor will kill you. I spend more on my dress than I intend, but it is very beautiful, and better than being dead. When I fold it into my hope chest, I think about the bride who played hide-and-go-seek on her wedding day and hid in the attic, in an old trunk that snapped shut around her and did not open. She was trapped there until she died. People thought that she had run away until years later, when a maid found her skeleton, in a white dress, folded inside that dark space. Brides never fare well in stories. Stories can sense happiness and snuff it out like a candle.

We marry in April, on an unseasonably cold afternoon. He sees me before the wedding, in my dress, and insists on kissing me deeply and reaching inside of my bodice. He becomes hard, and I tell him that I want him to use my body as he sees fit. I rescind my first rule, given the occasion. He pushes me against the wall and puts his hand against the tile near my throat, to steady himself. His thumb brushes my ribbon. He does not move his hand, and as he works himself in me he says, "I love you, I love you, I love you." I do not know if I am the first woman to walk up the aisle of St. George's with semen leaking down her leg, but I like to imagine that I am.

For our honeymoon, we go on a tour of Europe. We are not rich but we make it work. Europe is a continent of stories, and in between consummations, I learn them. We go from bustling, ancient metropolises to sleepy villages to Alpine retreats and back again, sipping spirits and pulling roasted meat from bones with our teeth, eating spaetzle and olives and ravioli and a creamy grain I do not recognize but come to crave each morning. We cannot afford a sleeper car on the train, but my husband bribes an attendant to permit us one hour in an empty room, and in that way we couple over the Rhine, my husband pinning me to the rickety frame and howling like something more primordial than the mountains we cross. I recognize that this is not the entire world, but it is the first part of it that I am seeing. I feel electrified by possibility.

(If you are reading this story out loud, make the sound of the bed under the tension of train travel and lovemaking by straining a metal folding chair against its hinges. When you are exhausted with that, sing the half-remembered lyrics of old songs to the person closest to you, thinking of lullabies for children.)

My cycle stops soon after we return from our trip. I tell my husband one night, after we are spent and sprawled across our bed. He glows with real delight.

"A child," he says. He lies back with his hands beneath his head. "A child." He is quiet for so long that I think that he's fallen asleep, but when I look over his eyes are open and fixed on the ceiling. He rolls on his side and gazes at me.

"Will the child have a ribbon?"

I feel my jaw tighten, and my hand fondles my bow involuntarily. My mind skips between many answers, and I settle on the one that brings me the least amount of anger.

"There is no saying, now," I tell him finally.

He startles me, then, running his hand around my throat. I put up my hands to stop him but he uses his strength, grabbing my wrists with one hand as he touches the ribbon with the other. He presses the silky length with his thumb. He touches the bow delicately, as if he is massaging my sex.

"Please," I say. "Please don't."

He does not seem to hear. "Please," I say again, my voice louder, but cracking in the middle.

He could have done it then, untied the bow, if he'd chosen to. But he releases me and rolls on his back as if nothing has happened. My wrists ache, and I rub them.

"I need a glass of water," I say. I get up and go to the bathroom. I run the tap and then frantically check my ribbon, tears caught in my lashes. The bow is still tight.

There is a story I love about a pioneer husband and wife killed by wolves. Neighbors found their bodies torn open and strewn around their tiny cabin, but never located their infant daughter, alive or dead. People claimed they saw the girl running with a wolf pack, loping over the terrain as wild and feral as any of her companions.

News of her would ripple through the local settlements upon each sighting. She menaced a hunter in a winter forest—though perhaps he was less menaced than startled at a tiny naked girl baring her teeth and howling so rawly it quaked the skin on his bones. A young woman, on the cusp of marriage age, trying to take down a horse. People even saw her ripping open a chicken in an explosion of feathers.

Many years later, she was said to be seen resting in the rushes along a riverbank, suckling two wolf cubs. I like to imagine that they came from her body, the lineage of wolves tainted human just the once. They certainly bloodied her breasts, but she did not mind, because they were hers and only hers. I believe that when their muzzles and teeth pressed against her she felt a kind of sanctuary, peace she would have found nowhere else. She must have been better among them than she would have been otherwise. Of that, I am certain.

. . .

Months pass and my stomach swells. Inside of me, our child is swimming fiercely, kicking and pushing and clawing. In public, I gasp and stagger to the side, clutching my belly and hissing through my teeth to Little One, as I call it, to stop. Once, I stumble on a walk in the park, the same park where my husband had proposed to me the year before, and go to my knees, breathing heavily and near weeping. A woman passing by helps me to sit up and gives me some water, telling me that the first pregnancy is always the worst, but they get better with time.

It is the worst, but for so many reasons besides my altered form. I sing to my child, and think about the old wives' tales of carrying the baby high or low. Do I carry a boy inside of me, the image of his father? Or a girl, a daughter who would soften the sons that followed? I have no siblings, but I know that eldest girls sweeten their brothers and are protected by them from the dangers of the world—an arrangement that buoys my heart.

My body changes in ways I do not expect—my breasts are large and hot, my stomach lined with pale marks, the inverse of a tiger's. I feel monstrous, but my husband seems renewed with desire, as if my novel shape has refreshed our list of perversities. And my body responds: in the line at the supermarket, receiving communion in church, I am marked by a new and ferocious want, leaving me slippery and swollen at the slightest provocation. When he comes home each day, my husband has made a list in his mind of things he desires from me, and I am willing to provide them and more, having been on the edge of coming since that morning's purchase of bread and carrots.

"I am the luckiest man alive," he says, running his hands across my stomach.

In the mornings, he kisses me and fondles me and sometimes

takes me before his coffee and toast. He goes to work with a spring in his step. He comes home with one promotion, and then another. "More money for my family," he says. "More money for our happiness."

I go into labor in the middle of the night, every inch of my insides twisting into an obscene knot before release. I scream like I have not screamed since the night by the lake, but for contrary reasons. Now, the pleasure of the knowledge that my child is coming is dismantled by the unyielding agony.

I am in labor for twenty hours. I nearly wrench off my husband's hand, howling obscenities that do not seem to shock the nurse. The doctor is frustratingly patient, peering down between my legs, his white eyebrows making unreadable Morse code across his forehead.

"What's happening?" I ask.

"Breathe," he commands.

I am certain that if any more time passes, I will crush my own teeth to powder. I look to my husband, who kisses my forehead and asks the doctor what's happening.

"I'm not satisfied this will be a natural birth," the doctor says. "We may have to deliver the baby surgically."

"No, please," I say. "I don't want that, please."

"If there's no movement soon, we're going to do it," the doctor says. "It may be best for everyone." He looks up and I am almost certain he winks at my husband, but pain makes the mind see things differently than they are.

I make a deal with Little One, in my mind. *Little One*, I think, *this is the last time that we are going to be just you and me. Please don't make them cut you out of me.*

Little One is born twenty minutes later. They do have to make a cut, but not across my stomach as I had feared. The doctor draws his scalpel down instead, and I feel little, just tugging, though perhaps it is what they have given me. When the baby is placed in my arms, I examine the wrinkled body from head to toe, the color of a sunset sky, and streaked in red.

No ribbon. A boy. I begin to weep, and curl the unmarked baby into my chest. The nurse shows me how to nurse him, and I am so happy to feel him drink, to touch the curls of his fingers, little commas, each of them.

(If you are reading this story out loud, give a paring knife to the listeners and ask them to cut the tender flap of skin between your index finger and thumb. Afterward, thank them.)

There is a story about a woman who goes into labor when the attending physician is tired. There is a story about a woman who herself was born too early. There is a story about a woman whose body clung to her child so hard they cut her to retrieve him. There is a story about a woman who heard a story about a woman who birthed wolf cubs in secret. When you think about it, stories have this way of running together like raindrops in a pond. Each is borne from the clouds separate, but once they have come together, there is no way to tell them apart.

(If you are reading this story out loud, move aside the curtain to illustrate this final point to your listeners. It'll be raining, I promise.)

They take the baby so that they may fix me where they cut. They give me something that makes me sleepy, delivered through a mask pressed gently to my mouth and nose. My husband jokes around with the doctor as he holds my hand.

"How much to get that extra stitch?" he asks. "You offer that, right?"

"Please," I say to him. But it comes out slurred and twisted and possibly no more than a small moan. Neither man turns his head toward me.

The doctor chuckles. "You aren't the first—"

I slide down a long tunnel, and then surface again, but covered in something heavy and dark, like oil. I feel like I am going to vomit.

"—the rumor is something like—"

"—like a vir—"

And then I am awake, wide awake, and my husband is gone and the doctor is gone. And the baby, where is—

The nurse sticks her head in the door.

"Your husband just went to get a coffee," she says, "and the baby is asleep in the bassinet."

The doctor walks in behind her, wiping his hands on a cloth.

"You're all sewn up, don't you worry," he said. "Nice and tight, everyone's happy. The nurse will speak with you about recovery. You're going to need to rest for a while."

The baby wakes up. The nurse scoops him from his swaddle and places him in my arms again. He is so beautiful I have to remind myself to breathe.

I recover a small amount every day. I move slowly and ache. My husband moves to touch me and I push him away. I want to return to our life as it was, but such things cannot be helped right now. I am already nursing and rising at all hours to take care of our son with my pain.

Then one day I take him in my hand, and afterward he is so content I realize that I can sate him, even if I remain unsated. Around our son's first birthday, I am healed enough to take my husband back into my bed. I weep with happiness as he touches me, fills me as I have wanted to be filled for so long.

My son is a good baby. He grows and grows. We try to have another child, but I suspect that Little One did so much ruinous damage inside of me that my body couldn't house another.

"You were a poor tenant, Little One," I say to him, rubbing shampoo into his fine brown hair, "and I shall revoke your deposit."

He splashes around in the sink, cackling with happiness.

My son touches my ribbon, but never in a way that makes me afraid. He thinks of it as a part of me, and he treats it no differently than he would an ear or a finger. It gives him delight in a way that houses no wanting, and this pleases me.

I do not know if my husband is sad that we cannot have another child. He keeps his sorrows as close to himself as he is open with his desires. He is a good father, and he loves his boy. Back from work, they play games of chase and run in the yard. He is too young to catch a ball, still, but my husband patiently rolls it to him in the grass, and our son picks it up and drops it again, and my husband gestures to me and cries, "Look, look! Did you see? He is going to throw it soon enough."

Of all the stories I know about mothers, this one is the most real. A young American girl is visiting Paris with her mother when the woman begins to feel ill. They decide to check into a hotel for a few days so the mother can rest, and the daughter calls for a doctor to assess her.

After a brief examination, the doctor tells the daughter that all her mother needs is some medicine. He takes the daughter to a taxi, gives the driver instructions in French, and explains to the girl that the driver will take her to his residence, where his wife will give her the appropriate remedy. They drive and drive for a very long time, and when the girl arrives, she is frustrated by the unbearable slowness of this doctor's wife, who meticulously assembles the pills from powder. When she gets back into the taxi, the driver meanders down the streets, sometimes doubling back on the same avenue. Frustrated, the girl gets out of the taxi to return to the hotel on foot. When she finally arrives, the hotel clerk tells her that he has never seen her before. When she runs up to the room where her mother had been resting, she finds the walls a different color, the furnishings different than her memory, and her mother nowhere in sight.

There are many endings to the story. In one of them, the girl is gloriously persistent and certain, renting a room nearby and staking out the hotel, eventually seducing a young man who works in the laundry and discovering the truth: that her mother had died of a highly contagious and fatal disease, departing this plane shortly after the daughter was sent from the hotel by the doctor. To avoid a citywide panic, the staff removed and buried her body, repainted and refurnished the room, and bribed all involved to deny that they had ever met the pair.

In another version of this story, the girl wanders the streets of Paris for years, believing that she is mad, that she invented her mother and her life with her mother in her own diseased mind. The daughter stumbles from hotel to hotel, confused and grieving, though for whom she cannot say. Each time she is ejected from another posh lobby, she weeps for something lost. Her mother is dead and she does not know it. She won't know it until she, herself, is also dead, assuming that you believe in paradise.

I don't need to tell you the moral of this story. I think you already know what it is.

·   ·   ·

Our son enters school when he is five, and I remember his teacher from that day in the park, when she had crouched to help me and predicted easy future pregnancies. She remembers me as well, and we talk briefly in the hallway. I tell her that we have had no more children since our son, and now that he has started school, my days will be altered toward sloth and boredom. She is kind. She tells me that if I am looking for a way to occupy my time, there is a wonderful women's art class at a local college.

That night, after my son is in bed, my husband reaches his hand across the couch and slides it up my leg.

"Come to me," he says, and I twinge with pleasure. I slide off the couch, smoothing my skirt very prettily as I shuffle over to him on my knees. I kiss his leg, running my hand up to his belt, tugging him from his bonds before swallowing him whole. He runs his hands through my hair, stroking my head, groaning and pressing into me. And I don't realize that his hand is sliding down the back of my neck until he is trying to loop his fingers through the ribbon. I gasp and pull away quickly, falling back and frantically checking my bow. He is still sitting there, slick with my spit.

"Come back here," he says.

"No," I say. "You'll touch my ribbon."

He stands up and tucks himself into his pants, zipping them up.

"A wife," he says, "should have no secrets from her husband."

"I don't have any secrets," I tell him.

"The *ribbon*."

"The ribbon is not a secret; it's just mine."

"Were you born with it? Why your throat? Why is it green?"

I do not answer.

He is silent for a long minute. Then,

"A wife should have no secrets."

My nose grows hot. I do not want to cry.

"I've given you everything you have ever asked for," I say. "Am I not allowed this one thing?"

"I want to know."

"You think you want to know," I say, "but you don't."

"Why do you want to hide it from me?"

"I'm not hiding it. It just isn't yours."

He gets down very close to me, and I pull back from the smell of bourbon. I hear a creak, and we both look up to see our son's feet vanishing up the staircase.

When my husband goes to sleep that night, he does so with a hot and burning anger that falls away as soon as he is truly dreaming. I am up for a long time listening to his breathing, wondering if perhaps men have ribbons that do not look like ribbons. Maybe we are all marked in some way, even if it's impossible to see.

The next day, our son touches my throat and asks about my ribbon. He tries to pull at it. And though it pains me, I have to make it forbidden to him. When he reaches for it, I shake a can full of pennies. It crashes discordantly, and he withdraws and weeps. Something is lost between us, and I never find it again.

(If you are reading this story out loud, prepare a soda can full of pennies. When you arrive at this moment, shake it loudly in the face of the people closest to you. Observe their expression of startled fear, and then betrayal. Notice how they never look at you exactly the same way for the rest of your days.)

I enroll in the art class for women. When my husband is at work and my son is in school, I drive to the sprawling green campus and the squat gray building where the art classes are held.

Presumably, the male nudes are kept from our eyes in some

deference to propriety, but the class has its own energy—there is plenty to see on a strange woman's naked form, plenty to contemplate as you roll charcoal and mix paints. I see more than one woman shifting forward and back in her seat to redistribute blood flow.

One woman in particular returns over and over. Her ribbon is red, and is knotted around her slender ankle. Her skin is the color of olives, and a trail of dark hair runs from her belly button to her mons. I know that I should not want her, not because she is a woman and not because she is a stranger, but because it is her job to disrobe, and I feel shame taking advantage of such a state. No small amount of guilt comes along with my wandering eyes, but as my pencil traces her contours, so does my hand in the secret recesses of my mind. I am not even certain how such a thing would happen, but the possibilities incense me to near madness.

One afternoon after class, I turn a hallway corner and she is there, the woman. Clothed, wrapped in a raincoat. Her gaze transfixes me, and this close I can see a band of gold around each of her pupils, as though her eyes are twin solar eclipses. She greets me, and I her.

We sit down together in a booth at a nearby diner, our knees occasionally brushing up against each other beneath the Formica. She drinks a cup of black coffee, which startles me, though I don't know why. I ask her if she has any children. She does, she says, a daughter, a beautiful little girl of eleven.

"Eleven is a terrifying age," she says. "I remember nothing before I was eleven, but then there it was, all color and horror. What a number," she says, "what a show." Then her face slips somewhere else for a moment, as if she has dipped beneath the surface of a lake, and when it comes back, she briefly speaks to her daughter's accomplishments in voice and music.

We do not discuss the specific fears of raising a girl-child.

Truthfully, I am afraid even to ask. I also do not ask her if she's married, and she does not volunteer the information, though she does not wear a ring. We talk about my son, about the art class. I desperately want to know what state of need has sent her to disrobe before us, but perhaps I do not ask, because the answer would be, like adolescence, too frightening to forget.

I am captivated by her, there is no other way to put it. There is something easy about her, but not easy the way I was—the way I am. She's like dough, how the give of it beneath kneading hands disguises its sturdiness, its potential. When I look away from her and then look back, she seems twice as large as before.

"Perhaps we can talk again sometime," I say to her. "This has been a very pleasant afternoon."

She nods to me. I pay for her coffee.

I do not want to tell my husband about her, but he can sense some untapped desire. One night, he asks what roils inside of me and I confess it to him. I even describe the details of her ribbon, releasing an extra flood of shame.

He is so glad of this development that he begins to mutter a long and exhaustive fantasy as he removes his pants and enters me, and I cannot even hear all of it, though I imagine that within its parameters she and I are together, or perhaps both of us are with him.

I feel as if I have betrayed her somehow, and I never return to the class. I find other amusements to occupy my days.

(If you are reading this story out loud, force a listener to reveal a devastating secret, then open the nearest window to the street and scream it as loudly as you are able.)

One of my favorite stories is about an old woman and her husband—a man mean as Mondays, who scared her with the violence of his temper and the shifting nature of his whims. She was only able to keep him satisfied with her cooking, to which he was a complete captive. One day, he bought her a fat liver to cook for him, and she did, using herbs and broth. But the smell of her own artistry overtook her, and a few nibbles became a few bites, and soon the liver was gone. She had no money with which to purchase a second one, and she was terrified of her husband's reaction should he discover that his meal was gone. So she crept to the church next door, where a woman had been recently laid to rest. She approached the shrouded figure, then cut into it with a pair of kitchen shears and stole the liver from her corpse.

That night, the woman's husband dabbed his lips with a napkin and declared the meal the finest he'd ever eaten. When they went to sleep, the old woman heard the front door open, and a thin wail wafted through the rooms. *Who has my liver? Whooooo has my liver?*

The old woman could hear the voice coming closer and closer to the bedroom. There was a hush as the door swung open. The dead woman posed her query again.

The old woman flung the blanket off her husband.

"*He* has it!" she declared triumphantly.

Then she saw the face of the dead woman, and recognized her own mouth and eyes. She looked down at her abdomen, remembering, now, how she carved into her belly. She bled freely there in the bed, whispering something over and over as she died, something you and I will never be privy to. Next to her, as the blood seeped into the very heart of the mattress, her husband slumbered on.

That may not be the version of the story you're familiar with. But I assure you, it's the one you need to know.

. . .

My husband is strangely excited for Halloween. I took one of his old tweed coats and fashioned one for our son, so that he might be a tiny professor, or some other stuffy academic. I even give him a pipe on which to gnaw. Our son clicks it between his teeth in a way I find unsettlingly adult.

"Mama," my son says, "what are you?"

I am not in costume, so I tell him I am his mother.

The pipe falls from his little mouth onto the floor, and he screams so loudly I am unable to move. My husband swoops in and picks him up, talking to him in a low voice, repeating his name between his sobs.

It is only as his breathing returns to normal that I am able to identify my mistake. He is not old enough to know the story of the naughty girls who wanted the toy drum and were wicked toward their mother until she went away and was replaced with a new mother—one with glass eyes and thumping wooden tail. He is too young for the stories and their trueness, but I have inadvertently told him anyway—the story of the little boy who only discovered on Halloween that his mother was not his mother, except on the day when everyone wore a mask. Regret sluices hot up my throat. I try to hold him and kiss him, but he only wishes to go out onto the street, where the sun has dipped below the horizon and a hazy chill is bruising the shadows.

I have little use for this holiday. I do not wish to walk my son to strangers' houses or to assemble popcorn balls and wait for trick-or-treat callers to show up at the door demanding ransom. Still, I wait inside with a whole tray of the sticky confections, answering the door to tiny queens and ghosts. I think of my son. When they leave, I put down the tray and rest my head in my hands.

Our son comes home laughing, gnawing on a piece of candy

that has turned his mouth the color of a plum. I am angry at my
husband. I wish he had waited to come home before permitting the
consumption of the cache. Has he never heard the stories? The pins
pressed into the chocolates, the razor blades sunk into the apples?
It is like him to not understand what there is to be afraid of in this
world, but I am still furious. I examine my son's mouth, but there is
no sharp metal plunged into his palate. He laughs and spins around
the house, dizzy and electrified from the treats and excitement. He
wraps his arms around my legs, the earlier incident forgotten. The
forgiveness tastes sweeter than any candy that can be given at any
door. When he climbs into my lap, I sing to him until he falls asleep.

Our son grows and grows. He is eight, ten. First, I tell him fairy
tales—the very oldest ones, with the pain and death and forced marriage pared away like dead foliage. Mermaids grow feet and it feels
like laughter. Naughty pigs trot away from grand feasts, reformed
and uneaten. Evil witches leave the castle and move into small cot-
tages and live out their days painting portraits of woodland creatures.

As he grows, though, he asks too many questions. Why would
they not eat the pig, hungry as they were and wicked as he had been?
Why was the witch permitted to go free after her terrible deeds? And
the sensation of fins to feet being anything less than agonizing he rejects outright after cutting his hand with a pair of scissors.

"It would hoight," he says, for he is struggling with his *r*'s.

I agree with him as I bandage the cut. It would. So then I tell
him stories closer to true: children who go missing along a particular stretch of railroad track, lured by the sound of a phantom train
to parts unknown; a black dog that appears at a person's doorstep
three days before her passing; a trio of frogs that corner you in the

marshlands and tell your fortune for a price. My husband, I think, would forbid these stories, but my son listens to them with solemnity and keeps them to himself.

The school puts on a performance of *Little Buckle-Boy*, and he is the lead, the buckle-boy, and I join a committee of mothers making costumes for the children. I am chief costume maker in a room full of women, all of us sewing together little silk petals for the flower-children and making tiny white pantaloons for the pirates. One of the mothers has a pale yellow ribbon on her finger, and it constantly tangles in her thread. She swears and cries. One day I even have to use the sewing shears to pick at the offending threads. I try to be delicate. She shakes her head as I free her from the peony.

"It's such a bother, isn't it?" she says. I nod. Outside the window, the children play—knocking each other off the playground equipment, popping the heads off dandelions. The play goes beautifully. Opening night, our son blazes through his monologue. Perfect pitch and cadence. No one has ever done better.

Our son is twelve. He asks me about the ribbon, point-blank. I tell him that we are all different, and sometimes you should not ask questions. I assure him that he'll understand when he is grown. I distract him with stories that have no ribbons: angels who desire to be human and ghosts who don't realize they're dead and children who turn to ash. He stops smelling like a child—milky-sweetness replaced with something sharp and burning, like a hair sizzling on the stove.

Our son is thirteen, fourteen. His hair is a little too long but I can't bear to cut it short. My husband scrambles the locks with his hand on his way to work, and kisses me on the side of the mouth. On his way to school, our son waits for the neighbor boy, who walks with a brace. He exhibits the subtlest compassion, my son. No instinct for cruelty, like some. "The world has enough bullies," I've told him over and over. This is the year he stops asking for my stories.

Our son is fifteen, sixteen, seventeen. He is a brilliant boy. He has his father's knack for people, my air of mystery. He begins to court a beautiful girl from his high school who has a bright smile and a warm presence. I am happy to meet her, but never insist that we should wait up for their return, remembering my own youth.

When he tells us that he has been accepted at a university to study engineering, I am overjoyed. We march through the house, singing songs and laughing. When my husband comes home, he joins in the jubilee, and we drive to a local seafood restaurant. His father tells him, over halibut, "We are so proud of you." Our son laughs and says that he also wishes to marry his girl. We clasp hands and are even happier. Such a good boy. Such a wonderful life to look forward to.

Even the luckiest woman alive has not seen joy like this.

There's a classic, a real classic, that I haven't told you yet.

A girlfriend and a boyfriend went parking. Some people say that means kissing in a car, but I know the story. I was there. They were parked on the edge of a lake. They were turning around in the backseat as if the world were moments from ending. Maybe it was. She offered herself and he took her, and after it was over, they turned on the radio.

The voice on the radio announced that a mad, hook-handed murderer had escaped from a local asylum. The boyfriend chuckled as he flipped to a music station. As the song ended, the girlfriend heard a thin scratching sound, like a paper clip over glass. She looked at her boyfriend and then pulled her cardigan over her bare shoulders, wrapping one arm around her breasts.

"We should go," she said.

"Nah," the boyfriend said. "Let's do that again. I've got all night."

"What if the killer comes here?" the girl asked. "The asylum is very close."

"We'll be fine, baby," the boyfriend said. "Don't you trust me?"

The girlfriend nodded reluctantly.

"Well, then—" he said, his voice trailing off in that way she would come to know so well. He took her hand off her chest and placed it onto himself. She finally looked away from the lakeside. Outside, the moonlight glinted off the shiny steel hook. The killer waved at her, grinning.

I'm sorry. I've forgotten the rest of the story.

The house is so silent without our son. I walk through it, touching all the surfaces. I am happy but something inside of me is shifting into a strange new place.

That night, my husband asks if I wish to christen the newly empty rooms. We have not coupled so fiercely since before our son was born. Bent over the kitchen table, something old is lit within me, and I remember the way we had desired before, how we had left love streaked on all of the surfaces, how he relished in my darkest spaces. I scream with ferocity, not caring if the neighbors hear, not caring if anyone looks through the window with its undrawn curtains and sees my husband buried in my mouth. I would go out on the lawn if he asked me, let him take me from behind in sight of the whole neighborhood. I could have met anyone at that party when I was seventeen—stupid boys or prudish boys or violent boys. Religious boys who would have made me move to some distant country to convert its denizens, or some such nonsense. I could have experienced untold numbers of sorrows or dissatisfactions. But as I straddle him on the floor, riding him and crying out, I know that I made the right choice.

We fall asleep exhausted, sprawled naked in our bed. When I wake up, my husband is kissing the back of my neck, probing the ribbon with his tongue. My body rebels wildly, still throbbing with the memories of pleasure but bucking hard against betrayal. I say his name, and he does not respond. I say it again, and he holds me against him and continues. I wedge my elbows in his side, and when he loosens from me in surprise, I sit up and face him. He looks confused and hurt, like my son the day I shook the can of pennies.

Resolve runs out of me. I touch the ribbon. I look at the face of my husband, the beginning and end of his desires all etched there. He is not a bad man, and that, I realize suddenly, is the root of my hurt. He is not a bad man at all. To describe him as evil or wicked or corrupted would do a deep disservice to him. And yet—

"Do you want to untie the ribbon?" I ask him. "After these many years, is that what you want of me?"

His face flashes gaily, and then greedily, and he runs his hand up my bare breast and to my bow. "Yes," he says. "Yes."

I do not have to touch him to know that he grows at the thought.

I close my eyes. I remember the boy of the party, the one who kissed me and broke me open by that lakeside, who did with me what I wanted. Who gave me a son and helped him grow into a man himself.

"Then," I say, "do what you want."

With trembling fingers, he takes one of the ends. The bow undoes, slowly, the long-bound ends crimped with habit. My husband groans, but I do not think he realizes it. He loops his finger through the final twist and pulls. The ribbon falls away. It floats down and curls on the bed, or so I imagine, because I cannot look down to follow its descent.

My husband frowns, and then his face begins to open with some other expression—sorrow, or maybe preemptive loss. My hand flies up in front of me—an involuntary motion, for balance or some other futility—and beyond it his image is gone.

"I love you," I assure him, "more than you can possibly know."

"No," he says, but I don't know to what he's responding.

If you are reading this story out loud, you may be wondering if that place my ribbon protected was wet with blood and openings, or smooth and neutered like the nexus between the legs of a doll. I'm afraid I can't tell you, because I don't know. For these questions and others, and their lack of resolution, I am sorry.

My weight shifts, and with it, gravity seizes me. My husband's face falls away, and then I see the ceiling, and the wall behind me. As my lopped head tips backward off my neck and rolls off the bed, I feel as lonely as I have ever been.

INVENTORY

One girl. We lay down next to each other on the musty rug in her basement. Her parents were upstairs; we told them we were watching *Jurassic Park*. "I'm the dad, and you're the mom," she said. I pulled up my shirt, she pulled up hers, and we just stared at each other. My heart fluttered below my belly button, but I worried about daddy longlegs and her parents finding us. I still have never seen *Jurassic Park*. I suppose I never will, now.

One boy, one girl. My friends. We drank stolen wine coolers in my room, on the vast expanse of my bed. We laughed and talked and passed around the bottles. "What I like about you," she said, "is your reactions. You respond so funny to everything. Like it's all intense." He nodded in agreement. She buried her face in my neck and said "Like this" to my skin. I laughed. I was nervous, excited. I felt like a guitar and someone was twisting the tuning pegs and my strings were getting tighter. They batted their eyelashes against my skin and breathed into my ears. I moaned and writhed, and hovered on the edge of coming for whole minutes, though no one was touching me there, not even me.

Two boys, one girl. One of them my boyfriend. His parents were out of town, so we threw a party at his house. We drank lemonade mixed with vodka and he encouraged me to make out with his friend's girlfriend. We kissed tentatively, then stopped. The boys made out with each other, and we watched them for a long time, bored but too drunk to stand up. We fell asleep in the guest bedroom. When I woke up, my bladder was tight as a fist. I padded down into the foyer, and saw someone had knocked a vodka lemonade onto the floor. I tried to clean it up. The mixture had stripped the marble finish bare. My boyfriend's mother found my underwear behind the bed weeks later, and handed them to him, laundered, without a word. It's weird to me how much I miss that floral, chemical smell of clean clothes. Now, all I can think about is fabric softener.

One man. Slender, tall. So skinny I could see his pelvic bone, which I found strangely sexy. Gray eyes. Wry smile. I had known him for almost a year, since the previous October, when we'd met at a Halloween party. (I didn't wear a costume; he was dressed as Barbarella.) We drank in his apartment. He was nervous and gave me a massage. I was nervous so I let him. He rubbed my back for a long time. He said, "My hands are getting tired." I said, "Oh," and turned toward him. He kissed me, his face rough with stubble. He smelled like yeast and the top notes of expensive cologne. He lay on top of me and we made out for a while. Everything inside of me twinged, pleasurably. He asked if he could touch my breast, and I clamped his hand around it. I took off my shirt, and I felt like a drop of water was sliding up my spine. I realized this was happening, really happening. We both undressed. He rolled the condom down and lumbered on top of me. It hurt worse than anything, ever. He came and I didn't. When he pulled out, the condom was covered in blood. He peeled it off and threw it away. Everything in me pounded. We slept on a too-small bed. He insisted on driving me back to the dorms the next day. In my room, I took off my clothes and wrapped myself in a towel. I still smelled like him, like the two of us together, and I wanted more. I felt good, like an adult who has sex sometimes, and a life. My roommate asked me how it was, hugged me.

One man. A boyfriend. Didn't like condoms, asked me if I was on birth control, pulled out anyway. A terrible mess.

One woman. On-and-off sort-of girlfriend. Classmate from Organization of Computer Systems. Long brown hair down to her butt. She was softer than I expected. I wanted to go down on her, but she was too nervous. We made out and she slipped her tongue into my mouth and after she went home I got off twice in the cool stillness of my apartment. Two years later, we had sex on the gravel rooftop of my office building. Four floors below our bodies, my code was compiling in front of an empty chair. After we were done, I looked up and noticed a man in a suit watching us from the window of the adjacent skyscraper, his hand shuffling around inside his slacks.

One woman. Round glasses, red hair. Don't remember where I met her. We got high and fucked and I accidentally fell asleep with my hand inside of her. We woke up predawn and walked across town to a twenty-four-hour diner. It drizzled and when we got there, our sandaled feet were numb from the chill. We ate pancakes. Our mugs ran dry, and when we looked for the waitress, she was watching the breaking news on the battered TV hanging from the ceiling. She chewed on her lip, and the pot of coffee tipped in her hand, dripping tiny brown dots onto the linoleum. We watched as the newscaster blinked away and was replaced with a list of symptoms of the virus blossoming a state away, in northern California. When he came back, he repeated that planes were grounded, the border of the state had been closed, and the virus appeared to be isolated. When the waitress walked over, she seemed distracted. "Do you have people there?" I asked, and she nodded, her eyes filling with tears. I felt terrible having asked her anything.

One man. I met him at the bar around the corner from my house. We made out on my bed. He smelled like sour wine, though he'd been drinking vodka. We had sex, but he went soft halfway through. We kissed some more. He wanted to go down on me, but I didn't want him to. He got angry and left, slamming the screen door so hard my spice rack jumped from its nail and crashed to the floor. My dog lapped up the nutmeg, and I had to force-feed him salt to make him throw up. Revved from adrenaline, I made a list of animals I have had in my life—seven, including my two betta fish, who died within a week of each other when I was nine—and a list of the spices in pho. Cloves, cinnamon, star anise, coriander, ginger, cardamom pods.

One man. Six inches shorter than me. I explained that the website I worked for was losing business rapidly because no one wanted quirky photography tips during an epidemic, and I had been laid off that morning. He bought me dinner. We had sex in his car because he had roommates and I couldn't be in my house right then, and he slid his hand inside my bra and his hands were perfect, fucking perfect, and we fell into the too-tiny backseat. I came for the first time in two months. I called him the next day, and left him a voicemail, telling him I'd had a good time and I'd like to see him again, but he never called me back.

One man. Did some sort of hard labor for a living, I can't remember what exactly, and he had a tattoo of a boa constrictor on his back with a misspelled Latin phrase below it. He was strong and could pick me up and fuck me against a wall and it was the most thrilling sensation I'd ever felt. We broke a few picture frames that way. He used his hands and I dragged my fingernails down his back, and he asked me if I was going to come for him, and I said, "Yes, yes, I'm going to come for you, yes, I will."

One woman. Blond hair, brash voice, friend of a friend. We married. I'm still not sure if I was with her because I wanted to be or because I was afraid of what the world was catching all around us. Within a year, it soured. We screamed more than we had sex, or even talked. One night, we had a fight that left me in tears. Afterward, she asked me if I wanted to fuck, and undressed before I could answer. I wanted to push her out the window. We had sex and I started crying. When it was over and she was showering, I packed a suitcase and got in my car and drove.

One man. Six months later, in my postdivorce haze. I met him at the funeral for the last surviving member of his family. I was grieving, he was grieving. We had sex in the empty house that used to belong to his brother and his brother's wife and their children, all dead. We fucked in every room, including the hallway, where I couldn't bend my pelvis right on the hardwood floors, and I jerked him off in front of the bare linen closet. In the master bedroom, I caught my reflection in the vanity mirror as I rode him, and the lights were off and our skin reflected silver from the moon and when he came in me he said, "Sorry, sorry." He died a week later, by his own hand. I moved out of the city, north.

One man. Gray eyes again. I hadn't seen him in so many years. He asked me how I was doing, and I told him some things and not others. I did not want to cry in front of the man to whom I gave my virginity. It seemed wrong somehow. He asked me how many I'd lost, and I said, "My mother, my roommate from college." I did not mention that I'd found my mother dead, nor the three days afterward I'd spent with anxious doctors checking my eyes for the early symptoms, nor how I'd managed to escape the quarantine zone. "When I met you," he said, "you were so fucking young." His body was familiar, but alien, too. He'd gotten better, and I'd gotten better. When he pulled out of me I almost expected blood, but of course, there was none. He had gotten more beautiful in those intervening years, more thoughtful. I surprised myself by crying over the bathroom sink. I ran the tap so he couldn't hear me.

One woman. Brunette. A former CDC employee. I met her at a community meeting where they taught us how to stockpile food and manage outbreaks in our neighborhoods should the virus hop the firebreak. I had not slept with a woman since my wife, but as she lifted her shirt I realized how much I'd been craving breasts, wetness, soft mouths. She wanted cock and I obliged. Afterward, she traced the indents in my skin from the harness, and confessed to me that no one was having any luck developing a vaccine. "But the fucking thing is only passing through physical contact," she said. "If people would just stay apart—" She grew silent. She curled up next

to me and we drifted off. When I woke up, she was working herself
over with the dildo, and I pretended I was still sleeping.

One man. He made me dinner in my kitchen. There weren't a lot of
vegetables left from my garden, but he did what he could. He tried
to feed me with a spoon, but I took the handle from him. The food
didn't taste too bad. The power went out for the fourth time that
week, so we ate by candlelight. I resented the inadvertent romance.
He touched my face when we fucked and said I was beautiful, and I
jerked my head a little to dislodge his fingers. When he did it a second time, I put my hand around his chin and told him to shut up.
He came immediately. I did not return his calls. When the notice
come over the radio that the virus had somehow reached Nebraska,
I realized I had to go east, and so I did. I left the garden, the plot
where my dog was buried, the pine table where I'd anxiously made
so many lists—trees that began with *m*: maple, mimosa, mahog-
any, mulberry, magnolia, mountain ash, mangrove, myrtle; states
that I had lived in: Iowa, Indiana, Pennsylvania, Virginia, New
York—leaving unreadable jumbles of letters imprinted in the soft
wood. I took my savings and rented a cottage near the ocean. After
a few months, the landlord, based in Kansas, stopped depositing
my checks.

Two women. Refugees from the western states who drove and drove
until their car broke down a mile from my cottage. They knocked
on my door and stayed with me for two weeks while we tried to
figure out how to get their vehicle up and running. We had wine
one night and talked about the quarantine. The generator needed
cranking, and one of them offered to do it. The other one sat down
next to me and slid her hand up my leg. We ended up jerking off

separately and kissing each other. The generator took and the power came back on. The other woman returned, and we all slept in the same bed. I wanted them to stay, but they said they were heading up into Canada, where it was rumored to be safer. They offered to bring me with them, but I joked that I was holding down the fort for the United States. "What state are we in?" one of them asked, and I said, "Maine." They kissed me on the forehead in turn and dubbed me the protector of Maine. After they left, I only used the generator intermittently, preferring to spend time in the dark, with candles. The former owner of the cottage had a closet full of them.

One man. National Guard. When he first showed up at my doorstep, I assumed he was there to evacuate me, but it turned out he'd abandoned his post. I offered him a place to stay for the night, and he thanked me. I woke up with a knife to my throat and a hand on my breast. I told him I couldn't have sex with him lying down like I was. He let me stand up, and I shoved him into the bookcase, knocking him unconscious. I dragged his body out to the beach and rolled it into the surf. He came to, sputtering sand. I pointed the knife at him and told him to walk and keep walking, and if he even looked back, I would end him. He obliged, and I watched him until he was a spot of darkness on the gray strip of shore, and then nothing. He was the last person I saw for a year.

One woman. A religious leader, with a flock of fifty trailing behind her, all dressed in white. For three days, I made them wait around the edge of the property, and after I checked their eyes, I permitted them to stay. They all camped around the cottage: on the lawn, on the beach. They had their own supplies and only needed a place to lay their heads, the leader said. She wore robes that made her look like a wizard. Night fell. She and I circled the camp in our bare feet, the light from the bonfire carving shadows into her face. We walked to the water's edge and I pointed into the darkness, at the tiny island she could not see. She slipped her hand into mine. I made her a drink—"More or less moonshine," I said as I handed her the tumbler—and we sat at the table. Outside, I could hear people laughing, playing music, children romping in the surf. The woman seemed exhausted. She was younger than she looked, I realized, but her job was aging her. She sipped her drink, made a face at the taste. "We've been walking for so long," she said. "We stopped for a while, somewhere near Pennsylvania, but the virus caught up with us when we crossed paths with another group. Took twelve before we got some distance between us and it." We kissed deeply for a long time, my heart hammering in my cunt. She tasted like smoke and honey. The group stayed for four days, until she woke up from a dream and said she'd had an omen, and they needed to keep going. She asked me to come with them. I tried to imagine myself with her, her flock following behind us like children. I declined. She left a gift on my pillow: a pewter rabbit as big as my thumb.

One man. No more than twenty, floppy brown hair. He'd been on foot for a month. He looked like you'd expect: skittish. No hope. When we had sex, he was reverent and too gentle. After we cleaned up, I fed him canned soup. He told me about how he walked through Chicago, actually through it, and how they had stopped bothering to dispose of the bodies after a while. He had to refill his glass before he talked about it further. "After that," he said, "I went around the cities." I asked him how far behind the virus was, really, and he said he did not know. "It's really quiet here," he said, by way of changing the subject. "No traffic," I explained. "No tourists." He cried and cried and I held him until he fell asleep. The next morning, I woke up and he was gone.

One woman. Much older than me. While she waited for the three days to pass, she meditated on a sand dune. When I checked her eyes, I noticed they were green as sea glass. Her hair grayed at the temples and the way she laughed tripped pleasure down the stairs of my heart. We sat in the half light of the bay window and the buildup was so slow. She straddled me, and when she kissed me the scene beyond the glass pinched and curved. We drank, and walked the length of the beach, the damp sand making pale halos around our feet. She told about her once-children, teenage injuries, having to put her cat to sleep the day after she moved to a new city. I told her about finding my mother, the perilous trek across Vermont and New Hampshire, how the tide was never still, my ex-wife. "What happened?" she asked. "It just didn't work," I said. I told her about the man in the empty house, the way he cried and the way his come shimmered on his stomach and how I could have scooped despair from the air by the handfuls. We remembered commercial jingles from our respective youths, including one for an Italian-ice chain that I went to at the end of long summer days, where I ate gelato, drowsy in the heat. I couldn't remember the last time I'd smiled so much. She stayed. More refugees filtered through the cottage, through us, the last stop before the border, and we fed them and played games with the little ones. We got careless. The day I woke up and the air had changed, I realized it had been a long time coming. She was sitting on the couch. She got up in the night and made some tea. But the cup was tipped and the puddle was cold, and I recognized the symptoms from the television and newspapers, and then the leaflets, and then the radio broadcasts, and then the hushed voices around the bonfire. Her skin was the dark purple of compounded bruises, the whites of her eyes shot through with red, and blood leaking from the misty beds of her fingernails. There was no time to mourn. I checked my own face in the mirror, and my eyes were still clear. I consulted my emergency list and its supplies. I took my bag and tent and I got into the dinghy and I rowed to the island, to this island, where I have been stashing food since I got to the cottage. I drank water and set up my tent and began to make lists. Every teacher beginning with preschool. Every job I've ever had. Every home I've ever lived in. Every person I've ever loved. Every person who has probably loved me. Next week, I will be thirty. The sand is blowing into my mouth, my hair, the center crevice of my notebook, and the sea is choppy and gray. Beyond it, I can see the cottage, a speck on the far shore. I keep thinking I can see the virus blooming on the horizon like a sunrise. I realize the world will continue to turn, even with no people on it. Maybe it will go a little faster.

MOTHERS

Here she is, on the porch, all straw hair and slumpy joints and a crack that passes through her lip like she is dirt that has never known rain. In her arms is a baby: genderless, red, not making any sort of noise.

"Bad," I say.

She kisses the baby on the ear and then hands it to me. I flinch when she extends her arms, but take the infant just the same.

Babies are heavier than you'd think.

"She's yours," Bad says.

I look down at the baby, who stares at me with wide eyes that shimmer like Japanese beetles. Her fingers curl around invisible locks of hair, and her sharp little nails dig into her skin. A feeling settles over me—a one-beer-deep feeling, a no-more-skittering-feet-after-the-trap-snaps feeling. I look back at Bad.

"What do you mean, she's mine?"

Bad looks at me as if I am unfathomably stupid, or possibly fucking with her, or both.

"I was pregnant. Now there's a baby. She's yours."

My brain doubles back on the sentence. For months, my head has been so fuzzy. Mail is stacked unread on my kitchen table, and my clothes are a giant mound on my once-immaculate floor. My uterus contracts in protest, confused.

"Look," Bad says. "There's only so much that I can do. I can't do any more than that. Right?"

I agree, but something feels wrong about following her down this line of reasoning. Dangerous.

"You can only do as much as you can do," I repeat anyway.

"Good," Bad says. "When the baby cries, she could be hungry or thirsty or angry or cranky or sick or sleepy or paranoid or jealous or she had planned something but it went horribly awry. So you'll need to take care of that, when it happens."

I look down at the baby, who is not crying now. She blinks sleepily, and I find myself wondering if dinosaurs ever blinked in the same way, before they were incinerated into dust. The baby relaxes—putting even more weight into her body than I thought possible—and curls her head against my breasts. She even purses her lips a little, as if she thinks she might be able to nurse.

"I am not your mother, baby," I say. "I can't feed you."

I am so hypnotized by her that I miss the receding footsteps, the crack of the slamming car door. But then Bad is gone, and for once, I am not alone, after.

Back inside, I realize I don't even know the baby's name. On the floor is a small cloth bag that I don't remember receiving. I go into the kitchen, where I sit down on a sagging cane chair. I imagine the chair breaking beneath me with the baby in my arms, and I stand back up and lean against the counter.

"Hello, baby," I say to the baby.

Her lids swing open again, and she fixes my face in her gaze.

"Hello, baby. What's your name?"

The baby doesn't respond, but she also doesn't cry, which surprises me. I am a stranger. She has never seen me before. If she cries, it is to be expected, there are reasons. But what does it mean that she doesn't cry? Is she afraid? She doesn't look afraid. Perhaps babies are not capable of terror.

She looks like she is working something out.

She smells clean, but chemical. And behind it, an edge of milk, bodily and sour, like something tipped askance. Her nose leaks a little, and she does not move to wipe it.

There is a crash, a shrill wail. I jump. The baby has reached out her hand and caught a banana in the fruit bowl, and taken down half a dozen pears. The hard pears roll, and the overripe ones splat. Now the baby does look terrified. She howls. I kiss the soft spot on her baby skull and carry her into the next room.

"Shhhh, baby."

Her mouth is an endless cavern, into which light and thought and sound descend, never to return. "Shhhh, baby." Why didn't Bad tell me her name?

"Shhhh, little thing, shhhh." My head throbs with the sound. Identical tears slide eye to ear on each side of her face, like a picture of a baby crying and not a baby at all. "Shhhh, little thing. Shhhh."

A brisk breeze whisks through the dust outside, and the screen door slams open. I jump. She screams.

When David and Ruth were married, they had a full Latin mass. Ruth's veil covered her face and the hem bumped over the floor as she walked down the aisle. A sea of hats and veils covered up women's updos, as per the request of the couple. The service was beautiful and old, connecting them to millennia.

At the reception, a woman in a cummerbund swept by me. I became very conscious of the way I chewed. I almost hadn't noticed her—in the crowd of relatives and friends, she'd registered as a very slight man—but no, her high cheekbones and feminine way of crossing her feet on an invisible line that ran on the floor gave her away. I watched her as the party wore on—through the toasts, through the chicken dance, through Ruth's twelve-year-old cousin doing a scandalous descent to the floor, butt first, upsetting her father—and when the dance floor cleared a bit the woman stepped out beneath the white Christmas lights wrapped in muslin, popped out her collar, rolled up her starched sleeves, and began to dance.

I'd always heard that weddings were supposed to make women horny, and for the first time, I understood. She moved with a flinty, masculine cool, such confidence, and I found myself unable to focus on anything else in the room. I got wet. I felt inadequate, too warm, inexplicably hungry.

When she approached me, my heart slowed. She spun me around like a good swing partner—assured, in control. I let myself go and laughed involuntarily. Gravity was gone.

Later, we danced so slowly we might as well have been standing. She bent her head toward my ear.

"You have the most beautiful hands I've ever seen," she said.

I called her two days later, never having believed more firmly in love at first sight, in destiny. When she laughed on the other end of the line, something inside of me cracked open, and I let her step inside.

This baby's head is bothering me because it's like a piece of fruit gone bad. I understand that, now, in the middle of this endless desert of sound. It's like the soft spot on the peach that you can just plunge your thumb into, with no questions asked, with not so much as a how-do-you-do. I'm not going to, but I want to, and the urge is so serious that I put her down. She screams louder. I pick her up and lean her against me, whispering, "I love you, baby, and I am not going to hurt you," but the first thing is a lie and the second thing might be a lie, but I'm just not sure. I should have the urge to protect her, but all I can think about is that soft spot, that place where I could hurt her if I tried, where I could hurt her if I wanted to.

A month after we met, Bad was packing a glass bowl as she straddled me, poking the weed gently with her finger. When she tipped the lighter to it and inhaled, her body shuddered along an invisible curve, and the smoke crawled out of her mouth one limb at a time; an animal.

"I haven't done this before," I told her.

She handed me the pipe, cupped her hand around the bowl, and lit. I inhaled; something flew into my windpipe and I coughed so hard I was certain there'd be blood.

"Let's try this," she said. She took a hit and put her mouth on mine, filling my lungs with heady smoke. I took it in, all of it, desire shooting straight through me. As we languished there, I felt my whole self loosening, my mind retreating to a place somewhere around my left ear.

She showed me around her old neighborhood, and I was so high that I let her take my hand and guide me like a child, and then we were in the Brooklyn Museum, and there was a long table that never seemed to end, suggestive and flowering plates for the Primordial Goddess, for Virginia Woolf. We were somewhere in Little Russia, and then a drugstore, and then a beach, and all I could feel was her hand and the warm hug of sand around my feet.

"I want to show you something," she said, and she walked me across the Brooklyn Bridge as the sun fell away.

We took some days. We drove to Wisconsin to see the Jellyman, who as it turned out was dead. We turned and drove to the ocean, an island off the coast of Georgia. We drifted in water warm as soup. I held her, and in the levity of the water, she held me.

"The ocean," she said, "is a big lez. I can tell."

"But not one of history," I said.

"No," she agreed. "Of space and time."

I considered this. My legs gently scissored through the water. My lips tasted like salt.

"Yes," I said.

In the distance, gray humps rolled out of the sea. I imagined sharks, and the mincemeat of our bodies.

"Dolphins," she breathed, and made it so.

We sank. She was so much older than I was, but rarely reminded me. She slid her hands high up my thighs in public places and told me her darkest story and asked about mine. I felt like she was seared into my time line, unchangeable as Pompeii.

She would shove me down onto the bed and hold herself upright with my pelvis. And I would let her be there, want her to be there, feel the weight of her, the clarity that settled over me. We'd peel off our clothes because they didn't belong between us. I would look over her smooth, pale skin, the pink shock of her labia, and kiss her mouth in a way that sent quakes straight to my fault lines, and think, *Thank god we cannot make a baby.* Because she seized something inside of me that delivered me straight from her bed, from her mouth, from her cunt and her angles and low voice and dropped me into my first domestic fantasy, our first joint daydream: the Uptown Café on

Kirkwood, wiping soft little gnocchi pieces from the gabbling chin of a baby, of our baby. We would joke and call her Mara, talk about her first words and her funny hair and her bad habits. Mara, a girl. Mara, our girl.

Back in Bad's bed, in the good bed, as she slid her hand into me, and I pulled and she gave and I opened and she came without touching herself, and I responded by losing all speech, I thought, *Thank god we cannot make a baby*. We can fuck senselessly and endlessly and come into each other, no condoms or pills or fear or negotiating days of the month or slumping against bathroom counters holding that stupid white stick up for inspection, *Thank god we cannot make a baby*. And when she said, "Come for me, come in me," *Thank god we cannot make a baby*.

We made a baby. Here she is.

We were in love, and I dreamt of our future. The home in the middle of the Indiana woods. An old chapel that once housed a cloister of nuns, nuns who prayed with their shoulders pressed against each other, and who took vows and called each other Sister. A stone exterior, dried mortar pinched and oozing. Narrow paths winding through old gardens, a new garden where we have turned the earth and put things into it, things that will grow if we care for them. A large circle of stained glass, as tall as me, depicting a pouting bleeding heart in slender slivers of smoky rose glass, two of the panels cracked from age.

Then a kitchen with dark wood cabinets that open to reveal long-stemmed wineglasses, teak boxes full of cloudy silverware, a stove littered with twenty-gallon pots and pans, a collection of six dozen mugs that we have found beautiful or ironic over the years, stacks of plates with chipped edges, a good set for company that we never have. Nearby, a small table with an empty wicker basket, an assortment of solid, unpainted chairs, and catching the light from the window, a collection of glass jars, the labels peeled away, bands of glue rubbed off with a persistent finger, all with the intent of reuse.

Beyond the table, there is an altar, with candles lit for Billie Holiday and Willa Cather and Hypatia and Patsy Cline. Next to it, an old podium that once held a Bible, on which we have repurposed an old chemistry handbook as the Book of Lilith. In its pages is our own liturgical calendar: Saint Clementine and All Wayfarers; Saints Lorena Hickok and Eleanor Roosevelt, observed in the summer with blueberries to symbolize the sapphire ring; the Vigil of Saint Juliette, complete with mints and dark chocolate; Feast of the Poets, during which Mary Oliver is recited over beds of lettuce, Kay Ryan over a dish of vinegar and oil, Audre Lorde over cucumbers, Elizabeth Bishop over some carrots; the Exaltation of Patricia Highsmith, celebrated with escargots boiling in butter and garlic and cliffhangers recited by an autumn fire; the Ascension of Frida Kahlo with self-portraits and costumes; the Presentation of Shirley Jackson, a winter holiday started at dawn and ended at dusk with a gambling game played with lost milk teeth and stones. Some of them with their own books; the major and minor arcana of our little religion.

In the fridge: pickled cucumbers and green beans crowding ridged jars, two glass containers of milk, one good, one sour, a carton of half-and-half, birth control from the age of men that I still haven't thrown away, a near-black eggplant, a jar of horseradish the shape of a bar of soap, olives, sweet Italian peppers tense as hearts, soy sauce, bloody steaks hidden away in the dry fold of paper, leaking shamefully, a cheese drawer with balls of fresh mozzarella floating in their own milky-water broth, and salami with a dusty white tubing that smells, Bad swears, like semen, rotting leeks that *will* be added to the compost pile, candied onions, shallots the size of fists. In the freezer, cracked plastic ice trays with cubes swollen past their banks, pesto made from the basil plants in the garden, cookie dough that will be eaten raw despite health warnings. The cupboards, when opened, are cluttered with extra-virgin olive oil, half a dozen bottles, some full of forests of rosemary and fat bulbs of peeled garlic, sesame oil whose glass bottle never seems to lose the greasy sheen on its outside, no matter how many times it is wiped clean, coconut oil half a waxy white solid, half like plasma, cans of black-eyed peas and cream of mushroom soup, boxes of almonds, a small sack of raw organic pine nuts, stale oyster crackers. Eggs on the counter, brown and pale green and speckled and irregular in size. (One of them has gone bad, but you can't tell from the outside; you'll only figure it out if you put it in a glass of water and it floats like a witch.)

In the bedroom there is a queen-size bed, a raft in the middle of a great stone ocean. On the dresser rolls a light bulb that, if held close to the ear and agitated, would reveal the broken filament rattling in the glass. Necklaces rope old wine bottles like nooses, frosted stoppers silence glass decanters. A nightstand that, when opened, reveals—shut that, please. In the bathroom, a mirror flecked with mascara from when Bad leans in close, the amoeba of her breath growing and shrinking. You never live *with* a woman, you live inside of her, I overheard my father say to my brother once, and it was, indeed, as if, when peering into the mirror, you were blinking out through her thickly fringed eyes.

And outside the door, nature. The spinning, breathtaking cathedral of the sky arches above the trees, trees that bend lush and neon green in spring—all buds, then bloom. Sudden rain breaks the tender leaves from their stems and lays the floor thick with a bright carpet. In the tangle of branches, baby birds—the gray and pink of half-cooked shrimp and with bones like dried spaghetti—scream for their mothers.

Then the hazy buzz of summer saunters in, and the air screeches and hums. Cicada-killing wasps catch the weakest and stab them motionless, hauling the weight of their bodies and their glass wings up and up and somewhere else. Fireflies drunkenly dazzle the dark. The leaves are full, dark green, the trees dense and folded in on themselves, catching secrets, and only the violent tear of thunder and the bleach-burn of lightning can pull the grove apart.

And then autumn, the first autumn, our first autumn, the first squash dish, the sweaters, the burning smell of the space heater, never leaving the heavy blankets, the scent of smoke that reminds me of being a Girl Scout and being twelve and camping with girls who hate me. The leaves catch fire, color burning away green like a disease. More rain, another carpet of leaves, yellow as dandelions, red as pomegranate skin, orange as carrot peels. There are strange evenings when the sun sets but it rains anyway, and the sky is gold and peach and also gray and purple like a bruise. Every morning, a fine mist coats the grove. Some nights, a bloody harvest moon rises over the horizon and stains the clouds like an alien sunrise.

And then the dry and curl, the slow approach of death on trillions of radial feet, peristalsis-perfect winterbeast, the ground more exposed than we thought possible, the trees alone, the howlgroan of the wind, the smell of the coming of snow. Blizzard throughout the night, illuminated by nothing out here in the woods and in the darkness, except for a flashlight beam from the other side of the window, which catches the fat flakes descending before they vanish beyond its reach. Inside, parched and itchy skin, cool lotion whorled onto backs. Fucking, muffling the cries, holding each other in a pocket of warmth beneath the quilts. And in the morning, we shove open the door, two bodies wrapped and huffing to free themselves into a world where they do not want to go. Snowdrifts turning the nuances of nature into bumps, reminding us to keep perspective, reminding us that everything has a season, reminding us that time passes and so will we, one day. And at the edge of the clearing, mittens turn our Mara's tiny hands into cartoons, her puffy jacket is zipped up to her small nose, and a woolen hat protects her fine brown hair, and we are reminded that we are alive, we love each other all of the time and like each other most of the time, and that women can turn children into this world like breathing. Mara reaches out and up, not for us but for some unseen presence, a voice, the shadow of a once-nun, un-ghosts of a future civilization that will populate this forest with a city long after we are dead. Mara reaches up, and we walk over to her and take her hand.

Our baby cries. I hold her up to me. She is too small for food, I think. Too small for—balancing her on my hip, I tear through my half-empty fridge, shoving aside Tupperware with velvety leftovers, a can wrapped in tinfoil. I find a jar of applesauce, but none of my spoons are small enough for her mouth. I dip my finger in the applesauce and offer it to her; she sucks hard. I rest my hand against the crown of her skull; kiss her skin delicate with baby oil. She snuffles and sobs, bits of applesauce bubbling out of her mouth.

"Egg?" I ask her.

She sneezes.

"Apple? Dog? Girl? Boy?"

The baby does look like me, and Bad—my pointy nose and brown hair, my sulky pout, her round chin and detached earlobes. The open, howling mouth—that's all Bad. I stop, the danger of this joke still firing in my brain even as I realize that Bad isn't here to hear it, to pause whatever she is doing to raise an eyebrow at me, maybe scold me for saying such a thing in front of our daughter, or maybe throw a glass at my head.

I pull my phone out of my pocket with my free hand and dial. Bad's voice echoes mechanically on other end and carves new spaces into me. Beep. I leave a message.

What I say: "Why did you leave her with me?"

What I want to say: "This almost broke me, but it didn't. It made me stronger than before. You have made me better. Thank you. I will love you until the end of time."

I wanted too much from her, I think. I demanded too much.

"I love you," I murmured while asleep, while awake, into her hair, into her neck.

"Please don't call me that," I reminded her. "I would never talk like that to you."

"I only want you, I swear," I said, when paranoia crept into her voice like an infection.

I believe in a world where impossible things happen. Where love can outstrip brutality, can neutralize it, as though it never was, or transform it into something new and more beautiful. Where love can outdo nature.

The baby nurses. I don't know on what. But she suckles just the same. Her gums catch and it hurts but I don't want her to stop, because I am her mother and she needs what she needs, even if it's not a true thing. She bites, and I cry out, but she is so small, and I cannot put her down.

"Mara," I whisper. She looks at me, directly at me, as if she recognized her name. I press my lips to her forehead and rock her back and forth, quietly gasping for air. She is real, she is real, she is solid in my arms, she smells clean and new. No mistakes. She is not yet a girl or a monster or anything. She is just a baby. She is ours.

I make Mara a crib by shoving my bed into a corner. I build walls with small embroidered pillows. I lay her down.

She starts to scream again. It comes from nowhere and goes on, endless and even as the horizon at sea. It doesn't taper, she doesn't inhale for breath, her flailing hands catch my face, cut it a little. I lay her down on the bed.

"Mara," I say. "Mara, please, please don't," and she doesn't stop, it goes on and on. For hours I bounce next to her on the bed, and the howling has filled the room and I cannot unhear it, and the clean smell of baby is replaced by something red-hot, like the burner of an electric stove with nothing on it. I touch her little feet and she screams and I blow raspberries on her belly and she screams and something inside of me is breaking; I am a continent but I will not hold.

A teacher overheard Bad screaming at me on the phone from the next bathroom stall. I knew she was there, I saw her high-heeled feet splayed on the tile, I heard her take in a breath as Bad's voice dropped low and cold and leaked through the receiver like gas. She waited until I was gone to leave. She awkwardly addressed it in the hallway that afternoon, her hands twisting around the cap of a ballpoint pen.

"I guess," she said, "all I am saying is that it's just not normal. I'm just worried for you."

"You are so kind to reach out," I said.

"I'm just saying that if it always sounds like that, then even if you think something is there, nothing is there." She accidentally flipped the cap out of her hands, and it went skittering down the long hallway. "Let me know if you want me to call someone, okay?"

I nodded, and she walked away. Even as she vanished around the corner, I was still nodding.

Mara pauses for breath. So much time has passed that light streaks the sky outside of the window. She takes me in again, my whole self into her eyes, all of my shame and pain and the truth of her mothers, the honest truth of them. I feel a jolt, my secrets slipping from me, unwilling. Then the screaming begins again, but I can endure it because of that precious moment, that break. My tolerance is fresh again, my love renewed. If she gives me one of those every day or so, I should be fine. I can do this. I can be a good mother.

I brush my finger along her curls and sing her a song from my childhood.

"Bill Grogan's goat, was feelin' fine, ate three red shirts, from off the line. Bill took a stick, gave him a whack, and tied him to, the railroad—"

My voice cracks and fades into silence. She pedals her feet in the air and howls and my ears are ringing and I crawl onto the bed next to her, my pleas swallowed by her voice.

I don't want to leave the room. I don't want to sleep. I am afraid that if I sleep, I will wake up and Mara will be gone, and in the silence entropy will take over, and my cells will expand and I will become one with the air. If I turn away, even for a second, I will look back and this will be just a mass of blankets and pillows, as empty a bed as it ever has been. If I blink, her form could dissolve beneath my fingers, and once again, I will be just me: undeserving, alone.

When I wake up, she is still here. It feels like a sign. If she cried in the night I did not hear it. I slept the kind of sleep where you wake up and know that you didn't flop around like a fucking hooked fish, you didn't keep me up all goddamned night with your sleep-weeping, Jesus Christ, you know that you were good and still. So my joints feel like the fat rubber bands used to bind broccoli, and my face is lined where I'd stupidly slept sleep-pressed against the seams of the quilt's patchwork. Mara is not crying. She's pumping her arms and legs around like pistons. Her eyes are opening and closing: morning glories screwing up tightly in the midday sun, Venus flytraps yawning wide to vibrations and heat.

I stand up and squint into the morning. Mara makes a squeak-ing noise. I pick her up. She seems heavier than yesterday. Is that possible?

As soon as I step out of the bedroom, she begins to scream again.

We take a bus to Indianapolis, transfer in a daze. She sleeps in my arms and does not stir, except to scream, decibels swallowing all conscious thought. The bodies around me, rumpled and stale, do not react appreciatively to the silence or angrily to the sound, for which I am grateful.

When we get off the bus in Bloomington, I realize— I remember—that it is spring. I find a ride with a kind woman who reminds me of someone I have forgotten. We drive along the highway until I ask her to stop.

"There's nothing here," she says. Her body language is almost purposefully relaxed.

The leaves rustle, as if in answer.

"Let me take you downtown," she says. "Or is there someone I can call for you?"

I get out, Mara in the crook of my arm.

It has rained recently. The mud is caking around my sneakers, more and more with each step. I walk like a colossal monster, ready to level a city.

There, up the slope of a hill, is a house. Our house. I recognize the stained glass, the smoke curling from the chimney and lacing up through the canopy of the trees. The picnic table outside needs a fresh coat of paint. An aging German shepherd, all bones and skin, is draped over the edge of a porch, his tail thumping in happiness as we approach.

"Otto," I say, and he lets me squeeze the ruff of his neck. He taps his jowls against my palm, and then licks it clean.

The door is unlocked because Bad and I trust our neighbors, the birds. Inside, the floors are stone.

I recognize the cabinets, the bed. Mara is silent in my arms. She does not even squirm. Perhaps she has been crying so much because she hasn't been home, but now she is home and now she is quiet. I sit down at a desk and roll a heavy pen across the wood. I run my fingers over the row of books alongside the wall. Behind the bookcase, a thin crack meanders through the plaster, deliberate. I touch it with my fingertip, trace it up, up, up until it is past my height. Part of me wants to move the bookshelf, look behind it, but there is no need. I know what's there.

I unwrap cured salmon from the fridge and examine it. The meat is drawn back from the forgotten pinbones like diseased gum

from teeth. I make a mark deep in the flesh with my finger, and
something inside of me is sated.

I press my cheek against the wavy glass windowpane. Otto has
followed us inside and is trailing behind me, bumping his cold nose
into Mara's foot. I pull a cookbook off the counter and flip it open.
The cover *thuds*. Aunt Julia's Bean Salad, I read. So much dill.

The last night of us, Bad threw me into a wall. I wish I could remember why. It seems like context would matter. She was all bone
and muscle and skin and light and laughter one minute and then a
tornado the next, a shadow passing over her face like a solar eclipse.
My head cracked the plaster. Light sparked behind my eyes.

"You cunt," she screamed. "I hate you. I fucking hate you. I have
always hated you."

I crawled to the bathroom and locked the door. From the outside, she rained punches into the wall like a hailstorm, and I turned
on the shower and undressed and stepped inside. I'm a Cancer. A
water baby, always. For a moment I was there, the Indiana woods,
the rain striking the leaves, the gentle Sunday-morning drizzle
during which we slept, only waking to see a sleepy, preteen Mara
come in, complain about a nightmare, and curl into our arms. This
will not always last, one day she will be too big for this, and for
us, her old mothers. Then the not-memory washed away like a wet
painting in a storm, and I was in the shower, shaking, and she was
outside, losing me, and there was no way for me to tell her not to.
There was no way for me to tell her that we are so close, we are so
close, please don't do this now, we are so fucking close.

"What do you think, Mara?" I ask her, spinning around a few times
before coming to rest against a wall. I lay her down on the heirloom

quilt that is snapped smartly over the big bed. One day I want to teach Mara to quilt like this, the way her grandmother did and the way that I am learning. We could start small. Baby quilts. You can do one of those in a night.

Otto barks.

The door opens, and around it curves a skinny arm. Then a face, and a bright yellow backpack. A little girl of ten or eleven, hair in an unraveling braid. It is Mara, old enough to walk, old enough to speak. Old enough to be bullied and then to face the bullies down. Old enough to ask questions without answers and have problems without solutions. Behind her, another child, a boy—her baby brother, Tristan. I remember his birth like it happened last week, like it is happening now, he was all blood and sideways, he was up in my ribs and refused the midwife's advances. Even now my stomach is still not the same, the walls once severed and pulled apart. And he will grow, and then he grew, and Tristan followed after Mara, and follows her still. She said she hated it but she loved it, I could tell she adored the attention. Mara and Tristan, brown-haired children. Brown like—someone's grandmother. Maybe mine.

A man behind them, and a woman. Both staring at me.

The woman tells Mara to stay away, the man clutches Baby Tristan across his chest. They ask me who I am, and I answer them. Otto barks. The woman calls him, but he barks at her and at me and does not cede his ground.

Mara, remember how you kicked sand into that neighbor child's eyes? I yelled at you and made you apologize in your best dress, and that night I cried by myself in the bathroom because you are Bad's child as much as you are mine. Remember when you ran into the plate glass window and cut your arms so badly we had to drive you to the nearest hospital in the pickup truck, and when it was over

Bad begged me to replace the backseat because of all the blood? Or when Tristan told us that he wanted to invite a boy to prom and you put your arm around him like this? Mara, remember? Your own babies? Your husband with his Captain Ahab beard and calloused hands and the house you bought in Vermont? Mara? How you still love your little brother with the ferocity of a star; an all-consuming love that will only end when one of you collapses? The drawings you handed us as children? Your paintings of dragons, Tristan's photographs of dolls, your stories about anger, his poems about angels? The science experiments in the yard, blackening the grass to gloss? Your lives sated and solid, strange but safe? Do you remember? Why are you crying, don't cry, don't. You cried a lot as a baby but you've been so stoic ever since.

Inside of me, a voice: *There was nothing tying you to her and you made it anyway, you made them anyway, fuck you, you made them anyway.*

To Mara and her brother, I say: Stop running, you'll fall, stop running, you'll break something, stop running, your mother will see, she will see and she will be so angry and she will yell and we cannot, we cannot, I cannot.

I say: Don't leave the faucet on. You'll flood the house, don't do it, you promised it would never happen again. Don't flood the house, the bills, don't flood the house, the rugs, don't flood the house, my loves, or we could lose you both. We've been bad mothers and have not taught you how to swim.

ESPECIALLY HEINOUS
272 Views of *Law & Order: SVU*

SEASON I

"PAYBACK": Stabler and Benson investigate the castration and murder of a New York City cab driver. They discover that the victim had assumed the identity of another man years before, because he was wanted by police. In the end, Stabler discovers that the stolen identity of the man in question was also stolen, and he and Benson have to begin the investigation all over again. That night, as he tries unsuccessfully to sleep, Stabler hears a strange noise. A deep drumming, two beats. It seems like it's coming from his basement. When he investigates the basement, it sounds like it's coming from outside.

"A SINGLE LIFE": The old woman couldn't bear getting dressed alone anymore. The solitary donning of shoes broke her heart over and over again. The unlocked front door, through which any neighbor could wander, would have been an afterthought, but there was no thought, after.

"OR JUST LOOK LIKE ONE": Two underage models are attacked while walking home from a club. They are raped and murdered. To add insult to injury, they are confused with two other raped and murdered underage models, who coincidentally are their respective twins, and both pairs are buried beneath the wrong tombstones.

"HYSTERIA": Benson and Stabler investigate the murder of a young woman who is initially believed to be a prostitute and the latest in a long line of connected victims. "I hate this goddamned city," Benson says to Stabler, dabbing her eyes with a deli napkin. Stabler rolls his eyes and starts the car.

"WANDERLUST": The old DA irons her hair before court, the way her mother showed her. After she loses the case, she packs three changes of clothes in a suitcase and gets into her car. She calls Benson from her cell phone. "Sorry, buddy. Hitting the road. Not sure when I'll be back." Benson pleads with her to stay. The old DA tosses the cell phone onto the road and pulls away from the curb. A passing taxi reduces it to splinters.

"SOPHOMORE JINX": The second time the basketball team covers up a murder, the coach decides that he's finally had enough.

"UNCIVILIZED": They find the boy in Central Park, looking like no one had ever loved him. "His body was crawling with ants," Stabler says. "Ants." Two days later, they arrest his teacher, who as it turns out had loved him just fine.

"STALKED": Benson and Stabler aren't allowed to notch any of the precinct's furniture, so they each have their own private system. Benson's headboard has eight scores that run along the curved oak edge like a spine. Stabler's kitchen chair has nine.

"STOCKS AND BONDAGE": Benson takes the bag of rotten vegetables out of the trunk when Stabler isn't looking. She throws it into a garbage can and it hits the empty bottom, wet and heavy. It splits open like a body that's been in the Hudson.

"CLOSURE": "It was inside of me," the woman says, pulling the bendy straw out of shape like a misused accordion. "But now it is outside of me. I would like to keep it that way."

"BAD BLOOD": Stabler and Benson will never forget the case where solving the crime was so much worse than the crime itself.

"RUSSIAN LOVE POEM": When they bring the mother up to the stand, the new DA asks her to state her name. She closes her eyes, shakes her head, rocks back and forth in her chair. She begins to sing a song softly under her breath, not in English, the syllables rolling out of her mouth like smoke. The DA looks to the judge for help, but he is staring at the witness, his eyes as distant as if he were lost in the forest of his own memory.

"DISROBED": A disoriented, naked, pregnant woman is discovered wandering around Midtown. She is arrested for indecent exposure.

"LIMITATIONS": Stabler discovers that even New York City ends.

"ENTITLED": "You can't do this to me!" the man shouts as he is escorted to the witness stand. "Don't you know who I am?" The DA closes her eyes. "Sir, I just need you to confirm that you did tell the police you saw a blue Honda fleeing the scene." The man pounds his open hand on the witness stand in defiance. "I do not recognize your authority!" The mother of the dead girl begins screaming so loudly that her husband carries her out of the courtroom.

"THE THIRD GUY": Stabler never told Benson about his little brother. But he also never told her about his older brother, which was understandable, because he didn't know about him, either.

"MISLEADER": Father Jones has never touched a child, but when he closes his eyes at night, he still remembers his high school girlfriend: her soft thighs, her lined hands, the way she dropped off that roof like a falcon.

"CHAT ROOM": Convinced that his teenaged daughter is in danger from cyberpredators, a father takes a crowbar to the family computer. He throws the pieces into the fireplace, strikes a match. His daughter complains of a light head, a burning in her chest. She calls him "Mom" with tears in her voice. She dies on a Saturday.

"CONTACT": Stabler discovers that his wife believes she saw a UFO, back when she was in her early twenties. He lies awake all night, wondering if this explains the memory loss, the PTSD, the night terrors. His wife wakes up weeping and screaming, on cue.

"REMORSE": At night, Stabler makes a list of the day's regrets. "Didn't tell Benson," he scrawls. "Ate more burrito than I had room for. Misspent that gift card. Hit that guy harder than I meant to." His wife comes up behind him and rubs his shoulder idly before crawling into bed. "Haven't told my wife today. Will probably not tell her tomorrow."

"NOCTURNE": The ghost of one of the murdered, misburied underage models begins to haunt Benson. She has bells for eyes, tiny brass ones dangling from the top of each socket, the hammers not quite touching her cheekbones. The ghost does not know her own name. She stands over Benson's bed, the right bell tinkling faintly, and then the left, and then the right again. This happens four nights in a row, at 2:07 a.m. Benson starts sleeping with a crucifix and pungent ropes of garlic, because she does not understand the difference between vampires and murdered teenagers. Not yet.

"SLAVES": The precinct's interns are monsters. When it's slow, they dick around on the phones. Into the dial tones, they chirp, "SVU, Manhattan's rapiest police department!" They have theories about Stabler and Benson. They place bets. They place lilacs (Benson's favorite) in her locker and daisies (Stabler's) in his. The interns drug Benson's and Stabler's coffees and then, after they fall asleep in the back room, the interns shove the cots close together and place both the detectives in compromising positions. Benson and Stabler wake up hours later, their hands on each other's cheeks, both wet with tears.

SEASON 2

"WRONG IS RIGHT": Benson wakes up in the middle of the night. She is not in her bed. She is in her pajamas, in the dark. Her hand is on a handle. A door is open. A confused-looking panda is watching her with dewy eyes. Benson shuts the door. She passes two llamas chewing thoughtfully on the sign for a hot dog stand. In the parking lot of the zoo, her car is idling against a cement post. She changes into the spare set of clothes she keeps in the trunk. She calls it in. "Ecoterrorists," she tells Stabler. He nods, jots down something in his notebook, then looks back up at her. "Do you smell garlic?" he asks.

"HONOR": Stabler dreams that a man at a Renaissance Faire insults Stabler's wife, and Stabler punches him in his self-satisfied face. When Stabler wakes up, he decides to tell his wife this story. He rolls over. She is gone. Stabler has never been to a Renaissance Faire.

"CLOSURE: PART 2": "It's not that I hate men," the woman says. "I'm just terrified of them. And I'm okay with that fear."

"LEGACY": Over breakfast, Stabler's daughter asks him about Benson's family. Stabler says that Benson doesn't have a family. "You always say that family is a man's one true wealth," says Stabler's daughter. Stabler thinks about this. "It's true," he says. "But Benson is not a man."

"BABY KILLER": Benson keeps the condoms in her nightstand drawer refreshed, and throws the expired ones away. She dutifully takes her pill at the same time every morning. She makes dates and always keeps them.

"NONCOMPLIANCE": The girl-with-bells-for-eyes tells Benson to go to Brooklyn. They can communicate, now, with the bells. (Benson taught herself Morse code.) Benson never goes to Brooklyn, but she agrees. She rides the train late at night, so late that there is only one man in her car, and he is sleeping on a duffel bag. As they shoot through the tunnels, the man looks blearily at Benson, then unzips his duffel bag and vomits into it, almost politely. The vomit is white, like Cream of Wheat. He rezips the bag. Benson gets off two stops too early, and ends up walking through Prospect Park for a very long time.

"ASUNDER": Stabler works out every morning at the precinct. He does tricep curls. He does crunches. He jogs on a treadmill. He thinks he hears his daughter's voice crying his name. Startled, he trips on the treadmill and his whole body slams against the cinder block wall. The path rolls toward him in endless loops.

"TAKEN": "It was dark," says Stabler's wife. "I was walking home alone. It was raining. Well, not really raining. Spitting, I guess. Misting. It was misting and the light from the street lamps was all pooled and golden and thick as oil. And I was breathing deeply and it felt healthy, healthy and right to be walking through that night." Stabler hears the drumming again. It shakes the water glass on the nightstand. Stabler's wife doesn't seem to notice.

"PIXIES": "Get out!" Benson screams, hurling pillows at the girl-with-bells-for-eyes. She's brought a friend this time, a small girl with hair in tight cornrows and her lips stitched shut. Benson gets out of bed and tries to push them away, but her hands and upper body go through both of them as if they were nothing. They taste like mildew in her mouth. She remembers being eight and kneeling before the humidifier in her room, taking in the steam as if it were the only way she could drink.

"CONSENT": "Stabler?" says Benson carefully. Stabler looks up from his raw knees. Benson unfolds the tiny square alcohol wipe and hands it to him. "Can I sit here? Can I help?" He nods wordlessly, lets her rub his knees. He hisses with pain through his teeth. "What did you do?" she asks. "The treadmill? Are these from the treadmill?" Stabler shakes his head. He can't say. He can't.

"ABUSE": More regrets. The lines crowd the page. "Showed Benson my skinned knees. Allowed her to assist me. Told my wife nothing was wrong. Let my wife tell me that nothing was wrong and didn't tell her that I could tell she was lying."

"SECRETS": The girls-with-bells-for-eyes tell Benson to go to Yonkers. Benson refuses and begins to burn sage in her apartment.

"VICTIMS": Her apartment is so crowded with ghosts that, for the first time since she can remember, Benson stays at someone else's place for the night. Her date is an investment banker, a boring and stupid man with a fat, piss-mean tabby who tries to suffocate Benson with her bulk. When she returns to her apartment the next morning, sore and angry and smelling like cat pee, the girls-with-bells-for-eyes are waiting for her, draped over every surface like Dalí's clocks. They crowd around her as she slowly brushes her teeth. She spits, rinses, and turns. "All right," she says. "What do you want me to do?"

"PARANOIA": "I'm not suppressing anything!" Stabler's wife yells at him. "Tell me about the night with the aliens," says Stabler. He is trying to learn. He is trying to figure it out. "It was misty," she says. "It was spitting." He hears the banging again, the tone, sounding from somewhere in the house. It makes his head ache. "Yes, I know, I know," Stabler says. "The light pooled around the lampposts. Like oil. There were so many iron gates. I walked past them and ran my fingers over their loops and whorls, and then my fingers smelled like metal." "Yes," says Stabler. "But then what?" But his wife is asleep.

"COUNTDOWN": The madman promises that there is a bomb hidden under a bench in Central Park. "Do you know how many benches there are in Central Park?" shouts Stabler, clutching an intern by his shirt collar. They send police officers to Central Park to chase people off benches as if they are pigeons, or the homeless. Nothing happens.

"RUNAWAY": The girl-with-bells-for-eyes sends Benson into every borough. Benson rides the subway. Eventually, she has seen every stop at least once. She is beginning to memorize the murals, the water stains, the smells. The Columbus Circle station smells like a urinal. Cortelyou smells, unnervingly, like lilacs. For the first time in a while, Benson thinks about Stabler. Back in her apartment, a girl-with-bells-for-eyes tries to tell Benson a story. *I was a virgin. When he took me, I popped.*

"FOLLY": "There is a case," says the captain. "A young boy has accused his mother of beating him into unconsciousness with a toilet plunger. This is a tricky one, though. The boy is the son of a political heavyweight with deep pockets. He golfs with the mayor. His wife is—Benson? Benson, are you listening?"

"MANHUNT": Stabler has determined that he is not even a little bit gay. He swallows his disappointment. His mouth tastes like orange peel.

"PARASITES": "Oh fuck," says Stabler's wife. "Fuck. Sweetie, the kids have lice. I need your help." They stand the kids in the tub. The oldest daughter rolls her eyes. Her mother helps them scrub their scalps, and the younger three whine that the shampoo burns. Stabler feels serene for the first time in months.

"PIQUE": "The victim has ties to the modeling industry," says the captain. "But we're having trouble tracking down where she lived. She might have come from another country. She was only fourteen." He hangs her autopsy photo on the bulletin board, her face flat and pale. The thumbtack pops into the cork and Benson jumps in her chair.

"SCOURGE": Stabler hears it again. The sound, the drumming. It seems to come from the break room. When he goes there, it sounds like it is coming from the interrogation room. Inside the interrogation room, he hears it again. He bangs his hands on the two-way mirror, imitating the sound, hoping to lure it to him, but all is quiet.

SEASON 3

"REPRESSION": In the middle of a sermon, Father Jones begins screaming. His parishioners look on in fear as he clings to the pulpit, wailing a name over and over. Convinced that this is an admission of guilt of some kind or another, the diocese calls Benson and Stabler. In his office, Benson knocks a pen off his desk, and Father Jones dives after it, howling.

"WRATH": Benson reaches up from her bed, like a baby. A girl-with-bells-for-eyes stands over her, like a mother. Benson grabs at the bells, pulls them as hard as she can. The girl-with-bells-for-eyes jerks violently, and every light bulb in Benson's apartment explodes, covering the carpet with glass.

"STOLEN": First it's a candy bar. The next day, a lighter. Stabler wants to stop, but he learned long ago to choose his battles.

"ROOFTOP": "Just tell me what you remember, Father." *Click.* "Okay. Her name was—well, I don't want to say it. She hated water and grass, so we picnicked on the top of her apartment building. She lived in that building with her mother. I loved her. I lost myself in her body. We lay a blanket over the gravel. I fed her orange slices. She told me she was a prophet, and that she had a vision that one day I would take an innocent life. I said no, no. She climbed up onto the cement wall that circled the roof. She stood there and declared her vision again. She said she was sorry. She didn't even fall like I expected. She simply knelt into the air."

"TANGLED": Stabler finds Benson sleeping on a sagging cot in the back room at the precinct. She wakes up when the door opens. She looks like she has "run the gauntlet," which is something Stabler's mother used to say before she left. Come to think of it, it's the last phrase Stabler can remember her speaking before that door swung shut.

"REDEMPTION": Benson accidentally catches a rapist when she Google-stalks her newest OkCupid date. She can't decide whether or not to mark this in the "success" ("caught rapist") or "failure" ("date didn't work out") column. She marks it in both.

"SACRIFICE": Benson leaves her handsome date at the table, in the restaurant, waiting for the drinks. She turns down an empty side street. She takes off her shoes and walks down the center of the road. It is too hot for April. She can feel her feet darkening from the blacktop. She should be afraid of broken glass but she is not. In front of a vacant lot, she stops. She reaches down and touches the pavement. It is breathing. Its two-toned heartbeat makes her clavicle vibrate. She can feel it. She is suddenly, irrevocably certain that the earth is breathing. She knows that New York is riding the back of a giant monster. She knows this more clearly than she has ever known anything before.

"INHERITANCE": The phrase *run the gauntlet* is stuck in Stabler's head, like water dripping and sluicing around his inner ear. He presses the muscles at the hinge of his jaw and cracks it. The crack takes the place of the single syllable of *run*. He does it again. *Crack* the gauntlet. Run the *crack*let. Run.

"CARE": Stabler is worried about Benson, but he cannot tell her.

"RIDICULE": Benson does her twice-monthly grocery trip. She drives her car to a grocery store in Queens and buys three hundred dollars' worth of produce. It will make her fridge look like the Garden of Eden. She will not eat it while she gnaws on chewy French toast in the Styrofoam container from the diner. The produce will, predictably, rot. Her fridge will smell overwhelmingly like dirt. She will collect it in garbage bags and throw it in the public trash can near the station before her next trip.

"MONOGAMY": Stabler wakes up one night to find his wife staring at the ceiling, tears soaking the pillow next to her head. "It was spitting," she says. "My fingers smelled like metal. I was so scared." For the first time, Stabler understands.

"PROTECTION": Benson crosses the street without looking. The taxi driver slams on his brakes, his bumper stopping a hair's width from Benson's shins. When she looks through the windshield, she sees a teenage boy in the passenger seat, eyes closed. When he opens them, the sun glints off the curves of the bells. The taxi driver screams at Benson as she stares.

"PRODIGY": "Look at me, Dad!" Stabler's daughter says, laughing, twirling. As clearly as if he were watching a movie, he sees her in two years' time, swatting a boyfriend's hands away in a backseat, harder and harder. She screams. Stabler starts. She has fallen to the ground and is clutching her ankle, crying.

"COUNTERFEIT": "You don't understand," says Father Jones to Benson. There are dark curves under his eyes, sacs the color of bruised apples. He is wearing a terry cloth bathrobe that says "Susan" in machine-stitched cursive letters on the breast pocket. "I can't help you. I'm having a crisis of faith." He tries to close the door, but Benson stops it with her hand. "I'm having a crisis of function," she says. "Tell me. What do you know about ghosts?"

"EXECUTION": The medical examiner pulls back the sheet from the dead girl's face. "Raped and strangled," she says, her voice hollow. "Your murderer pressed his thumbs into the girl's windpipe until she died. No prints, though." Stabler thinks that the girl looks a little like his wife's high school photo. Benson is certain she can see the jelly of the girl's eyes receding beneath their closed lids, certain she can hear the sound of bells. In the car, they are both quiet.

"POPULAR": They question everyone they can think of: her friends and enemies. The girls she bullied, the boys who loved her and hated her, the parents who thought she was wonderful and the parents who thought she was bad news. Benson stumbles into the precinct late, bleary-eyed. "My theory," she says, drinking her coffee slowly, with shaking hands, "my theory is that it was her coach, and my theory is that the missing underwear will be found in his office." The search warrant is issued so quickly that they find the underwear in his top desk drawer, still damp with blood.

"SURVEILLANCE": Benson doesn't know how to explain to Stabler the heartbeat beneath the ground. She is certain that she can hear it all the time now, deep and low. The girls-with-bells-for-eyes have taken to knocking before coming in. Sometimes. Benson takes taxis to faraway neighborhoods, gets down on her hands and knees on the street and the sidewalk and, once, in a woman's vegetable garden that took up her entire postage-stamp lawn. She can hear it everywhere. The drumming, echoing, echoing in the deep.

"GUILT": Benson can translate the bells so well, now. There is no delay between their chiming and her understanding. She pulls her pillow over her head until she can barely breathe. *Give us voices. Give us voices. Give us voices. Tell him. Tell him. Tell him. Find us. Find us. Find us. Please. Please. Please.*

"JUSTICE": Benson gets a pack of small children. Their bells are especially tiny, the ring higher than most. Benson is drunk. She holds her bed, which feels like an amusement park ride, pitching and rolling. *We will never ride the Tilt-A-Whirl again, ever. Get up! Get up!* they command her. She puts her head on her cell phone and uses speed dial. "My theory," she says to Stabler, "my theory is that I have a theory." Stabler offers to come over. "My theory," she says, "my theory is that there is no god." The children's bells ring so furiously that Benson can't even hear Stabler's reply over the din. When Stabler comes over and lets himself in with the spare key, he finds Benson bent over the toilet, heaving, crying.

"FREED": "It's the whole city," Benson says to herself as she drives. She imagines Stabler in the seat next to her. "I've been all over. It's the whole fucking city. The heartbeats. The girls." She clears her throat and tries again. "I know it sounds crazy. I just have a feeling." She pauses, then says, "Stabler, do you believe in ghosts?" Then, "Stabler, do you trust me?"

"DENIAL": Stabler finds the police report for his wife's rape. It's so old that he has to call in a favor from a guy in the records department. The sound of the paper scraping against the thin manila envelope slows Stabler's heart.

"COMPETENCE": Stabler and Benson respond to a report of a rape in Central Park. When they get there, the mutilated body has already been taken to the medical examiner's office. A confused junior cop is busy rolling yellow crime scene tape from tree to tree. "Weren't you just here?" he asks them.

"SILENCE": Benson and Stabler grab beers at a pub down the street from the station. They hold the frosted mugs tightly in their hands, leave glossy, sweating prints that look like angels. They say nothing.

SEASON 4

"CHAMELEON": Abler and Henson respond to a report of a rape in Central Park. They examine the mutilated body. "Cult," says Abler. "Occultists," says Henson. "A cult of occultists," they say in unison. "Take the body away."

"DECEPTION": Henson sleeps through every night. She wakes up refreshed. She eats a sesame seed bagel with chive cream cheese for breakfast, and with it a mug of green tea. Abler tucks in his kids and spoons his wife, who laughs in her sleep. When they get up, she relates to him the very funny joke from her dream, and he laughs, too. The children make pancakes. The hardwood floors are flooded with pools of light.

"VULNERABLE": For three days in a row, there is not a single victim in the entire precinct. No rapes. No murders. No rape-murders. No kidnappings. No child pornography made, bought, or sold. No molestations. No sexual assaults. No sexual harassments. No forced prostitution. No human trafficking. No subway gropings. No incest. No indecent exposures. No stalking. Not even an unwanted dirty phone call. Then, in the gloaming of a Wednesday, a man wolf-whistles at a woman on her way to an AA meeting. The whole city releases its long-held breath, and everything returns to normal.

"LUST": Abler and Henson are sleeping together, but no one knows. Henson is the best lay that Abler's ever had. Henson's had better.

"DISAPPEARING ACTS": "What are you doing here again?" the victim's grandmother asks them. Benson looks at Stabler, and Stabler at Benson, and they turn, confused, back to her. "I already told you everything I know," the old woman says, waving a gnarled hand at them dismissively. She slams the door so hard a flowerpot jumps off the porch railing and lands on the lawn. "Did you come and see her?" Benson asks Stabler. He shakes his head. "You?" he asks her. Inside, a Mills Brothers record starts up with pops and scratches. *Shine little glowworm, glimmer, glimmer.* "No," Benson says. "Never."

"ANGELS": Abler's sons bring home perfect grades and don't even need braces. Henson's many lovers bring her to increasingly ascending levels of ecstatic transcendence vis-à-vis the clitoris, vis-à-vis asking her what she wants, *yes*, what she, *yes*, what, *yes yes yes fuck yes.*

"DOLLS": The bells ring, ring, ring through the night, the peals stripping skin from Benson's body, or that's how it feels, anyway. *Faster, faster, go faster.* "I need to sleep," Benson says. "I need to sleep to go faster." *That makes no sense. We never get to sleep. We never sleep. We tirelessly pursue justice at all hours.* "Don't you remember needing sleep?" Benson asks wearily from her unwashed sheets. "You were human, once." *No no no no no no no no.*

"WASTE": There are so many notches in Benson's headboard—so many successes, so many failures, maybe she should have kept them apart?—that the wood looks like it's been chewed away by termites. When the two-tone beat sounds, the chips and shavings tremble on her carpet and nightstand.

"JUVENILE": "Five-year-olds murder six-year-olds," Benson says dully, the skin beneath her eyes dusky ash from lack of sleep.

"People can be monsters, or vulnerable as lambs. They—no, we—are perpetrators and victims at the same time. It takes so little to tip the scale one way or the other. This is the world we live in, Stabler." She sips noisily on her Diet Coke. She tries to look away from Stabler's wet eyes.

"RESILIENCE": Benson watches a lot of TV on her days off. She gets an idea. She spreads a line of salt along her threshold, on the windowsills. That night, for the first time in months, the girls-with-bells-for-eyes stay away.

"DAMAGED": Stabler rubs his wife's shoulders. "Can we talk?" She shakes her head. "You don't want to talk?" She nods. "You want to talk?" She shakes her head. "You don't want to talk?" She nods. Stabler kisses her hair. "Later. We'll talk later."

"RISK": Abler and Henson solve their ninth case in a row, and their captain takes them out for celebratory steaks and cocktails. Abler gnaws on hunks of steak too big for his gullet, Henson polishes off one dirty martini after another. Ten of them. Eleven. A man on the opposite side of the restaurant, who has been nibbling birdlike on a Caesar salad, begins to choke. He turns blue. A stranger delivers the Heimlich, and a half-chewed wad of meat lands on the table of a lifelong teetotaler who is starting to feel a little strange. "I feel like I've had twelve drinks," she says, giggling, hiccupping. She has. Henson drives Abler home, and they laugh. Thirteen blocks from the restaurant, they grope at each other, kissing as they stumble out of the car. Henson puts Abler's hand on her breast, and her nipple tightens.

"ROTTEN": Someone keeps leaving sacks of perfectly ripe produce in a trash can. Henson frequently finds herself pulling it out, taking it home, scrubbing the beets hard. How crazy. How weird to let a good thing go to waste.

"MERCY": The gunman lets all of the hostages go, including himself.

"PANDORA": Benson is lonely without the bells. Her apartment is so quiet. She stands in her doorway, staring down at the white line. She takes her big toe and probes it. She remembers being at the beach with her mother when she was a child and burning her feet on the hot, smooth sand. She pushes her toe, breaking the line, and says, "Oops," but doesn't really mean it. The children come rushing at her like a flash flood rolling through a narrow gorge. Their bells ring chaotic, gleeful and rapturous and angry, like a swarm of euphoric bees. They tickle her skin with their desperation. She has never felt so loved.

"TORTURED": *You are the only one we trust*, the girls-with-bells-for-eyes say to Benson. *Not that other one.* Benson assumes they mean Stabler.

"PRIVILEGE": Abler and Henson notice the bullet casing buried in the dirt. They notice the smear of blood near the door frame, the orientation of the street. They look at each other and know that they're each calculating the sunlight on this avenue at the time of the crime. By the time they get inside, they know to arrest the wife. They don't even have to ask her any questions.

"DESPERATE": "If you are dead, you can see everything," Benson says to the girls-with-bells-for-eyes. "Tell me who the others are. The—the doppelgängers. Why are they so much better at everything than me and Stabler? Tell me, please." The bells ring and ring and ring.

"APPEARANCES": Benson sees Henson coming out of the precinct. Her stomach gnarls. The same face, but prettier. The same hair, but bouncier. She must find out what kind of products she uses. Before she kills her.

"DOMINANCE": "You're a lunatic," Henson says, struggling against the handcuffs, and ropes, and chair, and chains. Benson leaves Stabler another message. "My partner is going to come and get me, you'll see," Henson says. "He'll come for me."

"FALLACY": "Stabler will come and back me up. He knows what you've been doing. Stealing our cases. Pretending to be us."

"FUTILITY": Stabler pulls out his cell phone as the ringtone dies. *14 New Voicemails.* He can't do it, he can't. The phone buzzes in his hand like an insect. *15.* He turns it off.

"GRIEF": Abler comes for Henson. Of course he does. He loves her. Benson watches as he gently unties the ropes, unwraps the chains, unlocks the handcuffs, and lets her stand up from the chair on her own. Benson is holding her gun in her hand. She unloads three bullets into each of them, not expecting much. They keep moving as if nothing were happening. They foxtrot down the street and out of sight.

"PERFECT": "Detective, how can you *not* account for bullets missing from your gun? What are you listening to? Benson! [. . .] No, I can't hear it. [. . .] There's no sound, what are you talking about?"

"SOULLESS": "Father Jones," Benson says, her forehead pressing into the rough carpet in his foyer, "something is really wrong with me." He puts his tumbler down, sits next to her. "Yeah," he says. "I know the feeling."

SEASON 5

"TRAGEDY": Miles away from the precinct, a teenage boy and his seven-year-old sister drop dead in the middle of their walk home from school. When they are autopsied, bullets are pulled from the purple meat of their organs, though there are no entrance wounds on either of their bodies. The medical examiner is baffled. The bullets *clink clink clink clink clink clink* in the metal dish.

"MANIC": The DA laughs and laughs. She laughs so hard she coughs. She laughs so hard she pees a little. She falls down onto the floor and does a little quarter-roll, still laughing. There is a knock on the bathroom door, and Benson pushes open the door, uncertainly. "Are you all right? The jury has come back. Are you—are you okay?"

"MOTHER": "Your mother called today," Stabler's wife says to him. "Please call her back so I don't have to make an excuse for you." Stabler looks up from his desk, where the manila envelope is resting, so anemically thin he wants to scream. He looks over at the mother of his children, the hollow at the base of her throat, the fine fringe of her eyelashes, the fat zit on her chin that she is probably minutes from popping. "I need to talk to you," he says.

"LOSS": "You have to understand," says Father Jones. "I loved her. I loved her more than I have loved everything. But she was sad, so sad. She couldn't bear to be here anymore. She saw too much."

"SERENDIPITY": Father Jones shows Benson how to pray. She clasps her hands together like a child, because that is the last time she tried it. He talks about opening her mind. She pulls her knees up to her chest. "If I open my mind any further, they'll crowd out everything." When he asks her what she means, she just shakes her head.

"COERCED": "I made it up," the woman says dully. Benson looks up from her yellow legal pad. "Are you certain?" she asks. "Yes," the woman says. "Start to finish. I certainly, definitely made it up from start to finish."

"CHOICE": Outside of the courtroom, protesters shove and shout, the wooden dowels of their signs knocking noisily against one another. It sounds like percussion. The worst percussion. Benson and Stabler use their bodies to shield the woman, who sobs and shuffles. Benson looks left, looks right. Shots. The woman crumples. Her blood runs down a storm drain, and she dies with her eyes half-open, an interrupted eclipse. Benson and Stabler feel the beat at the same time, down beneath the pavement, beneath the screaming and the panicked crowd and the signs and the woman dead, dead, there it is, the *one-two*, and they look at each other. "You can hear it, too," Stabler accuses hoarsely, but before Benson can answer, the shooter takes out another protester. Her sign falls face-down in the blood.

"ABOMINATION": The DA rolls down the hill in her dreams, stumbling, tumbling, rumbling down, down in the deep. In her dream, there is thunder, but the thunder is the color of rhubarb and it comes in twin booms. Every time the thunder sounds, the grass blades change shape. Then, beneath her body, the DA sees Benson, lying on her back, touching herself, laughing. The DA dreams her clothes off, and dreams herself rolling her body against Benson's, and the thunder rolls, too, except not really; it's more walking. *Dum-dum. Dum-dum. Dum-dum.* The DA comes, and wakes. Or maybe wakes, then comes. In the afterburn of the dream, she is alone in her bed, and the window is open, the curtains fluttering in the breeze.

"CONTROL": "Why did you look it up?" Stabler's wife asks. "Why? All I wanted was to bury it. I want it to be hidden. Why did you do it? Why?" She cries. She pummels her fists into a giant, over-stuffed throw pillow. She begins to walk from one end of the room to the other, holding her arms so tightly to her torso that Stabler is reminded of a man who once came to the precinct, covered in blood. He held his arms like this, too, and when he let them drop, his wounded abdomen opened up and his stomach and intestines peeked out, as if they were ready to be born.

"SHAKEN": "Hey," Benson says to the DA, smiling. The DA's hands squeeze tightly into themselves. "Hi," she says quickly before spinning on her heel and walk-running in the opposite direction.

"ESCAPE": The girl staggers into the precinct wearing nothing but a burlap sack. Stabler gives her a cup of water. She drinks it in a single gulp, and then vomits onto his desk. The contents: said water, four nails, splinters of plywood, and a laminated slip of paper with a code on one side that seems to indicate it came from a library book. The things she says are disjointed, but familiar; Benson recognizes a quote from *Moby-Dick*, and another from *The Price of Salt*. They put the girl in a foster home, where she continues to express her grief and lamentations through everyone else's words.

"BROTHERHOOD": Stabler only ever wanted daughters when he first married his wife. He'd had a brother. He knew. Now, he is paralyzed with fear for them. He wishes they were never born. He wishes they were still floating safely in the unborn space, which he imagines to be grayish-blue, like the Atlantic, studded with star-like points of light, and thick as corn syrup.

"HATE": Stabler's wife has not spoken to him since the manila folder. She chops vegetables with a large knife, and he would rather she stick it in his gut than continue the sparking silence. "I love you," he says to her. "Forgive me." But she keeps chopping. She puts clean slits in the stippled plastic cutting board. She lops off the heads of carrots. She undoes the cucumbers.

"RITUAL": Benson goes to a new age shop in the Village. "I need a spell," she says to the proprietor, "to find what I am seeking." He taps a pen against his chin for a few moments, and then sells her: four dried beans of unknown origin, a small white disk that proves to be a sliver of rabbit bone, a tiny vial that appears empty—"the memory of a young woman losing her virginity," he says—a granite basin, a wedge of dried clay from the banks of the Hudson.

"FAMILIES": Stabler invites Benson over to his house for Thanksgiving. Benson offers to help pull the guts from the turkey, something she always wanted to do as a child. Stabler's wife gives her a bright orange bowl, leaves to attend to her squabbling children. Benson notices that Stabler's wife is not speaking to Stabler. She sighs, shakes her head. Benson sticks her hand deep into the turkey's guts. Her fingers push through gristle and meat and bones and close around something. She pulls. Out of the turkey comes a string of entrails, on which are suspended tiny bells, slick with blood. The meal is a great success. There is a photo of it on Stabler's hard drive. Everyone is smiling. Everyone is having a very nice time.

"HOME": Benson and Stabler go to the New York Public Library. They show the feral girl's photo to the librarians. One of them says she doesn't know her, but her eyes drift upward when she says this. Benson knows that she is lying. She follows the librarian to the break room and shoves her up against a vending machine. Inside, bags of chips and pretzels rustle. "I know you know her," Benson says. The woman bites her lip, then takes Benson and Stabler down to the basement. She pushes open a metal door to an old boiler room, from which hangs a broken padlock. A cot stands against a far wall, stacks and stacks of books make a tiny metropolis all over the floor. Benson flips open a cover, then another. All of them have a red stamp: WITHDRAWN. The librarian pulls the gun out of Stabler's holster. Stabler shouts. Benson turns around just in time for a fine red mist to paint her skin.

"MEAN": "How could you possibly let her get your gun?" Benson yells at Stabler. "How could you be looking at books when there was a kidnapping librarian in the room?" he yells back. "Sometimes—" she starts angrily, but her voice trails off.

"CARELESS": The captain takes the last photo down from the bulletin board. He wants a drink more than he has in many years. "All it would have taken," he says, his voice rising with every syllable, "for ONE WOMAN to survive would have been my detectives not being ASLEEP," here he slams the photo down on the desk with more force than had actually killed her, "on the JOB." Benson looks down at her legal pad, where she has anagrammed and anagrammed the serial killer's clue, never succeeding.

"SICK": This is how it went. The girl was sick with prophecy. She touched the arm of young Ben Jones, later to be Father Jones, before she knelt herself to death off a Brooklyn rooftop. He carried it inside of his body for decades. Stabler was the one to restrain him when he freaked out during Mass, and now had it, too. He sees his children, projected into their terrifying futures. He sees his wife, living long and always remembering. He cannot see Benson, though. Something shades his vision. She is smoke, elusive.

"LOWDOWN": Stabler is grocery shopping with his oldest daughter when he sees a man picking up apples, examining them closely, and setting them back down on the pile. He recognizes him. The man looks up. He recognizes Stabler, too. He calls him by his first name, except it's not his first name, really. "Bill!" he says. "Bill!" He looks at Stabler's daughter. Stabler grabs her arm and pulls her into the next aisle. "Bill," the man says, sounding excited, knocking over a display of corn tortillas. "Bill! Bill! Bill!"

"CRIMINAL": A man in a ski mask robs a bank with a plastic gun and gets fifty-seven dollars. The teller saves the day by slicing off his face with the machete that he keeps under his counter.

"PAINLESS": "Don't you worry," the gynecologist says to Stabler's wife. "This isn't going to hurt one bit."

"BOUND": Benson decides to try the spell. She combines the ingredients like the man had shown her. She crushes the beans and the bone. She uncorks the bottle. "Tip it fast," he'd told her, "and catch it under your pestle, or else it'll float up and away." She turns the bottle toward the mortar, but suddenly her brain convulses and she is remembering something that never happened, a screaming, burning pain, a dark room lined with windows, curtains drawn, a cold, black table. She stumbles blindly backward and knocks over the mortar and pestle. She falls to the floor and trembles, shakes. When it finally passes, she sees a girl-with-bells-for-eyes staring back at her. Ringing back at her. *The first of many times*, she says. All night, Benson dreams, dreams, dreams.

"POISON": One afternoon, at her desk, Benson feels the telltale tickling. She shifts in her chair. She crosses and uncrosses her legs. On the way home, she stops at the drugstore on the corner. In her bathroom, she squats. She walks carefully to her bed and gets horizontal. She feels the bullet melting inside of her, making her better. A girl-with-bells-for-eyes comes to the side of her bed, bells swinging wildly like she is a church caught in a stiff wind. *Come on.* "I can't." *Why not?* "I can't get up. I can't move. I can't even cough." *What is happening to you?* "You wouldn't understand." *Get up.* "I *can't*." The core of her is soothed and calmed and she cannot move or else everything will come out. The girl-with-bells-for-eyes gets as close to the bed as she can without walking through it. She begins to glow. Benson's bedroom is filling with light. Across the street, a man with a telescope lifts his head from the eyepiece, gasps.

"HEAD": "Okay, so, here's my theory," Stabler says to Benson when she gets back into the car with the coffees. "Human organs. They are wet and thick and fit together like pieces of a puzzle. It's almost like someone zipped open every body before birth and slopped them in there like oatmeal. Except that's not possible." Benson looks at Stabler and squeezes her cup so hard a little fart of scalding coffee runs down her hand. She looks behind her. She looks back at him. "It's almost like," he says thoughtfully, "they were grown on the inside, and are meant to be shaped together." Benson blinks. "It's almost like," she says, "we grow. In the womb. And keep growing." Stabler looks excited. "Exactly!" he says. "And then, we die."

SEASON 6

"BIRTHRIGHT": Two of Stabler's daughters get into a fight over a bowl of soup. When Stabler gets home, the oldest daughter has an ice pack on her forehead and the youngest is kicking her feet above the tiled kitchen floor. Stabler goes into the bedroom, where his wife is lying on her back on the bed, staring at the ceiling. "They're your daughters," she says to Stabler. "Not mine."

"DEBT": Benson and Stabler don't play Monopoly anymore.

"OBSCENE": Benson buys twice as much produce as normal, and doesn't even wait for it to rot. She throws a ripe vegetable into every garbage can in a twenty-block radius. It feels good to spread it out like this, the wasting.

"scavenger": After the body is removed, Benson and Stabler stand around the dried pool of blood. A police officer comes into the bedroom. "The landlord is outside," she says. "He wants to know when he can get to cleaning up the apartment for rental." Benson pokes the stain with her foot. "You know what'd get this out?" Stabler looks at her, his eyebrows knit. "OxiClean. It'd get this stain right out," she continues. "You could rent this place next week." Stabler looks around. "The landlord isn't here yet," he says, slowly. "OxiClean would get this right out," she says again.

"outcry": Only after the sixth small black girl goes missing does the police commissioner finally make a statement, interrupting the season finale of a popular soap opera. The enraged letters start coming soon after. "Are *you* going to tell me if Susan's baby belongs to David or not, Mister Police Commissioner??????" says one. Another person sends anthrax.

"conscience": The drumming won't stop. Stabler considers that it's his conscience making that horrible, horrible sound.

"charisma": Benson likes her Tuesday-night date too much to go home with him.

"doubt": Father Jones prepares to deliver the Eucharist. The first people in line look like Stabler and Benson, except different. Wrong, somehow. When he lays the wafer on the first one's tongue, the man closes his mouth, smiles. Father Jones feels forgiveness melting down the back of his own throat. The woman, then, too, takes it, smiles. Father Jones almost chokes this time. He excuses himself. In the bathroom, he rocks back and forth on his feet, clutching the counter and weeping.

"WEAK": Stabler works out three times a day, now. He insists on jogging to crime scenes instead of using the squad car. Whenever he takes off from the station, his button-down and tie tucked into bright red running shorts, Benson goes and gets herself a coffee from the bodega, reads a newspaper, and then drives to the crime scene. Stabler always arrives a few minutes later, his fingers pressed against his pulse, shoes striking the pavement in an even rhythm. He jogs in place while they interview witnesses.

"HAUNTED": On the subway, Benson thinks she sees Henson and Abler on a train running in the opposite direction. They blast past each other in a blaze of butter-yellow light, the windows flashing by like frames on a filmstrip, and Henson and Abler appear to be in every one, moving jerkily as if they are rotating through a phenakistoscope. Benson tries to call Stabler, but there's no signal below the earth. Across from her, a little girl playing a video game on her mother's phone kicks off one of her flip-flops. Benson realizes, with utter certainty, that this girl is going to die soon. She gets off the train and vomits into a garbage can.

"CONTAGIOUS": Benson stays home with swine flu. Her fever reaches 104; she hallucinates that she is two people. She reaches over to the opposite pillow, years empty, and feels for her own face. The girls-with-bells-for-eyes try to make her soup, but their hands pass through the cupboard handles.

"IDENTITY": Stabler offers to take the children out for Halloween. He goes as Batman, buys a hard plastic mask. The children roll their eyes. Before they go out, his wife faces him. She reaches up and snatches the mask off his face. He seizes it back from her and slides it back on. She pulls it off again, so hard the band snaps and catches his face. "Ow," he says. "What are you doing that for?" She shoves the mask into his chest. "Doesn't feel very nice, does it?" she hisses through clenched teeth.

"QUARRY": The man takes out his rifle, braces it against his good shoulder, and squeezes the trigger with all the seductive force of a beckoning. The bullet strikes the missing woman's neck, and she goes down, loosed of her life before she lands in the leaves and sends them up like ashes.

"GAME": The man lets out another sobbing woman. As she begins to run for the woods, he realizes he's tired and wants to go make some dinner. He takes a few steps toward the tree line, and she joins her sister.

"HOOKED": "I choose this life," the prostitute says to the social worker with the worried eyes. "I do. Please put your energy into helping girls who aren't here by choice." She is so right. She is murdered anyway.

"GHOST": A prostitute is murdered. She is too tired to become a spirit.

"RAGE": A prostitute is murdered. She is too angry to become a spirit.

"PURE": A prostitute is murdered. She is too sad to become a spirit.

"INTOXICATED": The girl-with-bells-for-eyes—the first one who had sought Benson's sour sleep breath and twitching eyelids all that time ago—comes into Benson's bedroom. She walks up to the bed. She presses her fingers into Benson's mouth. Benson does not wake up. The girl pushes herself in and in, and when Benson's eyes open, Benson is not opening them. Benson is curled up in the corner of her mind, and she sees through her eyes distantly, as if they were windows on the opposite side of a lengthy living room. Benson-who-is-not-Benson walks around the apartment. Benson-who-is-not-Benson takes off her nightgown and touches her grown woman's body, inspecting every inch. Benson-who-is-not-Benson puts on clothes, hails a cab, and knocks on Stabler's door, and even though it is 2:07 a.m., Stabler does not look even a little bit sleepy, though he is confused. "Benson," he says. "What are you doing here?" Benson-who-is-not-Benson grabs his T-shirt in her hand and pulls him toward her, kissing him with more force and hunger than Stabler has ever felt in his own mouth. She releases his shirt. Benson cries into the darkened walls of her own skull. Benson-who-is-not-Benson wants more. Stabler wipes his mouth with his hand and then looks at his fingers, as if expecting to see something. Then he shuts the door. Benson-who-is-not-Benson returns to her apartment. Benson looks up from her knees to see the girl-with-bells-for-eyes standing in front of her. "Who is driving?" she asks thickly. The bells ring. *No one.* And indeed, Benson's body is lying heavy as an unanimated golem on the bed. The bells ring. *I'm sorry.* The girl-with-bells-for-eyes sinks her fingers into Benson's head, and

"NIGHT": Benson wakes up. Her head is throbbing. She rolls over onto the cool side of the pillow, her dream ebbing away from her like a rubber duck bobbing gently out to sea.

"BLOOD": The butcher takes a hose to the floor, and the blood spirals and sinks down the drain. It wasn't animal blood, but he has no way of knowing what it was that his assistant was cutting up. The evidence is destroyed. The girls remain lost forever.

"PARTS": "Is it me, or is this steak kind of gamey?" Benson's date says to Benson. She shrugs and looks down at her scallops. She prods one with a knife and it parts a little in the center, like a mouth opening, or worse. "It's just . . . a weird flavor," he says. Another bite. "But good, I guess. Good." Benson can't remember what he does for a living. Is this their second date, or their third? He chews with his mouth open. She invites herself to his apartment.

"GOLIATH": Stabler takes another long pull of his whiskey. He slumps in his armchair. Upstairs his wife sleeps, dreams, wakes up, sleeps more, hates him, wakes, hates him, sleeps. He thinks of Benson, the way she stood there, the way her clothes looked put on funny, the way she drank from him as if she were dying of thirst, the dreamy way her hand ran over the metal fence, over the iron-tipped gate as if she was asleep, as if she was high, as if she was a woman in love, in love, in love.

SEASON 7

"DEMONS": Shadows pass over the marbled halls of justice, through the police station, across crowded and empty streets. They slide up walls and through grates and under doors and arc through glass windowpanes. They take what they want, leave what they want. Life is created and destroyed. Mostly destroyed.

"DESIGN": "If this child is part of the Plan, then the Plan was that I would be raped. If this child is not part of the Plan, then my rape was a violation of the Plan, in which case the Plan is not a Plan at all, but a Polite Fucking Suggestion." Benson reaches out for the survivor's hand, but the woman looks down at the water, kneels from the railing, and is gone.

"911": "Look, it's just that I'm walking around feeling like I'm going to vomit out my own toenails, and I want to die, and I want to kill someone, sometimes, and I feel like I'm on the verge of dissolving into a puddle of organs and slop. Organ slop." A pause. "Um, that's—that's—I'm sorry. Look, I just called to report a vandal in my neighborhood."

"RIPPED": They find the actress hours after her disappearance, tied to the mast of a ship in New York Harbor, a reproduction musket laced between the coils of rope and wedged between her voluminous breasts. Her Renaissance Faire corset is half-unlaced, her shirt torn. He wanted her to fight back, she tells Stabler. He wanted her to slap him, and call him a scoundrel, and then to marry him. He called himself Reginald.

"STRAIN": Benson gets the flu. She vomits up: spinach, paint shavings, half a golf pencil, and a single bell the size of her pinky nail.

"RAW": Benson and Stabler's favorite sushi restaurant has stopped using plates and started using models. Benson pinches a red swatch of tuna from the hip bone of a brunette who seems to be trying very hard not to breathe. The owner stops by the table, and seeing Benson's frown, says, "It's more cost-effective." Stabler reaches for a piece of eel, and the model takes a sudden breath. The meat eludes his chopsticks—once, twice.

"NAME": All over the city, pedestrians stop midstride, a small weight lifted from bodies, a memory snuffed. A barista, marker poised over a cup, asks a man the same question in ten seconds. He stares at her, blinks. "I don't know," he says. In graves and ditches, in morgues and mortuaries, in rushes and bogs, dipping and rolling on the skins of rivers, names trace the bodies of the dead like flames along kindling, like electricity. For four minutes, the city becomes filled with the names, with their names, and though the man cannot tell the barista that Sam wants his latte, he can tell her that Samantha is not coming home but she is somewhere, though she is nowhere, and she knows nothing, and everything.

"STARVED": Stabler tries to convince his oldest daughter to eat something, anything. She takes the paper napkin in seven small bites.

"ROCKABYE": After the children are asleep, Stabler sits next to his wife, who is cocooned under the blankets of their bed. Even her face is swaddled. Stabler gently pokes at the opening in the comforter, and soon the tip of her nose is revealed, a heart of skin around her eyes. She is crying. "I love you," she says. "I do. I am so angry with you. But I do love you." Stabler takes her into his arms, her whole cloth burrito self, and rocks her in his arms, whispering *sorry, sorry* into her ear. After he turns out the light, she asks him to cover her face again. He lays the tucked bits back over her, lightly.

"storm": The air roils. The clouds rush at the city as if they have been waiting.

"alien": A new police commissioner rides into town. He makes big promises. His teeth are the color and shape of Chiclets, too even. Stabler keeps trying to tally the number of teeth that show when the police commissioner smiles for the camera, but he loses count every time.

"infected": When the girls-with-bells-for-eyes come to Benson's door, they are silent. When Benson finally opens the door to go to the gym, they are there, filling the hallway. Their bells rock, but no sound comes out. When Benson gets close, she realizes that someone has unhooked the hammers. The bells swing back and forth and back and forth, and they are quieter than they have ever been.

"blast": Stabler takes his wife dancing. He is surprised that she agrees. Past the doors of the salsa club, she is lithe and hot, sweating, spinning. He has not seen her this way since they were young, since just before they were married. The glaze of sweat and the smell of her turns him on, cracks open his want in a way that he'd forgotten existed. They dance close. She slides her hand down the front of his pants, bites her lip, kisses him. Deep inside his body, something beats. *Dum-dum. Dum-dum. Dum-dum.* A heartbeat, almost. They take a cab home, and in their bedroom rip her dress getting it off, and they have not done this in years, this, this, and she digs her nails into his back and whispers his name, and they have not been like this since those years before, since that time long ago, before before, but after. He calls her name.

"TABOO": After she comes, Benson's arm cramps hard, like her muscle is folding itself in half. She rubs her forearm and bites her lip. She listens to the distant throbbing of salsa music coming from an apartment across the street. A film of sweat seals her guilt like Saran Wrap.

"MANIPULATED": The precinct's interns sense that something has changed between Benson and Stabler, but they don't know what. They track their movements in a repurposed notebook from a bio-chem class. They take photos of them with their cell phones. They sprinkle Spanish fly into the coffee machine. They summon a demon with blood from their own bodies and ash from a cathedral votive and a squirrel bone and white chalk and bundles of dried sage. They beg the demon for his help. Annoyed, he takes one of them back to hell with him, punishment for making him come so far.

"GONE": "Lucy, do you know where Evan is?" Stabler asks her. "He's never this late."

"CLASS": "Lucy, do you know where Evan is? He's never missed biochem before."

"VENOM": Benson drains her coffee. Her mouth burns a little. She feels woozy. She lies down in the back room.

"FAULT": In her dream, Benson hears the heartbeat. She is on an empty New York City street. There is no breeze. The pavement does move, though, as if something is breathing. Benson begins to follow the sound of the heartbeat down the street. She sees a dark door-way, a sign above it that reads SHAHRYAR BAR & GRILL. Inside, the counters are polished and dark red. The bottles and glasses gleam like the surface of a river, and every time the beat sounds they tremble. There is a door tucked in the corner, a strip of light glowing beneath it. Laughter. Benson thinks it sounds like it did when she was a girl, and her mother had a cocktail party and Benson had to sit in her bedroom, a plate of tiny appetizers and half a cup of apple juice resting on her nightstand. She nibbled a mushroom that was full of something melted, and then drank her juice, and she could hear laughter on the other side of the door, glasses clinking, voices going loud and soft and loud again. She tried to read a book but ended up in her bed in the dark, listening to the voices that were so far and so close, picking out her mother's bray in the din like pulling a loose thread of elastic from the band of your underpants, pulling, tightening, ruining them. That is what she feels now, the voices on the other side of the door. She reaches for the handle, the distance between her hand and it halving with each passing nanosecond, the metal cold even before her hand touches it. When Benson wakes up, she is screaming.

"FAT": "Just one more bite," Stabler begs his oldest daughter. "Just one, baby. Just one carrot. Let's start with one carrot." He sees her being carved away, the way the wind shapes a dune into nothing. "One. Just one."

"WEB": Benson googles. <<dead girls bells eyes missing hammers>> <<girls bells eyes>> <<girl ghost bells eyes>> <<ghosts broken>> <<what happens if I see a ghost?>> <<what makes a ghost?>> <<ghost fixing>> For months, the ads in her browser try to sell her: brass bell sets, ghost-hunting equipment, video cameras, CDs of bell choirs, dolls, shovels.

"INFLUENCE": The new police commissioner looks up from his blotter. Across from him, Abler and Henson are not taking notes. They have perfect memories. "Make it so," says the new police commissioner. "Make it so."

SEASON 8

"INFORMED": Benson is sure that her smartphone is smarter than she is, and she finds it deeply upsetting. When it gives her information, she puts it close to her face, says, "NO," and does the opposite.

"CLOCK": The DA watches the hour and minute hands pinching time between them. When the judge asks her if she has any questions for the witness, she shakes her head. At home, Henson is waiting for her, curled up on the couch with a copy of *Madame Bovary*, chewing on a piece of hair, laughing at all the right places. They make dinner together. They watch the rain.

"RECALL": A story is delivered over and over again on the twenty-four-hour news channels. Tainted vegetables, they say. Bok choy, broccoli, celery, brussels sprouts, all dirty, bad, wrong. Benson catches the tail end of a report as she forks stir-fry straight out of the pan. "Return produce to your local stores for a full refund," the reporter says, looking grave. Benson looks down at the pan. She finishes every scrap of green. She goes to her fridge and begins to prepare more.

"UNCLE": "Dad," says Stabler's youngest, "who is Uncle E?" He looks up from his newspaper. "Uncle E?" "Yes," she says. "A man came up to me after school today. He said his name was Uncle E and that he was my uncle." Stabler hasn't spoken to his younger brother, Oliver, in ten years. He's pretty sure Oliver still lives in Switzerland. He doesn't even know if Oliver knows he's an uncle.

"CONFRONTATION": At the courthouse, Stabler looks up from the bathroom sink and sees Abler standing behind him. Abler smirks. Stabler swings around, half-soaped fists raised. The bathroom is empty.

"INFILTRATED": "Look, Benson," Henson says from the other end of the line. Her voice sounds tinny and far away, as if she is standing over Benson's body while Benson dies. "The thing is, you are suffering. You don't want to suffer anymore, do you?" Benson leans the earpiece harder against her shoulder, and the plastic casing slips along the grease of her unwashed face. She does not answer. "It's just that," Henson continues, "we could make this all stop, you know. The girls. The sounds. The wanting." Benson looks up. Stabler is shuffling through a stack of folders, absently scratching his jaw, humming under his breath. "All you have to do is bring him to us. Bring him to us, and we can all call a truce."

"UNDERBELLY": Benson traces the call to a warehouse in Chelsea. Once there, she and Stabler use bolt cutters to get inside. The hallway is dark. A single light bulb, the filament struggling to burn, hangs from the ceiling. Benson and Stabler pull out their guns. They grope along the walls with their free hands until they reach another door. A big room, now, big as an airplane hangar, empty. Their footsteps echo. Benson sees another door on the other side of the room. It looks different. The strip beneath it glows red. She can feel her heart knocking loudly in her chest. *Dum-dum. Dum-dum.*

Dum-dum. She realizes that the sound is bigger than she is, that it is coming from outside of her, around her. She looks at Stabler, panicked, and he looks confused. "Are you all right?" he asks her. She shakes her head. "We have to go. We have to go *now*." He gestures to the door on the other side of the room. "Let's check out that door." "No." "But Benson—" "No!" She grabs his arm, and pulls him. They erupt into the sunshine.

"CAGE": The rapist is raped. The raped are rapists. "Some days," the prison doctor says to a resident as they stitch up another torn rectum, "I wonder if the bars make the monsters, and not the other way around."

"CHOREOGRAPHED": The courtroom. A hallway. Six doors. In and out of each set—detectives, police officers, lawyers, judges, the damned. People go in one set of doors and come out another. Benson and Stabler miss Henson and Abler every single time.

"SCHEHERAZADE!": "Let me tell you a story," Henson whispers to the DA as they curl up in her bed, the air heavy with the smell of sex. "When it's over, I'll tell you what you want to know about Benson, about Stabler, about all of it. Even about the sounds." The DA mumbles her assent, feeling drowsy. "The first story," Henson whispers, "is about a queen and her castle. A queen, her castle, and a hungry beast that lives below."

"BURNED": Father Jones senses the demon, though he cannot see it. From his bed, he smells sulfur, he feels the evil sitting on his chest. "What do you want?" he asks. "Why are you here?"

"OUTSIDER": The forensic psychologist is asked to come in on a case involving a serial rapist and murderer who dismembers his victims as if they are middle school frog dissections. "It makes more sense to him than you might think," he says evenly as he watches the man laugh from the other side of the two-way mirror. Stabler frowns. He distrusts the psychologist's judgment.

"LOOPHOLE": Benson buys a thousand bells and removes their hammers. She tries to give them to the girls-with-bells-for-eyes, but the hammers don't take. She tries drawing them on a piece of paper, but the ink runs when pressed into their faces. The girls crowd into her kitchen, so many of them, and so bright that the neighbor who spies on Benson with his telescope is certain that her apartment is on fire, and calls the fire department. Benson sits in her wicker chair, her hands resting on her knees. "All right," she says. "Come in." And they do. They walk into her, one at a time, and once they are inside she can feel them, hear them. They take turns with her vocal cords. "Hello," Benson says. "Hello!" Benson says. "This feels really good," Benson says. "What should we do first?" Benson says. "Now, wait," Benson says. "I'm still me." "Yes," Benson says, "but you are legion, too." In the distance, sirens tear up the night.

"DEPENDENT": "Did you know that Evan was kidnapped?" Benson asks the captain. He taps his sobriety coin on the varnished wood. "Who's Evan?" "The intern! The intern. The intern who used to sit at that desk!" She points at Lucy, who is weeping softly in her rolling chair. Every sniffle pushes her back a millimeter until she is almost in the hall.

"HAYSTACK": Benson promises Lucy that she will look for Evan. She visits all of his normal haunts. The girls crowd in her head, talk to her. "He's not here," they say. "He's Elsewhere. He's swallowed." When Benson tells Stabler about her search, he sighs deeply. "He'll get spit up somewhere," he says knowingly. "Just not here."

"PHILADELPHIA": Evan the intern was annoying everyone in hell, so the demon sent him back. He overshot his target, though, and accidentally deposited him in Pennsylvania. Evan decides to stay. He never liked New York, anyway. Too expensive. Too sad.

"SIN": Father Jones absolves the blooming trees and flowers. As their pollen is carried off, and begins to clog people's lungs, Father Jones smiles. The coughs of redemption.

"RESPONSIBLE": Lucy the intern looks down at the slip of paper in her hand, where Benson had scribbled Father Jones's address. When she looks up again, the front door opens, and Father Jones leans against the frame, looking exhausted. "Come in, child," he says. "It seems we have a lot to talk about."

"FLORIDA": Over the course of three weeks, five different people catch and cut open five different gators in the Everglades. Inside each belly, an identical left arm—sparkling purple jelly bracelet, chipped green polish, thin white scar where the pinky meets the palm. When they run the prints, they trace the arm back to a missing girl in New York. The medical examiner looks at the five arms lined up next to each other. Spooked, she discards four of them. "Remaining body unrecovered," she writes in her notes. "Victim presumed deceased."

"ANNIHILATED": Benson finally sits down and counts. She goes through files, paper and computer. She tallies, hatch marks in groups of five, and covers pages and pages and pages. She goes home, flipping the blade out of her pocketknife as soon as the door closes behind her. She begins to dig into the kitchen table, the edges of the cupboards, counting, counting, counting, losing count, finding it again.

"PRETEND": Stabler pushes open Benson's door. She is lying on the kitchen floor, arms outspread, facing the ceiling. Around her, the chairs and tables and footstool are all chewed to pieces. "There are so many of them," Benson whispers. Stabler kneels down next to her. He strokes her hair gently. "It will be okay," he says. "It will be okay."

"SCREWED": The DA calls in sick, again. "The sixty-fifth story," Henson whispers into her ear, "is about a world that watches you and me and everyone. Watches our suffering like it is a game. Can't stop. Can't tear themselves away. If they could stop, we could stop, but they won't, so we can't."

SEASON 9

"ALTERNATE": On a Tuesday, Stabler's wife returns from the store to find a man sitting on the stoop. He turns out his palms apologetically. "I lost my keys," he says. She sets down the sack of groceries on the ground, fumbles for her own. She watches him out of the corner of her eye. He looks just like Stabler. His smile leaves the same tiny indent to the left of his mouth. But something in her brain is screaming: he is not my husband. The door swings open. Inside, her youngest comes out of her bedroom and wipes sleep from her eyes. She points to the man. "That's Uncle E!" she shouts.

Stabler's wife grabs a heavy vase from the side table and whirls around, but he is already out the door, down the street, running full speed, and then gone.

"AVATAR": In the back row of the movie theater, Henson's arm creeps over the DA's shoulder. The DA looks at Henson's face in the flickering half dark. Here, more than anywhere, she looks just like Benson. She kisses her mouth.

"IMPULSIVE": In the cop bar, Wilson Phillips plays. Stabler looks annoyed, but Benson grins at the memory from her adolescence. She mouths the words while training her eyes on her beer. She bobs her head at every mention of "reckless" and "kiss."

"SAVANT": The boy turns out lists and lists of the missing, dating back to before his birth, chronologically by the date of their disappearances. He draws thick black lines through most of them, though not all. His mother doesn't understand the names, or the lines, and burns the lists on the grill in their backyard.

"HARM": When Stabler's wife tells him about Uncle E, he instructs her to take the kids and go to her mother's house in New Jersey. He sits on the stoop and waits for Abler to come back. He fantasizes about taking a brick to Abler's head. His cell phone rings. "You think I'd ever visit the same place twice?" Abler purrs. Stabler tries to think, hard, about where Abler and Henson will be. But has no idea.

"SVENGALI": The DA kisses Henson, their twelfth hour of fucking, sleep, fucking, sleep. She hums promises into her ear. Father

Jones shows Lucy how to keep demons away. Stabler stalks New York, searching for Abler, tense as piano wire, vibrating with rage. Benson takes herself and the girls inside her out on the town for dancing, for sweaty bottles of beer, to show them a good time.

"BLINDED": Benson dreams that Henson and Abler seize her eyeballs and pull them out slowly, the nerve bundles stretching and drooping like Silly Putty.

"FIGHT": Stabler would just straight-up challenge them, but he doesn't even know where to throw down his gloves.

"PATERNITY": The dirty truth is, Benson doesn't have a father.

"SNITCH": Without the interns to do their nefarious bidding, the gods turn to other tricks.

"STREETWISE": All Benson knows is that she's sure the street is breathing. The girls tell her what she needs to know. She is right to be afraid.

"SIGNATURE": Full of girls, Benson finds scrawling her own name to be almost impossible.

"UNORTHODOX": "I don't care what the evidence says," the judge chuckles. "You're obviously innocent. Obviously! Get out of here, you. Say hi to your dad for me."

"INCONCEIVABLE": Stabler goes and visits his wife and kids at his mother-in-law's. They watch *The Princess Bride*, and fall asleep before the end. Together on the couch, piled high with pillows, dark but for the glow of the screen, Stabler and his wife look at what they have made.

"UNDERCOVER": "What have you learned?" the new police commissioner asks Henson and Abler. He is not a religious man, but the expressions on their faces so unnerve him that he crosses himself, which he has not done since he was a child.

"CLOSET": The DA steps out into the sunshine, blinking, shielding her face. She almost bumps into Benson, who is strolling down the sidewalk. Benson smiles at her. "Haven't seen you around in a while. Have you been sick?" The DA blinks and reflexively wipes her mouth, catching the smear of lipstick that doesn't belong to her. "Yes," she says. "No. Well, yes, a little."

"AUTHORITY": Alone in his family's house, Stabler drinks five old-fashioneds. He is disturbed by how easy it is. He thinks about his children, his wife. His brother, suddenly, his baby brother. He struggles to remember his baby brother, who flits through his synapses like a sketch. Suddenly certain of something, Stabler runs out into the street and stares up at the sky. "Stop," he begs. "Stop reading. I don't like this. Something is wrong. I don't like this."

"TRADE": In a graveyard, Benson begins to dig. Her spine aches and her muscles freeze and twitch and burn. She digs up the first girl, then the second, then the third, then the fourth. She slides one coffin left, one coffin right, one coffin up, one coffin down. She drops them under their correct, respective names. Inside of her, four girls speak. "Thank you," Benson says. "Yes, thank you," Benson says. Her mind clears a fraction. She breathes. It is easier.

"COLD": Stabler meets Benson in her apartment. She is sitting in a pile of wood chips that used to be her kitchen table. She takes a long, languorous swallow of beer and smiles a watery smile. "My theory," she says. "Our theory. Our theory is that there is a god, and he is hungry."

SEASON 10

"TRIALS": "I am so tired," the DA confesses to her boss. "I'm tired of losing cases. I'm tired of turning rapists back out onto the street. I'm tired of winning, too. I'm tired of justice. Justice is exhausting. I am a one-woman justice machine. It's too much to ask of me. Can we stage my death? Or something?" She does not tell the truth: she wants to see what Benson will do at her funeral.

"CONFESSION": Stabler and his wife go for a walk, in New Jersey. They walk along a dirty beach—with shoes, so as not to cut their feet on broken bottles. "He locked me in the room," she says to him. "He turned the lock and smiled at me. I couldn't move. He hadn't tied me up, but I couldn't move. That's the worst part. No excuse. You fight to put names on all of your dead, but not every victim wants to be known. Not all of us can deal with the illumination that comes with justice." She dips her head, and he remembers the first time he met her. "Also," she says softly, "you should know that Benson loves you."

"SWING": Stabler pushes his youngest higher and higher. He thinks about what his wife said. "Off, Daddy! I said off!" He realizes she is shrieking at the top of her lungs. She, his daughter, not his wife. And certainly not Benson. Definitely not Benson.

"LUNACY": Benson doesn't think about the moon very often, but when she does, she always undoes her top four buttons, tilts her throat up to the sky.

"RETRO": An old woman kills a local deli owner. She tells Benson and Stabler that he raped her when they were teenagers. They don't have the heart to tell her that he was a twin.

"BABES": All of the Hooters waitresses get pregnant at once. No one will say why. "This is not really a case," Benson says, exasperated. Stabler doodles on his pad—a picture of a tree. Or maybe it's a tooth?

"WILDLIFE": Deer, raccoons, rats, mice, cockroaches, flies, squirrels, birds, spiders, all of them, gone. Scientists take notice immediately. The state pours money into research. Where did they go? What does it mean that they are missing? What would it take for their return?

"PERSONA": Benson likes her date, but the girls inside her screw it up by referring to themselves in the collective. "It's the *royal* 'we'!" she howls after his retreating back.

"PTSD": Every night, Benson dreams about the girls' deaths. She slips in and out of stabbings and shootings and stranglings and poisonings and gags and ropes and *No, no, no*s, all lucid, and cut with Benson's normal dreams: sex with Stabler, apocalypses, teeth falling out, teeth falling out of Benson onto Stabler while they fuck on a boat as the Flood wipes everything away.

"SMUT": The DA watches the twenty-four-hour news networks for twenty-four hours.

"STRANGER": "What do you mean?" Stabler breathes into the phone. "Three birth certificates to Joanna Stabler in that ten-year stretch," the clerk says. "Oliver, you, and an Eli." "I don't have a brother Eli," Stabler says. "According to this, you do," she says, sucking noisily on a large wad of gum. Stabler hates it when people chew gum.

"HOTHOUSE": Benson covers her apartment in flowerpots and long troughs full of black dirt, laying them among the destroyed remnants of her furniture. She plants basil and thyme and dill and oregano and beets and spinach and kale and rainbow chard. The sound of pattering water released from a watering can is so beautiful she wants to cry. Time to make something grow.

"SNATCHED": A tiny Dominican girl is taken off the street by a man in a gray coat. She is never seen again.

"TRANSITIONS": Every time Benson flips her bedroom light on and off, she hears the sound. *Dum-dum.* She feels it in her teeth.

"LEAD": When she is tired, Benson lets the girls take over. They run her body all over town, buying hard lemonades and shimmying her chest at bouncers and, once, before Benson can take over again, kissing a busboy sweetly on his mouth, a mouth that tastes like metal and spearmint.

"BALLERINA": She dances four nights a week for two years. He buys a ticket for every show, sits in the mezzanine, never goes backstage for an autograph. She always gets the uneasy sensation that she is being watched, aggressively, but never knows who it is.

"HELL": Father Jones sends Lucy the intern out into the world, infected as Stabler was. He kneels from the rooftop of his building, and takes the demon with him.

"BAGGAGE": "Yes," Stabler's mother says to him over the phone, carefully. "I did have an older son, Eli. But I haven't seen him since you were a child." "Where did he go?" Stabler asked. "Why did you never say?" "Some things," she says, her voice thick with tears, "are better left unsaid."

"SELFISH": The medical examiner can't bring herself to admit that sometimes, *she's* the one who wants to be cut open, to have someone tell her all of her own secrets.

"CRUSH": "I really care about you," Stabler says. "And I know how you feel. I'm sorry that I've led you on. I'm sorry I haven't been forthright. But I love my wife. We were going through a patch, but I love her. I should have told you after we kissed. I should have said that it wouldn't go anywhere." "We kissed?" Benson says. She probes her memories, and only comes up with dreams.

"LIBERTIES": "I mean, not . . . not *everybody*," the constitutional scholar scoffed, looking equal parts amused and scandalized. "Can you imagine if *everyone* had those rights? Anarchy." Abler smiles, and pours him another drink.

"ZEBRAS": Benson wakes up in the zoo again. She scales the wall, not caring that she trips the alarm, not caring that as she runs, cop cars are cruising, flashing, looking for her and only her. She is barefoot, her feet bleed, the street breathes, the street heats, the street is waiting, and what else is waiting? Beneath, beneath, beneath.

SEASON 11

"UNSTABLE": Stabler listens to Benson. She tells him everything—the girls and their now-silent bells—and things he already knows—the heartbeats from the ground, and its breathing, and her love. He looks around at the apartment full of plants, more greenhouse than home. "You're saying they're inside of you now." "Yes." "Right this minute." "Yes." "Do they tell you things?" "Sometimes." "Like what?" "They say, 'Ow, yes, no, stop it, that one, help us, there, but why, but when, I'm hungry, we're hungry, kiss him, kiss her, wait, okay . . .' Also, I bought some bells." She points to a ravaged cardboard box, overflowing with packing peanuts and glints of brass. Stabler frowns. "Benson, how can I help?"

"SUGAR": The handsome older gentleman folds his cloth napkin in half before dabbing his mouth. "What I'm saying," he says to Benson, who can't stop staring, "is that if this continues, I will expect you to quit your job. Naturally, you'll be compensated above and beyond your current salary. I'll just expect you to always be available."

"SOLITARY": Benson trims her plants, and bats away regret over saying no.

"HAMMERED": Benson wakes up to see Henson standing over her bed. She is holding a garbage bag, and she is grinning. She dumps the contents over Benson's bed, and they tumble out like ghostly river shrimp. The stolen hammers from the girls' bells. They weigh nothing and yet Benson can feel them, somehow. Inside her head, the girls explode in chatter. When the points of light stop flashing in Benson's eyes, she realizes that Henson has left. She tries to pick up the hammers, and they dissolve in her fingers like fog.

"HARDWIRED": The DA comes over to Benson's apartment to talk about a case. "I like your greenhouse," she says. Benson blinks, disbelieving. Then, she smiles shyly, offers to show her the plants. She shows the DA how to rewire a heat lamp. They laugh into the night.

"SPOOKED": "You just gotta learn to live with it," the bored officer says to the woman sitting in the chair across from him, shaking.

"USERS": Everyone on the web forum wakes up to find a jagged crack up the length of their bathroom mirrors.

"TURMOIL": Abler and Henson reverse the stoplights, flood bathrooms, and steal the interior workings of all deadbolts.

"PERVERTED": "You can't stop me," the note, pinned to the body, reads. "I control everything. —THE WOLF." Benson and Stabler start a new file. Stabler cries.

"ANCHOR": They can't prove that the naval officer was responsible, because the evidence isn't waterproof.

"QUICKIE": The DA finally throws Henson out of her bed. "You're not her," she says, her voice heavy with sadness. "One more story,"

Henson says, leaning against the door frame. "Don't you want to hear just one more? It's a good one. It's a real doozy."

"SHADOW": If the day had been sunny and not overcast, she would have seen him coming. Everyone blames the weatherman.

"P.C.": "It's just that," the guy says, pumping his head confidently, "my sense of humor is pretty subversive, you know? I, like, don't submit to the P.C. brigade. I'm, like, a rebel. An independent thinker. Y'know?" For the first time in ages, Benson leaves her date. She's desperate, but not that desperate.

"SAVIOR": One night, Lucy knocks on Benson's door. "Your gun," she says. Benson frowns at her. "What?" Lucy seizes the gun from Benson's holster. Benson makes a grab for it, but not before Lucy smears something on the handle. "A gift from Father Jones," she says, handing it back to her.

"CONFIDENTIAL": "It's been nice having her come around," Benson says to her plants, referring to the DA. Benson hates diaries. "She's really great company. Really great." She imagines that the plants are arching toward her voice.

"WITNESS": There isn't one. The DA can't try the case.

"DISABLED": Stabler goes to visit his wife and children. He worries that Abler is following him. He stops his car. He drives back to New York. He takes a train. He hitchhikes to the house.

"BEDTIME": Stabler's wife curls against him. She breathes into his ear. "When do you think we can leave my mother's place?" she asks. "When we catch Uncle E," he says. He feels her face pull into a sleepy smile. "What do you think Uncle E stands for, anyway?" she asks blearily.

"CONNED": Stabler tackles Abler to the ground. "I know who you are!" Stabler says into his ear. "You're my brother, Eli. Uncle E, indeed." Abler chuckles from beneath him. "No," he says. "I'm not. I just called myself that to fuck with you. Eli died in prison, years ago. Your brother was a rapist. Your brother was a monster." Benson pulls Stabler off. "Don't listen to him," she says. "Don't." Abler grins. "Do you want me to tell you who Henson is? She's—"

"BEEF": The hamburger doesn't give a fuck who it kills.

"TORCH": A girl is raped and lit on fire. She comes into Benson's head screaming, smoke curling off her burned skin, not under-standing. It is the longest night of Benson's life thus far.

"ACE": Abler and Henson sense what is coming. They fuck, they eat, they drink, they smoke. They go dancing, tangoing on the chairs; a gavotte across the finished walnut. When the Beasley family comes home, there are heel marks in the soft wood of their dining room table, and half of the plates are broken.

"WANNABE": Copycat mischief-makers reverse street signs and tie people's shoelaces together. When Stabler falls over a fifth time, he slams his fist down on his floor. "THAT. IS. IT."

"SHATTERED": "Don't you understand?" Abler howls as Benson and Stabler struggle to their feet. Henson laughs and laughs. "You think this is all some vast conspiracy, but it's not. It's just the way it is." Benson pulls her gun from her holster and unloads a clip into both of them. Abler falls over immediately, an expression of surprise on his face. Blood gurgles from Henson's mouth, drips in a long stream down her chin. "Just like in the movies," Benson breathes.

SEASON 12

"LOCUM": Without Henson and Abler, Benson and Stabler don't know what to do with themselves. They go back, slowly, to old files. The missing girls and women. The dead. "Let's get them out," Stabler says, newly confident. "Let's set them free."

"BULLSEYE": "The reason we didn't catch him before is that his alibi was foolproof. But now, we know."

"BEHAVE": They start responding to no.

"MERCHANDISE": They arrest the madam who had permitted so many of her girls to be drowned. "Not by my hands!" she howls as they drag her to the squad car. "Not by my hands!"

"WET": Benson doesn't know how she knows, but she does. They walk the length of the Hudson. They locate eight missing bodies—different murderers, different years. She names them as the gurneys go rumbling past her.

"BRANDED": They catch the serial brander. His victims pick him out of a lineup, strange smiles pushing through their burned faces.

"How did you catch him?" one woman asks Benson. "Good old-fashioned police work," she says.

"TROPHY": "I'm looking for a wife," Benson's date says. He is handsome. He is brilliant. She stands up, folds her napkin on the table, and pulls three twenties from her wallet. "I have to go. I just . . . I have to go." She runs down the street. She breaks a heel on her shoe. She skips the rest of the way.

"PENETRATION": "No." "Yes." "No." "No?" "No." "Oh."

"GRAY": Benson plants some flowers.

"RESCUE": Benson and Stabler take out the kidnapper even before he reaches his destination.

"POP": Benson and Stabler think they hear gunfire, but when they come bursting out of the diner, it's just tiny fireworks lighting up windows three stories over their heads.

"POSSESSED": "Not for much longer," Benson says, to herself, in her sleep.

"MASK": Stabler and his wife dance all over the house, mouse masks on their faces. The kids stare at the scene in horror, and run to their room, where one is busy forgetting and the other is remembering what will, one day, be a chapter in her well-received memoir. Father Jones didn't touch just Stabler and Lucy, you know.

"DIRTY": The DA comes and helps Benson sweep up the wood chips from her floor. They clean the windows. They order pizza and talk about first loves.

"FLIGHT": The city is still hungry. The city is always hungry. But tonight, the heartbeat slows. They fly, they fly, they fly.

"SPECTACLE": On a Wednesday, they catch so many bad guys that Benson throws up seventeen girls in one afternoon. She laughs as they spill out of her, tumble into her vomit like oil slicks, and dissipate into the air.

"PURSUIT": They chase. They catch. No one gets away.

"BULLY": The last girl clings to the inside of Benson's skull. "I don't want to be alone," Benson says. "I don't, either," Benson says, "but you need to go." Stabler comes into Benson's apartment. "Her name is Allison Jones. She was twelve. She was raped by her father, and her mother didn't believe her. He killed her and buried her on Brighton Beach." Inside, the girl shakes her head, as if to dislodge the sand in her hair. "Go," Benson says. "Go." The girl smiles and doesn't, her bells barely rocking. "Thank you," Benson says. "You're welcome," Benson says. There is a sound—a new sound. A sigh. And then, she is gone. Stabler hugs Benson. "Good-bye," he says, and then, so is he.

"BOMBSHELL": The DA comes to Benson's door. Benson's head, newly clear, feels like a vacant airplane hangar, a desert. Expansive, but empty. She knows there are more—there will always be more— but for now she relishes the space. The DA reaches her hand up to Benson's face, and traces her jaw with the barest weight. "I want you," she says to Benson. "I've wanted you since the first time I met you." Benson leans forward and kisses her. The heartbeat is a hunger. She pulls her inside.

"TOTEM": "In the beginning, before the city, there was a creature. Genderless, ageless. The city flies on its back. We hear it, all of us, in one way or another. It demands sacrifices. But it can only eat what we give it." Benson strokes the DA's hair. "Where did you hear that story?" she asks. The DA bites her lip. "From someone who always seemed to be right," she says.

"REPARATIONS": Stabler and his wife talk it over. They decide to take the kids and go far, far away. "A new place," he says, "where we can have any names we want. Any histories."

"BANG": A bomb goes off in Central Park. It was beneath a park bench the whole time. No one is sitting on the bench when it detonates, and the only casualty is a passing pigeon. The serial killer sends a note to Benson and Stabler. All it says is "Oops."

"DELINQUENT": Benson and the DA are both late to work, and smell like each other. Stabler sends in his resignation by express post.

"SMOKED": The DA and Benson roast vegetables on the grill, laughing. The smoke rises up and up, drifts over the trees, curls past birds and rot and blooms. The city smells it. The city takes a breath.

REAL WOMEN HAVE BODIES

I used to think my place of employment, Glam, looked like the view from inside a casket. When you walk through the mall's east wing, the entrance recedes like a black hole between a children's photography studio and a white-walled boutique.

The lack of color is to show off the dresses. It terrifies our patrons into an existential crisis and then, a purchase. This is what Gizzy tells me, anyway. "The black," she says, "reminds us that we are mortal and that youth is fleeting. Also, nothing makes pink taffeta pop like a dark void."

At one end of the store is a mirror easily twice as tall as I am, rimmed by a baroque gold frame. Gizzy is so tall that she can dust the top of the giant mirror with only a small step stool. She is my mother's age, maybe a little older, but her face is strangely youthful and unlined. She paints her mouth matte peach every day, so evenly and cleanly that if you look at her too hard, you feel faint. I think her eyeliner is tattooed on her lids.

My coworker Natalie thinks that Gizzy runs this store because she's pining after her lost youth, which is her answer for why any "real adult" does anything she thinks is stupid. Natalie rolls her eyes behind Gizzy's back and always rehangs the dresses a little roughly, like they're to blame for the minimum wage or useless degrees or student debt. I follow behind her, smoothing out the skirts because I hate to see them ruffled any more than they have to be.

I know the truth. Not because I'm particularly perceptive or anything. I just overheard Gizzy talking on the phone once. I've seen the way she runs her hands over the dresses, the way her fingers linger on people's skin. Her daughter is gone like the others, and there isn't anything that she can do about it.

"I really like this," says the girl with the seal hair. She looks like she has just emerged from the ocean. The dress is the color of Dorothy's shoes and has a plunging back. "But I don't want to get a reputation," she murmurs, to no one in particular. She puts her hands on her hips, spins around, and flashes a smile. For a moment she looks like Jane Russell from *Gentlemen Prefer Blondes*, and then she is seal girl again, and then she is just a girl.

Her mother brings her another dress, this one gold with a cobalt shimmer on its surface. It's the first day of the season, and there's still a lot to choose from: bright teal slips and dusky pink thunderpuff, the *Bella* series, the one the color of bees. Mermaid cuts in salt-flat white; trumpet-style in algae red; princess gowns in liver purple. The Ophelia, which looks perpetually wet. Emma Wants a Second Chance, the exact shade of a doe standing in a shadow. The Banshee, with its strategically shredded, milk-colored silk. The skirts curl, ruffled, with layers of taffeta, except when they drag and slink. Their busts are crunchy with coral hand-stitched sequins, or studded with pebbles, or stretched with netting the color of frosted sea glass or neon early-morning buttercream or overripe cantaloupe. There is one that is just thousands of jet-black beads in midnight-black settings, that moves with every breath. The most expensive dress costs more than I make in three months; the least expensive two hundred, down from four because a strap is broken and Petra's mother has been too busy to come fix it.

Petra delivers the dresses to Glam. Her mother is one of our biggest suppliers. The Sadie's Photo crew has taken to skulking around Glam's entrance to gawk at the customers and shout rude comments, but Chris and Casey and a rotating assortment of other assholes leave Petra alone. She always wears a baseball cap over her short brown hair and tightly laced combat boots. When she's hauling the gauzy dresses wrapped up in plastic, she looks like she's battling a giant prom monster—all petticoat undersides and rhinestone tentacles—with her bare hands, and that is not the kind of woman you idly mess with. Casey referred to her as a dyke once during a smoke break, but he's too afraid of her to say anything to her face.

She makes me nervous, in an excess-salivation kind of way. We've had exactly two exchanges since I started working at Glam. The first one went like this:

"Do you need any help?"

"No."

And, three weeks later:

"It must be raining," I said, as the prom dress creature trembled in her hands and the plastic sheeting sent off drops of water.

"Maybe if it rains enough, we'll all drown. That'll be a nice change."

She is very cute when she comes out from underneath all of that fabric.

The first reports started at the height of the recession. The first victims—the first women—had not been seen in public for weeks. Many of the concerned friends and family who broke into their homes and apartments were expecting to find dead bodies.

I guess what they actually found was worse.

There was a video that went viral a few years back: amateur footage from a landlord in Cincinnati who brought a video camera with him in order to cover his ass as he evicted a woman who had fallen behind on the rent. He walked from room to room, calling her name, swinging the camera this way and that and making wisecracks. He had lots of things to say about her artwork, her dirty dishes, the vibrator on her nightstand. You could almost miss the punch line to the whole meandering affair if you were not looking closely enough. But then the camera spun around, and there she was, in the most sun-drenched corner of her bedroom, hidden by the light. She was naked, and trying to conceal it. You could see her breasts through her arm, the wall through her torso. She was crying. The sound was so soft that the inane chatter of the landlord had covered it until then. But then you could hear it—miserable, terrified.

No one knows what causes it. It's not passed in the air. It's not sexually transmitted. It's not a virus or a bacteria, or if it is, it's nothing scientists have been able to find. At first everyone blamed the fashion industry, then the millennials, and, finally, the water. But the water's been tested, the millennials aren't the only ones going incorporeal, and it doesn't do the fashion industry any good to have women fading away. You can't put clothes on air. Not that they haven't tried.

During our shared fifteen-minute break behind the emergency exit, Chris hands his cigarette to Casey. They pass it back and forth, the smoke curling out of their mouths like goldfish.

"Hips," Chris says. "That's what you want. Hips and enough flesh for you to grab onto, you know? What would you do without something to hold? That's like—like—"

"Like trying to drink water without a cup," Casey finishes.

I am always surprised at the poetry with which boys can describe boning.

They offer me the cigarette, like always. Like always, I decline. Casey grinds it against the wall and lets the butt drop; the ash clings to the brick like a bad cough.

"All I'm saying is," says Chris, "if I want to fuck mist, I'll just wait for a foggy night and pull my dick out."

I pinch the muscle between my shoulder and neck. "Apparently some guys like that."

"Who? No one I know," Chris says. He reaches out and presses his thumb into my collarbone, quickly. "You're like a stone."

"Thanks?" I knock his hand away.

"I mean, you're solid."

"Okay."

"Those other girls—" Chris begins.

"Man, did I ever tell you about the time I photographed a woman who had started to fade?" Casey says. Sadie's Photo specializes mostly in children's portrait photography, handing them props and planting them in these hellish little dioramas—a farmhouse, a tree house, a gazebo by a pond that's actually a piece of glass surrounded by green felt—but occasionally they get teenagers, even adult couples.

Chris shakes his head.

"When I was trying to clean up her portrait on the computer, there were all these weird reflections, like the lens was dirty or busted. Then I realized that I was just seeing what was behind her."

"Shit, dude. Did you tell her?"

"Fuck no. I figured she'd find out soon enough."

"Hey, stone girl," Casey shouts above the rumble of a forklift. "You coming?"

.   .   .

When I come back in from break, Natalie is glowering, stomping around the interior of Glam like a tiger stalking in its cage. Gizzy rolls her eyes as I sign in.

"I don't know why I keep her around," she says in a dry voice. "Petra will be in later with some new dresses. Don't let Natalie take off anyone's head."

Natalie unwraps four sticks of gum and folds them into her mouth one at a time, rolling the mass around in there as she chews, slowly and without apparent pleasure. Chris and Casey stop by, but when she glares at them, they take off like she's spitting acid.

"Fuckers," she mutters. "I have a goddamn photography degree, and I can't even get a job at Sadie's taking pictures of screaming babies. How the hell do those two assholes get to work there?" She flips the hanger of the first dress she sees. The mountain-blue bustle trembles. I turn it back.

"Do you ever wonder if the girls who come in here realize they're gonna grow up exactly as fucked as we are?" she says. I shrug, and she flips another dress. After that, I let her rage through the empty store. I stand near the closest rack, a collection ranging from pale, silky seafoam to dense moss, smoothing the skirts and watching the front door. The dresses look even sadder than normal tonight, even more like stringless marionettes. I hum under my breath as I fix twisted sequins. One of them pops off and flutters through the air. I kneel down and press the tip of my finger to it; then I tug at the hems so that they skim an even inch over the black carpeting. When I look up, I see a pair of combat boots, a bouquet of Technicolor skirts.

"You getting off soon?" Petra asks me. I stare up at her for a long moment, my crooked index finger bearing a gleaming sequin, and feel the heat of a blush creeping up my neck.

"I'm, uh, done at nine."

"It's nine now."

I stand. Petra lays the dresses gently over the counter. Natalie is back at the register, watching us curiously. "Are you okay to close up?" I ask her. She nods, her left eyebrow so sharply arched, it's in danger of touching her hairline.

We sit at a small table in the food court, across from Glam and the ice skating rink. The mall has just closed, so the space is empty except for clerks turning out the lights and rolling down the clattering grates at the storefronts.

"We could get a coffee or something, or—"

She touches my arm, and a shock of pleasure bolts from my cunt to my breastbone. She is wearing a necklace I've never seen before: a smoky quartz encased in a tangled sprawl of copper vines. Her lips are a little chapped.

"I hate coffee," she says.

"What about—"

"I hate that, too."

Petra's mother runs a motel off the highway, taken over from her father when he died a few years back. The patrons are mostly truckers, Petra explains as she drives, which is why it's set so far off the road. Between the entrance and the distant building is a tundra of thick, knobbly ice, over which Petra's ancient station wagon rocks like a canoe against the lapping tide. Slowly, we move closer and closer to the motel, which looms like a haunted house. A sign on the dilapidated building next to the motel blinks through a set of letters, B-A-R, three times before illuminating in its entirety and going dark. Petra drives with one hand on the wheel, the other rubbing a slow circle on my hand.

Petra parks the car along a deserted strip of spaces. The numbered doors are shut against the cold, quiet. "I need to get a key," she says. She gets out and walks around to my side of the car. She opens the door. "Are you coming?"

Inside the lobby, a large woman in a peach nightgown is using a sewing machine behind the counter. She looks like a melting ice cream cone—loose. Long hair spills off her head and disappears behind her back. The air is warm and soft and filled with a mechanical purring.

"Hey, Mama," says Petra. The woman doesn't respond.

Petra bangs on the counter with her hand. "Mama!" The woman behind the desk looks up briefly before returning to her work. She smiles but does not say anything. Her fingers flit like honeybees emerging from a hive on a too-warm winter day—dizzy, purposeful, punch-drunk. She moves a piece of heavy cotton through the machine, creating a hem.

"Who is this?" she asks. Her eyes don't break from her work.

"She's from Gizzy's store at the mall," Petra says, rifling through a drawer. She pulls out a white keycard and runs it through a small gray machine, pressing a few buttons. "I'm going to send her back with some of the new dresses."

"Sounds good, baby girl."

Petra pockets the card.

"We're going to take a walk."

"Sounds good, baby girl."

Petra fucks me in room 246, which is around the back of the building. She turns on the light and fan over the bed, and takes her shirt off by grabbing it behind the collar. I lie down on the bed, and she straddles me.

"You're really beautiful," she says into my skin. She grinds her pelvis hard against mine, and I moan, and at some point the cold charm of her necklace dips into my mouth and knocks against my teeth. I laugh, she laughs. She takes off the necklace and sets it down on the nightstand, the chain slithering like sand. When she sits up again, the ceiling fan frames her head like a glowing halo, like she's a Madonna in a medieval painting. There is a mirror on the opposite side of the room, and I catch fragments of her reflection. "May I—" she starts, and I nod before she finishes. She puts her hand over my mouth and bites my neck and slips three fingers into me. I laugh-gasp against her palm.

I come fast and hard, like a bottle breaking against a brick wall. Like I've been waiting for permission.

Afterward, Petra pulls a blanket over me, and we lie there listening to the wind. "How are you doing?" she asks, after a while.

"Okay," I say. "I mean, good. I wish every workday ended like that. I'd never miss a shift."

"Do you like working there?" she asks.

I snort, but don't know how to continue after that.

"That bad?"

"I mean, it's fine, I guess?" I draw my hair up into a bun. "It could be worse. It's just that I'm broke as hell and it's not like this is what I wanted to be doing with my life, but a lot of people have it worse."

"You're very kind to the dresses," she says.

"I just don't like it when Natalie fucks with them, even if she's half-joking. It seems—I don't know. Undignified."

Petra studies me. "I knew it. I knew you could tell."

"What?"

"Come on." She gets up and slips her shirt on, her underwear, her pants. It takes her a moment to lace her boots up as tightly as they were before. I hunt around for my shirt for a minute before finding it trapped between the mattress and the headboard.

Petra leads me through the parking lot and into the lobby. Her mother is not there. She steps behind the counter and pushes open the door.

At first, the room appears strangely lit—studded with patches of iridescent blue, like will-o'-the-wisps misleading us through a swamp. Dress forms stand at attention, an army with no purpose, surrounded by long tables scattered with pincushions and spools of thread, baskets of sequins, beads, and charms, an unspiraling measuring tape that looks like a snail, bolts of fabric. Petra takes my hand and guides me along the wall.

We are not alone in the room. Petra's mother is hovering near a dress, a bracelet pincushion wrapped around her wrist. As my eyes adjust to the dark, the lights coalesce into silhouettes, and I realize the room is full of women. Women like the one in the viral video, see-through and glowing faintly, like afterthoughts. They drift and mill and occasionally look down at their bodies. One of them, with a hard and sorrowful face, is standing very close to Petra's mother. She moves toward the garment slung over the dress form—butter yellow, the skirt gathered in small places like a theater curtain. She presses herself into it, and there is no resistance, only a sense of an ice cube melting in the summer air. The needle—trailed by thread of guileless gold—winks as Petra's mother plunges it through the girl's skin. The fabric takes the needle, too.

The girl does not cry out. Petra's mother makes tight, neat stitches along the girl's arm and torso, skin and fabric binding together as tightly as two sides of an incision. I realize that I am digging my fingers into Petra's arm, and she is letting me.

"Let me out," I say, and Petra pulls me through the door. We are standing in the middle of the well-lit vestibule. A sign resting on an easel reads CONTINENTAL BREAKFAST, 6 A.M.–8 A.M.

"What—" I point to the door. "What is she doing? What are they doing?"

"We don't know." Petra begins to pick at a bowl of fruit. She takes out an orange and rolls it around under her hand. "My mother has always been a seamstress. When Gizzy approached her about making dresses for Glam, she agreed. The women started showing up a few years ago—they would just fold themselves into the needlework, like it was what they wanted."

"Why would they do that?"

"I don't know."

"Didn't she tell them to stop?"

"She tried, but they kept coming. We don't even know how they know about this place." The orange begins to leak, and the air fills with the bite of citrus oil.

"Did you tell Gizzy?"

"Of course. But she said that as long as they sought us out, it was all right. And those dresses do so well—they sell more than anything my mother has ever made before. It's like people want them like that, even if they don't realize it."

I leave the motel on foot. I walk slowly over the ice, falling frequently. Once, I turn and look back and see Petra's outline in the lobby window. My hands go numb with cold. My cunt throbs, my head aches, and I can still feel her necklace in my mouth. I can taste the metal, and the stone. At the main road, I call a cab.

·   ·   ·

I go to Glam early the next morning. My key is missing—I must have left it on the dresser at the motel, I realize, swearing under my breath—so I wait for Natalie to arrive. Inside the store, I leave her to the morning tasks and search through the dresses. They rustle beneath my fingers, groan on their hangers. I press my face into their skirts, shape the bodices beneath my hands to give them room.

I wander the mall on my lunch break. I wonder about the merchandise I pass. Who's in there? The wooden picture frame samples arranged in descending v's down a felt display case look askew, as if they've been invaded. The glass-and-steel chess set in the window of the game store—are those the reflections of passersby in the fat curve of the queen and the pawns, or faces peering out? There's an ancient Pac-Man machine that takes everyone's quarters, seemingly on purpose. I walk past the heavily scented entrance of a JCPenney cosmetics counter, and imagine customers uncapping tubes of lipstick and twisting the color free, and faded women squeezing up around the makeup, thumbs first.

In front of the Auntie Anne's, I stand and watch as the dough is pulled, heavy and wet. I imagine toddlers, faded girls (they were fading younger and younger, weren't they? That's what they said on the news) pressed into the dough, and, yes, isn't that a curled hand? A pouting lip? A little girl standing in front of the counter asks her mother for a pretzel.

"Susan," the mother admonishes. "Pretzels are junk food. They will make you fat." And she drags her away.

A posse of teenagers squeezes into Glam after I get back. The girls pull dresses off hangers and slip them on carelessly, not even pulling the modesty curtains closed enough to conceal their dressing and undressing. When they come out, I can see the faded women all bound up in them, fingers laced tightly through the grommets. I cannot tell if they are holding on for dear life or if they are trapped. The rustling and trembling of the fabric could be weeping or laughter. The girls spin and lace and tighten. From the doorway of the store, Chris and Casey are gnawing on Slurpee straws. They hoot and holler but never cross the threshold. Their mouths are stained blue.

"Fuck you!" I run toward the entrance, a stapler's comforting weight deep in my palm. My arm is ready to sling it, if I have to. "Get out. Go the fuck away."

"Jesus," Chris says, blinking. He takes a step back. "What's your problem?"

"Hey, Lindsay, nice!" Casey yells into the store. A blonde turns and grins, popping her hip to the side like she's about to balance an infant on it. Deep in the thick folds of the satin, I see lidless eyes.

In Glam's black bathroom, I throw up everything.

"I can't stay," I tell Gizzy. "I just can't."

She sighs. "Look," she says, "I really like you a lot. The economy is shit, and I know you don't have another job lined up. Can you at least stay on until the end of the season? I can even give you a little raise."

"I can't."

"Why not?" She hands me a tissue, and I blow my nose.

"I just can't."

She looks genuinely sad. She digs a piece of paper out of her desk and starts to write on it. "I'm not sure how long Natalie will last without you," she says. "I like Natalie."

I let out a bark of laughter.

"Come on, Natalie's great, but she's the worst."

"She's not the worst."

"She called a customer a 'sanctimonious twat' today. To her face."

Gizzy looks up at me and sighs. "She reminds me of my daughter, all piss and vinegar. Isn't that stupid? What a stupid reason." She smiles sadly.

"Gizzy, is your daughter—is she here? In the—in the store?"

Gizzy turns her face away and finishes writing. She hands the paper to me. "Sign this?"

I do.

"Your final check will come in the mail," she says, and I nod. "Bye, kiddo. If you ever want your job back, you know how to find me." She squeezes my hand lightly and puts the pen in a drawer.

Through the narrowing gap of the closing office door, I see Gizzy staring at the far wall.

Petra is waiting next to my car.

"You forgot this." She hands me the missing key. I take it and slide it into my pocket. I look away from her.

"I just quit," I say. "I'm leaving." I open the driver's-side door and drop into the seat. She gets in next to me. "Look, what do you want?" I say.

"You like me, right?"

I rub my neck. "Yes. I guess."

"Why don't we go out? For real this time." She slings a heavy boot up on the dashboard. "No faded women. No dresses. Just, I dunno, movies and food and fucking."

I hesitate.

"Promise," she says.

I find a cleaning job at the local condiment factory, a late-night shift. The pay is shit, but no worse than Glam. One job is the same as another. I move out of my apartment and into the motel, where

I can stay for free. The rooms are never entirely full and Petra assures me her mother will never know the difference.

I spend most of my time in the factory sweeping, mopping, walking past large rooms where hot, acrid blasts of cooking wine take the air out of my lungs. Barbecue sauce is brewing and the smell saturates my hair and clothes. I rarely catch a glimpse of another human being, and I like it that way. I often find myself searching the dark corners, but why would they come here? I am always afraid that I will find one trying to cook herself into the mustard, but I never do.

Months fall away. I consider going to grad school, if the government doesn't shut the universities down like they're threatening to. We binge-watch medical procedural shows and eat lo mein and kiss and fuck and sleep odd hours tangled up together like coat hangers.

One night, I find her standing in front of the bathroom mirror, pulling at her face in the fluorescent light. I come up behind her and kiss her shoulder. "Hey," I say. "Sorry, I really smell like a steak today. I'll wash up."

I step into the shower. The water heats my skin, and I moan from the sensation. The shower curtain rustles, and Petra joins me, her skin drawn up into goose bumps. She puts her hand behind my head, heating it up in the water, and then slips it between my legs. The other one loops through my hair, pulls me against the tile.

After I come, she steps out of the shower. When I leave the bathroom, drying my hair, she's lying spread-eagled on the bed, and I know.

"I'm fading," she says, and as she says it, I can see that her skin is more like skim milk than whole, that she seems less there. She breathes and the impression blinks, like she's fighting it. I feel like my feet are trapdoors that have sprung open, and my insides are hurtling out of my body. I want to hold her, but I'm afraid that if I do, she'll give way beneath my arms. "I don't want to die," she says.

"I don't think—they're not dead," I say, but the statement feels like a lie and is unhelpful in every way.

I have never seen Petra cry, not until now. She brings her hands to her face—the outline of her lips visible, ever so faintly, through their jail bars of tendons, muscle, and bone. A shudder runs the length of her body. I touch her, and still she has mass. A stone.

"A few months," she says. "Or something like that. That's what the news says, right?" She pinches the bridge of her nose, tugs her earlobes, presses her fingers tightly into her stomach.

That first night, Petra just wants to be held, so that's what I do. We line up our bodies and press them together, every inch. She wakes up ravenous—for food, for me.

A few days later, my eyes open at dawn and Petra is not there. I flip back the covers, stalk into the bathroom, shove the shower curtain open with a slinking rattle. A chill moves through my body, and I check the drawers, the space beneath the TV, the inside of the radiator. Nothing.

As the mattress creaks beneath my sinking body, she comes though the door, her shirt sticking to her through patches of sweat. She bends over and puts her hands on her knees, still trying to catch her breath. Only when she looks up does she see me, shaking.

"Oh god, oh god, I'm so fucking sorry." She sits down next to me and I bury my face in her shoulder, where she smells like loam.

"I thought it'd happened already," I whisper. "I thought you were gone."

"I just needed to get out into the morning," she says. "I wanted to feel my body running." She kisses me. "Let's do something tonight."

When the sun sets, we go to the trucker bar behind the motel. The beer tastes watery and the glasses sweat. We sit at a table with pictures of fox heads and people's names carved into the scarred wood. Petra has discovered that she can pass small objects through her fingers sometimes, so she drops coins into her hand as we sip our beers. I can't watch.

"Let's play darts or something," I say.

Petra lifts her fingers and tries to grab the quarter on the table. Her fingers pass through it once, twice, but on the third try her hand seems to blink into the physical universe again and she gets it. She sinks the quarter into the jukebox. I ask the bartender for darts and he hands them to me in an old cigar box.

We take turns throwing them at the target. Neither of us is very good, and I bury one in the wall. Petra's laugh is dark and liquid.

"My aim has never been good," I confess. "When I was a kid, we used to have a beanbag toss game that my aunt bought us, and I literally never once got a beanbag into the hole. Not a single time. We're talking literally years of my life. My brother thought it was the goddamn funniest thing he'd ever seen."

Petra stares at me. A handsome smile pulls at the edge of her mouth and then vanishes, replaced by a flattened expression. Then she says, "Your family sounds really fucking nice." The word *nice* is like a splinter of glass.

I have been picking up my phone every few days, intending to explain to my family that women are sewn into dresses and I'm working at a factory and am living in a motel with the daughter of a seamstress who is also dying though not exactly dying. I can't. The last time I talked to my mother, I assured her I was solid and safe, though I confessed to her that I'd had to delay my student loan payments again. I made up stories about the day's clients, and it must have been believable because she sounded relieved.

"They are," I say. "Maybe you'll get to meet them one day."

"I wouldn't bother. I'm on the way out, right?"

"Jesus fuck, Petra. Don't talk like that. And don't talk to me like that."

She falls into a sullen silence; absently picks at a zit on her chin. She finishes her beer, buys another, her dart tosses becoming less precise, yawning wider and wider from the center target. I don't like the way she is pulling the darts out of the board—like she's yanking on an opponent's ponytail. After the fourth game, her hand blinks out mid-drink and the glass falls, beer and shards of glass asterisking on the wooden floorboards.

Petra walks over to the board. I can see her opening and closing her fist, feeling for substance. In the moment that matter returns to her, she rests her hand, flat and palm down, on the wall. Pulling the dart from the target, she plunges it deep into the back of her hand, just below the knuckles.

From the back of the bar, someone yells, "Holy shit."

I crash past the table and grab Petra, though not before she has plunged the needle of the dart into her hand twice more. She is screaming. Blood streams down her arm like maypole ribbons. Men get up quickly from their stools and chairs, some of which clatter to the floor. Petra flails, howling. Her blood spatters the wall like rain. A stocky man in a black baseball cap helps me drag her out the front door. I half-carry, half-haul her across the icy parking lot. After we have gone a few dozen yards, she seems to soften in my arms. For a moment, I am terrified she is fading again, but no, she is still solid, just limp with exhaustion and stubbornness. A dark trail marks the path we have taken.

She refuses the hospital. In our room, I disinfect her wound, wrap it in gauze.

We have never fucked with such urgency as we do in these weeks, but she is fading more and feeling less. She comes infrequently. She withdraws for longer and longer periods of time—one minute, four, seven. Each episode shows a different view of her—a skeleton, ropy muscles, the dark shapes of her organs, nothing. She wakes up sobbing, and I rope my arm tightly around her torso, shushing gently into her ear. She reads rumors on the Internet about how you can slow fading. One message board talks about a high-iron diet, so she steams enough spinach to feed a large family and chews on it wordlessly. Another recommends ice-cold showers, and I find her trembling and goosebumped in the bathtub. She lets me dry her off, like she's a child.

On a warm Sunday, Petra wants to go for a hike, so we do. Spring seizes the valley in fits and spurts, and today the paths through the woods are muddy. Snow melts and drips water into our hair. We follow a creek that is practically a living thing, surging messily through its own curves and bends.

We take a break in a sunny clearing and eat oranges and cold chicken. Petra has taken to treating every meal as her last, so she peels the skins off the pieces of chicken and chews on them with her eyes closed, and then on the meat itself, and then she sucks hard on every bone before throwing it off into the trees. She sets each wedge of orange in her mouth reverently, as if it is the Eucharist, bites into the meat, and pulls the rinds away like hangnails. She rubs the peels against her skin.

"I've been doing some reading," says Petra in between pulls of ice water. "It turns out that they think that the faded women are doing this sort of—I don't know, I guess you'd call it terrorism? They're getting themselves into electrical systems and fucking up servers and ATMs and voting machines. Protesting." She still refers to them in the third person. "I like that."

The woods are quiet but for the hum of insects and twittering of birds. We peel off our clothes and soak in the sun. I examine my fingertips against the light, pink-amber halos around the shadows of my bones.

I lean over Petra and kiss her bottom lip, the top. I kiss her throat. I bury my hand between her thighs.

Around us, minutes inch over the dirt like ants, tumble into the swollen stream, are carried away.

We find a chapel among the trees. The pews are even and rigid, and stained glass windows line the walls. Our footfalls echo along the stone floor. The air is hot and we kick up dust that weaves through the light.

We sit down in a pew that groans beneath our weight. Petra lays her head on my shoulder. "Do you think faded women ever die?"

"I guess I don't know."

"Or age?"

I shrug and press my nose into her hair.

"So I might be twenty-nine for all of eternity."

"Maybe. You'll be haunting me when I'm a hundred and you'll look fantastic and I'll look like shit."

"Nah, you'll be a beautiful crone. You'll have a cabin in the forest and there will be rumors that you're a witch, but the kids who are brave enough to get close will get to listen to your stories." She shudders so hard I feel it in my skeleton.

I see movement out of the corner of my eye and I stand. In the window depicting Saint Rita of Cascia, a faded woman is clinging to the lead, her fingers curled around the cames as if they were monkey bars. She is watching us, rocking on her heels, popping in and out of the glass as if she were treading water. Petra notices her and stands next to me. In her hand, I see the votive of a prayer candle.

"Petra, don't."

I can see her throw muscles twitching. "I can set her free," she says. "If I break it, I can set her free."

"We don't know that."

"Don't tell me what to do. You're not my fucking mother."

I gently circle her wrist and lean into her hair. "I love you," I say. It's the first time I've said it, and it tastes strange in my mouth—real but not ready, like a too-hard pear. I ease the votive from her hand and slide it into my jacket pocket. I kiss her temple, her jaw. She turns into my body. I think she's going to cry, but she doesn't.

"I miss you already," she says.

I run my hand along her back, and as I do I am certain I see a flash of my own muscle. My stomach tightens. The chicken and oranges protest, press up my esophagus. "We should go back," I say. "I think it's gonna be dark soon."

The faded woman won't look away. She smiles. Or maybe she is grimacing.

We come out of the woods like we're being born.

· · ·

In our room, we watch the news, our bodies curled together in the soft blue glow of the television. Pundits point fingers at each other, screaming as the cohost between them shimmers and wavers under the studio lights. They are talking about how we can't trust the faded women, women who can't be touched but can stand on the earth, which means they must be lying about something, they must be deceiving us somehow.

"I don't trust anything that can be incorporeal and isn't dead," one of them says.

The woman blinks away midbroadcast, a microphone tumbling to the floor. The camera scrambles to look away.

Before we go to bed, I set the votive from the chapel on the nightstand and light the candle. It flickers comfortingly, casting the furniture against the wall like shadow puppets.

I dream that we go to a restaurant that serves only soup. I can't decide what to order, and she laughs and stirs the bowl she's already received. When she pulls the spoon out, there is a jellied, ghostly hand twirled tightly around the handle, and she pulls the faded woman up and up. The woman's mouth is open as if she's crying out, but I can't hear anything.

When I wake, I am sure Petra has gone for a run, before I realize that my hand has sunk into the luminous cavern of her chest.

I tip into her completely, choke like I'm being waterboarded. She wakes up and screams as I flail around inside her.

After a minute, we calm down. She moves away from me, to the edge of the bed. We wait. Seven minutes go by. Ten. Half an hour.

"Is this it?" I ask her. "Is this it?"

I don't want to leave, but she is turned away from me. I stand up. She does not look at anything except her own hands.

After a long time, she says, "It's time to go."

I cry. I slip on my boots, their heels chewed up by my uneven footsteps. I look at her there, gone, and she finally turns and I know she can see my body, still solid enough to be limned in light, moving about the watery afterbirth of the sunrise.

I close the door behind me, and I feel my nerves fire on and off. Soon, I'll be nothing more, too. None of us will make it to the end.

Only half of the mannequins in Glam's windows are clothed. It's the end of the season. The shop will rotate, soon. The stock will go—somewhere. The lights go out, the gate rattles down halfway. Natalie stoops beneath it and pulls it shut.

She stands up and sees me. She looks thinner than I remember. She nods ever so slightly and then takes off into the cavernous interior of the mall. I hold my old key tightly in my hand. It fits the lock—Gizzy never bothered to change it. The gate slides up loudly. The pinking shears are stuck in the back of my jeans, where I could carry a gun, if I cared to.

I cut the places where one thing is stitched to another. I unlace bodices. I can see them, the women, loosened from their moorings, blinking up at me. "Get out," I tell them. I tear at the hems and seams. The dresses are coming apart, looking more alive than I have ever seen them, the fabric splitting away from the form like so many banana peels, flaps of gold and peach and wine. "Get out," I say again. They are blinking, unmoving.

"Why aren't you going?" I scream. "Say something!" They do not.

I pull away the panel of a bodice. A woman stares back at me. She could be Gizzy's daughter. She could be Petra or Natalie, or my mother, or even me. "No, fuck it. You don't even have to say anything. Just get out. The gate is open. Please."

A flashlight beam dances over the far wall. I hear a deep voice. "Hello? Who's there? I've called the police."

"Please, go!" I scream, even as the security guard tackles me to the ground. From the blackness of the floor, I see them all, faintly luminous, moving about in their husks. But they remain. They don't move, they never move.

EIGHT BITES

As they put me to sleep, my mouth fills with the dust of the moon. I expect to choke on the silt but instead it slides in and out, and in and out, and I am, impossibly, breathing.

I have dreamt of inhaling underneath water and this is what it feels like: panic, and then acceptance, and then elation. I am going to die, I am not dying, I am doing a thing I never thought I could do.

Back on earth, Dr. U is inside me. Her hands are in my torso, her fingers searching for something. She is loosening flesh from its casing, slipping around where she's been welcomed, talking to a nurse about her vacation to Chile. "We were going to fly to Antarctica," she says, "but it was too expensive."

"But the penguins," the nurse says.

"Next time," Dr. U responds.

Before this, it was January, a new year. I waded through two feet of snow on a silent street, and came to a shop where wind chimes hung silently on the other side of the glass, mermaid-shaped baubles and bits of driftwood and too-shiny seashells strung through with fishing line and unruffled by any wind.

The town was deep dead, a great distance from the late-season smattering of open shops that serve the day-trippers and the money savers. Owners had fled to Boston or New York, or, if they were lucky, farther south. Businesses had shuttered for the season, leaving their wares in the windows like a tease. Underneath, a second town had opened up, familiar and alien at the same time. It's the same every year. Bars and restaurants made secret hours for locals, the rock-solid Cape Codders who've lived though dozens of winters. On any given night you could look up from your plate to see round bundles stomp through the doorway; only when they peeled their outsides away could you see who was beneath. Even the ones you knew from the summer were more or less strangers in this perfunctory daylight; all of them were alone, even when they were with each other.

On this street, though, I might as well have been on another planet. The beach bunnies and art dealers would never see the town like this, I thought, when the streets are dark and a liquid chill roils through the gaps and alleys. Silence and sound bumped up against each other but never intermingled; the jolly chaos of warm summer nights was as far away as it could be. It was hard to stop moving between doorways in this weather, but if you did you could hear life pricking the stillness: a rumble of voices from a local tavern, wind livening the buildings, sometimes even a muffled animal encounter in an alley: pleasure or fear, it was all the same noise.

Foxes wove through the streets at night. There was a white one among them, sleek and fast, and she looked like the ghost of the others.

I was not the first in my family to go through with it. My three sisters had gotten the procedure over the years, though they didn't say anything before showing up for a visit. Seeing them suddenly svelte after years of watching them grow organically, as I have, was like a palm to the nose, more painful than you'd expect. My first sister, well, I thought she was dying. Being sisters, I thought we all were dying, noosed by genetics. When confronted by my anxiety—"What disease is sawing off this branch of the family tree?" I asked, my voice crabwalking up an octave—my first sister confessed: a surgery.

Then, all of them, my sisters, a chorus of believers. Surgery. A surgery. As easy as when you broke your arm as a kid and had to get the pins in—maybe even easier. A band, a sleeve, a gut rerouted. *Rerouted*? But their stories—*it melts away, it's just gone*—were spring-morning warm, when the sun makes the difference between happiness and shivering in a shadow.

When we went out, they ordered large meals and then said, "I couldn't possibly." They always said this, always, that decorous insistence that they *couldn't possibly*, but for once, they actually meant it—that bashful lie had been converted into truth vis-à-vis a medical procedure. They angled their forks and cut impossibly tiny portions of food—doll-sized cubes of watermelon, a slender stalk of pea shoot, a corner of a sandwich as if they needed to feed a crowd loaves-and-fishes-style with that single serving of chicken salad—and swallowed them like a great decadence.

"I feel so good," they all said. Whenever I talked to them, that was what always came out of their mouths, or really, it was a mouth, a single mouth that once ate and now just says, "I feel really, really good."

Who knows where we got it from, though—the bodies that needed the surgery. It didn't come from our mother, who always looked normal, not hearty or curvy or Rubenesque or Midwestern or voluptuous, just normal. She always said eight bites are all you need to get the sense of what you are eating. Even though she never counted out loud, I could hear the eight bites as clearly as if a game show audience were counting backward, raucous and triumphant, and after *one* she would set her fork down, even if there was food left on her plate. She didn't mess around, my mother. No pushing food in circles or pretending. Iron will, slender waistline. Eight bites let her compliment the hostess. Eight bites lined her stomach like insulation rolled into the walls of houses. I wished she was still alive, to see the women her daughters had become.

And then, one day, not too soon after my third sister sashayed out of my house with more spring in her step than I'd ever seen, I ate eight bites and then stopped. I set the fork down next to the plate, more roughly than I'd intended, and took a chip of ceramic off the rim in the process. I pressed my finger into the shard and carried it to the trash can. I turned and looked back at my plate, which had been so full before and was full still, barely a dent in the raucous mass of pasta and greens.

I sat down again, picked up my fork, and had eight more bites. Not much more, still barely a dent, but now twice as much as necessary. But the salad leaves were dripping vinegar and oil and the noodles had lemon and cracked pepper and everything was just so beautiful, and I was still hungry, and so I had eight more. After, I finished what was in the pot on the stove and I was so angry I began to cry.

I don't remember getting fat. I wasn't a fat child or teenager; photos of those young selves are not embarrassing, or if they are, they're embarrassing in the right ways. Look how young I am! Look at my weird fashion! Saddle shoes—who thought of those? Stirrup pants—are you joking? Squirrel barrettes? Look at those glasses, look at that face: mugging for the camera. Look at that expression, mugging for a future self who is holding those photos, sick with nostalgia. Even when I thought I was fat, I wasn't; the teenager in those photos is very beautiful, in a wistful kind of way.

But then I had a baby. Then I had Cal—difficult, sharp-eyed Cal, who has never gotten me half as much as I have never gotten her—and suddenly everything was wrecked, like she was a heavy-metal rocker trashing a hotel room before departing. My stomach was the television set through the window. She was now a grown woman and so far away from me in every sense, but the evidence still clung to my body. It would never look right again.

As I stood over the empty pot, I was tired. I was tired of the skinny-minny women from church who cooed and touched each other's arms and told me I had beautiful skin, and having to rotate my hips sideways to move through rooms like crawling over someone at the movie theater. I was tired of flat, unforgiving dressing room lights; I was tired of looking into the mirror and grabbing the things that I hated and lifting them, clawing deep, and then letting them drop and everything aching. My sisters had gone somewhere else and left me behind, and as I always have, I wanted nothing more than to follow.

I could not make eight bites work for my body and so I would make my body work for eight bites.

Dr. U did twice-a-week consultations in an office a half-hour drive south on the Cape. I took a slow, circuitous route getting there. It had been snowing on and off for days, and the sleepy snowdrifts caught on every tree trunk and fencepost like blown-away laundry. I knew the way because I'd driven past her office before—usually after a sister's departure—and so as I drove this time I daydreamt about buying clothes in the local boutiques, spending too much for a sundress taken off a mannequin, pulling it against my body in the afternoon sun as the mannequin stood, less lucky than I.

Then I was in her office, on her neutral carpet, and a receptionist was pushing open a door. The doctor was not what I expected. I suppose I had imagined that because of the depth of her convictions, as illustrated by her choice of profession, she should have been a slender woman: either someone with excessive self-control or a sympathetic soul whose insides had also been rearranged to suit her vision of herself. But she was sweetly plump—why had I skipped over the phase where I was round and unthreatening as a panda, but still lovely? She smiled with all her teeth. What was she doing, sending me on this journey she herself had never taken?

She gestured, and I sat.

There were two Pomeranians running around her office. When they were separated—when one was curled up at Dr. U's feet and the other was decorously taking a shit in the hallway—they appeared identical but innocuous, but when one came near the other they were spooky, their heads twitching in sync, as if they were two halves of a whole. The doctor noticed the pile outside of the door and called for the receptionist. The door closed.

"I know what you're here for," she said, before I could open my mouth. "Have you researched bariatric surgery before?"

"Yes," I said. "I want the kind you can't reverse."

"I admire a woman of conviction," she said. She began pulling binders out of a drawer. "There are some procedures you'll have to go through. Visiting a psychiatrist, seeing another doctor, support groups—administrative nonsense, taking up a lot of time. But everything is going to change for you," she promised, shaking a finger at me with an accusing, loving smile. "It will hurt. It won't be easy. But when it's over, you're going to be the happiest woman alive."

My sisters arrived a few days before the surgery. They set themselves up in the house's many empty bedrooms, making up their side tables with lotions and crossword puzzles. I could hear them upstairs and they sounded like birds, distinct and luminously choral at the same time.

I told them I was going out for a final meal.

"We'll come with you," said my first sister.

"Keep you company," said my second sister.

"Be supportive," said my third sister.

"No," I said, "I'll go alone. I need to be alone."

I walked to my favorite restaurant, Salt. It hadn't always been Salt, though, in name or spirit. It was Linda's, for a while, and then Family Diner, then The Table. The building remains the same, but it is always new and always better than before.

I thought about people on death row and their final meals, as I sat at a corner table, and for the third time that week I worried about my moral compass, or lack thereof. They aren't the same, I reminded myself as I unfolded the napkin over my lap. Those things are not comparable. Their last meal comes before death; mine comes before not just life, but a new life. *You are horrible*, I thought, as I lifted the menu to my face, higher than it needed to be.

I ordered a cavalcade of oysters. Most of them had been cut the way they were supposed to be, and they slipped down as easily as water, like the ocean, like nothing at all, but one fought me: anchored to its shell, a stubborn hinge of flesh. It resisted. It was resistance incarnate. Oysters are alive, I realized. They are nothing but muscle; they have no brains or insides, strictly speaking, but they are alive nonetheless. If there were any justice in the world, this oyster would grab hold of my tongue and choke me dead.

I almost gagged, but then I swallowed.

My third sister sat down across the table from me. Her dark hair reminded me of my mother's: almost too shiny and homogenous to be real, though it was. She smiled kindly at me, as if she were about to give me some bad news.

"Why are you here?" I asked her.

"You look troubled," she said. She held her hands in a way that showed off her red nails, which were so lacquered they had horizontal depth, like a rose trapped in glass. She tapped them against her cheekbones, scraping them down her face with the very lightest touch. I shuddered. Then she picked up my water and drank deeply of it, until the water had filtered through the ice and the ice was nothing more than a fragile lattice and then the whole construction slid against her face as she tipped the glass higher and she chewed the slivers that landed in her mouth.

"Don't waste that stomach space on water," she said, *crunch-crunch-crunch*ing. "Come on now. What are you eating?"

"Oysters," I said, even though she could see the precarious pile of shells before me.

She nodded. "Are they good?" she asked.

"They are."

"Tell me about them."

"They are the sum of all healthy things: seawater and muscle and bone," I said. "Mindless protein. They feel no pain, have no verifiable thoughts. Very few calories. An indulgence without being an indulgence. Do you want one?"

I didn't want her to be there—I wanted to tell her to leave—but her eyes were glittering as if she had a fever. She ran her finger-nail lovingly along an oyster shell. The whole pile shifted, doubling down on its own mass.

"No," she said. Then, "Have you told Cal? About the procedure?"

I bit my lip. "No," I said. "Did you tell your daughter, before you got it?"

"I did. She was so excited for me. She sent me flowers."

"Cal will not be excited," I said. "There are many daughter duties Cal does not perform, and this will be one, too."

"Do you think she needs the surgery, too? Is that why?"

"I don't know," I said. "I have never understood Cal's needs."

"Do you think it's because she will think badly of you?"

"I've also never understood her opinions," I said.

My sister nodded.

"She will not send me flowers," I concluded, even though this was probably not necessary.

I ordered a pile of hot truffle fries, which burned the roof of my mouth. It was only after the burn that I thought about how much I'd miss it all. I started to cry, and my sister put her hand over mine. I was jealous of the oysters. They never had to think about themselves.

At home, I called Cal to tell her. My jaw was so tightly clenched, it popped when she answered the phone. On the other end I could hear another woman's voice, stopped short by a finger to the lips unseen; then a dog whined.

"Surgery?" she repeated.

"Yes," I said.

"Jesus Christ," she said.

"Don't swear," I told her, even though I am not a religious woman.

"What? That's not even a fucking swear," she yelled. "*That* was a fucking swear. And this. *Jesus Christ* is not a swear. It's a proper name. And if there's ever a time to swear, it's when your mom tells you she's getting half of one of her most important organs cut away for no reason—"

She was still talking, but it was growing into a yell. I shooed the words away like bees.

"—occur to you that you're never going to be able to eat like a normal human—"

"What is wrong with you?" I finally asked her.

"Mom, I just don't understand why you can't be happy with yourself. You've never been—"

She kept talking. I stared at the receiver. When did my child sour? I didn't remember the process, the top-down tumble from sweetness to curdled anger. She was furious constantly, she was all accusation. She had taken the moral high ground from me by force, time and time again. I had committed any number of sins: Why didn't I teach her about feminism? Why did I persist in not understanding anything? And *this*, this takes the cake, no, *don't* forgive the pun; language is infused with food like everything else, or at least like everything else should be. She was so angry, I was glad I couldn't read her mind. I knew her thoughts would break my heart.

The line went dead. She'd hung up on me. I set the phone on the receiver and realized my sisters were watching me from the doorway, two looking sympathetic, the other smug.

I turned away. Why didn't Cal understand? Her body was imperfect but it was also fresh, pliable. She could sidestep my mistakes. She could have the release of a new start. I had no self-control, but tomorrow I would relinquish control and everything would be right again.

The phone rang. Cal, calling back? But it was my niece. She was selling knife sets so she could go back to school and become a— well, I missed that part, but she would get paid just for telling me about the knives, so I let her walk me through, step-by-step, and I bought a cheese knife with a special cut-out center—"So the cheese doesn't stick to the blade, see?" she said.

In the operating room, I was open to the world. Not that kind of open, not yet, everything was still sealed up inside, but I was naked except for a faintly patterned cloth gown that didn't quite wrap around my body.

"Wait," I said. I laid my hand upon my hip and squeezed a little. I trembled, though I didn't know why. There was an IV, and the IV would relax me; soon I would be very far away.

Dr. U stared at me over her mask. Gone was the sweetness from her office; her eyes looked transformed. Icy.

"Did you ever read that picture book about Ping the duck?" I asked her.

"No," she said.

"Ping the duck was always punished for being the last duck home. He'd get whacked across the back with a switch. He hated that. So he ran away. After he ran away he met some black fishing birds with metal bands around their necks. They caught fish for their masters but could not swallow the fish whole, because of the bands. When they brought fish back, they were rewarded with tiny pieces they could swallow. They were obedient, because they had to be. Ping, with no band, was always last and now was lost. I don't remember how it ends. It seems like a book you should read."

She adjusted her mask a little. "Don't make me cut out your tongue," she said.

"I'm ready," I told her.

The mask slipped over me and I was on the moon.

Afterward, I sleep and sleep. It's been a long time since I've been so still. I stay on the couch because stairs, stairs are impossible. In the watery light of morning, dust motes drift through the air like plankton. I have never seen the living room so early. A new world.

I drink shaking sips of clear broth, brought to me by my first sister, who, silhouetted against the window, looks like a branch stripped bare by the wind. My second sister checks in on me every so often, opening the windows a crack despite the cold—to let some air in, she says softly. She does not say the house smells stale and like death but I can see it in her eyes as she fans the door open and shut and open and shut as patiently as a mother whose child has vomited. I can see her cheekbones, high and tight as cherries, and I smile at her as best I can.

My third sister observes me at night, sitting on a chair near the sofa, where she glances at me from above her book, her brows tightening and loosening with concern. She talks to her daughter—who loves her without judgment, I am sure—in the kitchen, so softly I can barely hear her, but then forgets herself and laughs loudly at some joke shared between them. I wonder if my niece has sold any more knives.

I am transformed but not yet, exactly. The transformation has begun—this pain, this excruciating pain, it is part of the process—and will not end until—well, I suppose I don't know when. Will I ever be done, transformed in the past tense, or will I always be transforming, better and better until I die?

Cal does not call. When she does I will remind her of my favorite memory of her: when I caught her with a chemical depilatory in the bathroom in the wee hours of morning, creaming her little tan arms and legs and upper lip so the hair dissolved like snow in sunlight. I will tell her, when she calls.

The shift, at first, is imperceptible, so small as to be a trick of the imagination. But then one day I button a pair of pants and they fall to my feet. I marvel at what is beneath. A pre-Cal body. A pre-me body. It is emerging, like the lie of snow withdrawing from the truth of the landscape. My sisters finally go home. They kiss me and tell me that I look beautiful.

I am finally well enough to walk along the beach. The weather has been so cold that the water is thick with ice and the waves churn creamily, like soft serve. I take a photo and send it to Cal, but I know she won't respond.

At home, I cook a very small chicken breast and cut it into white cubes. I count the bites and when I reach eight I throw the rest of the food in the garbage. I stand over the can for a long while, breathing in the salt-and-pepper smell of chicken mixed in with coffee grounds and something older and closer to decay. I spray window cleaner into the garbage can so the food cannot be retrieved. I feel a little light but good; righteous, even. Before, I would have been growling, climbing up the walls from want. Now I feel only slightly empty, and fully content.

That night, I wake up because something is standing over me, something small, and before I slide into being awake I think it's my daughter, up from a nightmare, or perhaps it's morning and I've overslept, except even as my hands exchange blanket warmth for chilled air and it is so dark, I remember that my daughter is in her late twenties and lives in Portland with a roommate who is not really her roommate and she will not tell me and I don't know why.

But something is there, darkness blotting out darkness, a person-shaped outline. It sits on the bed, and I feel the weight, the mattress springs creaking and pinging. Is it looking at me? Away from me? Does it look, at all?

And then there is nothing, and I sit up alone.

As I learn my new diet—my forever diet, the one that will end only when I do—something is moving in the house. At first I think it is mice, but it is larger, more autonomous. Mice in walls scurry and drop through unexpected holes, and you can hear them scrabbling in terror as they plummet behind your family portraits. But this thing occupies the hidden parts of the house with purpose, and if I drop my ear to the wallpaper it breathes audibly.

After a week of this, I try to talk to it.

"Whatever you are," I say, "please come out. I want to see you."

Nothing. I am not sure whether I am feeling afraid or curious or both.

I call my sisters. "It might be my imagination," I explain, "but did you also hear something, after? In the house? A presence?"

"Yes," says my first sister. "My joy danced around my house, like a child, and I danced with her. We almost broke two vases that way!"

"Yes," says my second sister. "My inner beauty was set free and lay around in patches of sunlight like a cat, preening itself."

"Yes," says my third sister. "My former shame slunk from shadow to shadow, as it should have. It will go away, after a while. You won't even notice and then one day it'll be gone."

After I hang up with her, I try to take a grapefruit apart with my hands, but it's an impossible task. The skin clings to the fruit, and between them is an intermediary skin, thick and impossible to separate from the meat. Eventually I take a knife and lop off domes of rinds and cut the grapefruit into a cube before ripping it open with my fingers. It feels like I am dismantling a human heart. The fruit is delicious, slick. I swallow eight times, and when the ninth bite touches my lips I pull it back and squish it in my hand as if I am crumpling an old receipt. I put the remaining half of the grapefruit in a Tupperware. I close the fridge. Even now I can hear it. Behind me. Above me. Too large to perceive. Too small to see.

When I was in my twenties, I lived in a place with bugs and had the same sense of knowing invisible things moved, coordinated, in the darkness. Even if I flipped on the kitchen light in the wee hours and saw nothing, I would just wait. Then my eyes would adjust and I would see it: a cockroach who, instead of scuttling two-dimensionally across the yawn of a white wall, was instead perched at the lip of a cupboard, probing the air endlessly with his antennae. He desired and feared in three dimensions. He was less vulnerable there, and yet somehow more, I realized as I wiped his guts across the plywood.

In the same way, now, the house is filled with something else. It moves, restless. It does not say words but it breathes. I want to know it, and I don't know why.

"I've done research," Cal says. The line crackles as if she is somewhere with a bad signal, so she is not calling from her house. I listen for the voice of the other woman who is always in the background, whose name I have never learned.

"Oh, you're back?" I say. I am in control, for once.

Her voice is clipped, but then softens. I can practically hear the therapist cooing to her. She is probably going through a list that she and the therapist created together. I feel a spasm of anger.

"I am worried because," she says, and then pauses.

"Because?"

"Sometimes there can be all of these complications—"

"It's done, Cal. It's been done for months. There's no point to this."

"Do you hate my body, Mom?" she says. Her voice splinters in pain, as if she were about to cry. "You hated yours, clearly, but mine looks just like yours used to, so—"

"Stop it."

"You think you're going to be happy but this is not going to make you happy," she says.

"I love you," I say.

"Do you love every part of me?"

It's my turn to hang up and then, after a moment's thought, disconnect the phone. Cal is probably calling back right now, but she won't be able to get through. I'll let her, when I'm ready.

I wake up because I can hear a sound like a vase breaking in reverse: thousands of shards of ceramic whispering along hardwood toward a reassembling form. From my bedroom, it sounds like it's coming from the hallway. From the hallway, it sounds like it's coming from the stairs. Down, down, foyer, dining room, living room, down deeper, and then I am standing at the top of the basement steps.

From below, from the dark, something shuffles. I wrap my fingers around the ball chain hanging from the naked light bulb and I pull.

The thing is down there. In the light, it crumples to the cement floor, curls away from me.

It looks like my daughter, as a girl. That's my first thought. It's body-shaped. Prepubescent, boneless. It is one hundred pounds, dripping wet.

And it does. Drip.

I descend to the bottom and up close it smells warm, like toast. It looks like the clothes stuffed with straw on someone's porch at Halloween—the vague person-shaped lump made from pillows to aid a midnight escape plan. I am afraid to step over it. I walk around it, admiring my unfamiliar face in the reflection of the water heater even as I hear its sounds: a gasping, arrested sob.

I kneel down next to it. It is a body with nothing it needs: no stomach or bones or mouth. Just soft indents. I crouch down and stroke its shoulder, or what I think is its shoulder.

It turns and looks at me. It has no eyes, but still, it looks at me. *She* looks at me. She is awful but honest. She is grotesque but she is real.

I shake my head. "I don't know why I wanted to meet you," I say. "I should have known."

She curls a little tighter. I lean down and whisper where an ear might be.

"You are unwanted," I say. A tremor ripples her mass.

I do not know I am kicking her until I am kicking her. She has nothing and I feel nothing except she seems to solidify before my foot meets her, and so every kick is more satisfying than the last. I reach for a broom and I pull a muscle swinging back and in and back and in, and the handle breaks off in her and I kneel down and pull soft handfuls of her body out of herself, and I throw them against the wall, and I do not know I am screaming until I stop, finally.

I find myself wishing she would fight back, but she doesn't. Instead, she sounds like she is being deflated. A hissing, defeated wheeze.

I stand up and walk away. I shut the basement door. I leave her there until I can't hear her anymore.

· · ·

Spring has come, marking the end of winter's long contraction.

Everyone is waking up. The first warm day, when light cardigans are enough, the streets begin to hum. Bodies move around. Not fast, but still: smiles. Neighbors suddenly recognizable after a season of watching their lumpy outlines walk past in the darkness.

"You look wonderful," says one.

"Have you lost weight?" asks another.

I smile. I get a manicure and tap my new nails along my face, to show them off. I go to Salt, which is now called The Peppercorn, and eat three oysters.

I am a new woman. A new woman becomes best friends with her daughter. A new woman laughs with all of her teeth. A new woman does not just slough off her old self; she tosses it aside with force.

Summer will come next. Summer will come and the waves will be huge, the kind of waves that feel like a challenge. If you're brave, you'll step out of the bright-hot day and into the foaming roil of the water, moving toward where the waves break and might break you. If you're brave, you'll turn your body over to this water that is practically an animal, and so much larger than yourself.

Sometimes, if I sit very still, I can hear her gurgling underneath the floorboards. She sleeps in my bed when I'm at the grocery store, and when I come back and slam the door, loudly, there are padded footsteps above my head. I know she is around, but she never crosses my path. She leaves offerings on the coffee table: safety pins, champagne bottle corks, hard candies twisted in strawberry-patterned cellophane. She shuffles through my dirty laundry and leaves a trail of socks and bras all the way to the open window. The drawers and air are rifled through. She turns all the soup can labels forward and wipes up the constellations of dried coffee spatter on the kitchen tile. The perfume of her is caught on the linens. She is around, even when she is not around.

I will see her only one more time, after this.

I will die the day I turn seventy-nine. I will wake up early because outside a neighbor is talking loudly to another neighbor about her roses, and because Cal is coming today with her daughter for our annual visit, and because I am a little hungry, and because a great pressure is on my chest. Even as it tightens and compresses I will perceive what is beyond my window: a cyclist bumping over concrete, a white fox loping through underbrush, the far roll of the ocean. I will think, *it is as my sisters prophesied.* I will think, *I miss them, still.* I will think, *here is where I learn if it's all been worth it.* The pain will be unbearable until it isn't anymore; until it loosens and I will feel better than I have in a long time.

There will be such a stillness, then, broken only by a honeybee's soft-winged stumble against the screen, and a floorboard's creak.

Arms will lift me from my bed—her arms. They will be mother-soft, like dough and moss. I will recognize the smell. I will flood with grief and shame.

I will look where her eyes would be. I will open my mouth to ask but then realize the question has answered itself: by loving me when I did not love her, by being abandoned by me, she has become immortal. She will outlive me by a hundred million years; more, even. She will outlive my daughter, and my daughter's daughter, and the earth will teem with her and her kind, their inscrutable forms and unknowable destinies.

She will touch my cheek like I once did Cal's, so long ago, and there will be no accusation in it. I will cry as she shuffles me away from myself, toward a door propped open into the salty morning. I will curl into her body, which was my body once, but I was a poor caretaker and she was removed from my charge.

"I'm sorry," I will whisper into her as she walks me toward the front door.

"I'm sorry," I will repeat. "I didn't know."

THE RESIDENT

Two months after receiving my acceptance letter to Devil's Throat, I kissed my wife good-bye. I left the city and drove north, toward the P—— Mountains, where I had attended Girl Scout camp in my youth.

The letter sat beside me on the passenger seat, pinned down by my pocketbook. Nearly as thick as fabric, the paper did not flutter like lighter, cheaper stock would have; occasionally it spasmed with the wind. The crest at the top was embossed with gold leaf, the silhouette of a hawk that has just plucked the writhing body of a fish from the water. "Dear Ms. M——," it said.

"Dear Ms. M——," I murmured as I drove.

The landscape changed. Soon I passed suburbs and malls, and then stretches of trees and low hills, and then I went through a tunnel steeped in tungsten light and began a slow, meandering ascent. These mountains were so close, only two hours and fifteen minutes from our home, but I saw them rarely nowadays.

The trees dropped away from the roadside, and I passed a sign: WELCOME TO Y——! WE'RE GLAD YOU'RE HERE. The town was rundown and gray, like so many of the old coal and steel towns that dotted the state. I'd describe the houses that lined the main thoroughfare as ramshackle, but *ramshackle* suggests a charm that these lacked. A traffic light hung above the lone intersection, and except for a cat that darted behind a garbage can, there was no movement.

I stopped at a gas station whose prices were a full eighty cents above the state average—I had consulted the price before my departure. I went inside the minimart to pay for my gas, and picked up a bottle of water.

"'S two for one," said the morose-looking adolescent behind the counter. There was a tiny television suspended from the ceiling, playing a program I did not recognize.

"What?" I said.

"You can get one more bottle, for free," he said. A constellation of pustules clustered at his jaw in the elliptical shape of the Andromeda galaxy. They were tipped in yellowish-green domes. How he resisted lancing them was anyone's guess.

"I don't want one more bottle," I said, pushing my money across the counter.

He looked puzzled, but picked up the bills. "You heading up the mountain?" he said.

"Yes," I said, relieved that he had asked me. "To the residency at Devil's Throat."

His finger faltered over the register's buttons, his hand crimped as if he were experiencing pain. He rubbed his jaw and then looked up at me with an unreadable expression; one of his pimples had opened and left a comet's trail of pus across his skin.

I was about to ask him if he'd ever been to that part of the mountain, when a trill of music sounded from the television above us. On the screen, a young woman in a nightgown stood barefoot in a stand of trees. She slowly lifted her arms out to the side, groping at the air, then flapping listlessly like a stunned bird that's just struck a window. She opened her mouth, as if to call out for help, but then soundlessly closed and opened it again, like a patient with a secret on her deathbed.

The camera cut to behind the trees, where a group of girls watched the unfortunate young woman take one stumbling step, then another. One of them, leaning into her neighbor's ear, whispered: "Not everybody's cut out for this, I guess."

Then a laugh track ripped open the audio, and the youth guffawed as he punched numbers into the cash register. "What is this?" I whispered, disturbed.

"Rerun," he grunted. The change he returned to me was damp with sweat. Outside, I touched my face and was startled to discover tears the temperature of blood.

Soon, my car tipped upward and I was climbing the mountain again.

In my adolescence, I had a standing obligation to attend Girl Scout camp for a long weekend every autumn with the rest of my troop. Since we left after school, and in late October, by the time we arrived in these mountains we were beset by an inky darkness. In the backseat of Mrs. Z——'s minivan, the girls fell into silence and sleep, having been so long on the road, and having exhausted conversation well before leaving civilization. After the incident, I always sat in the passenger seat. It was fine, as I preferred the company of adults to that of my peers.

In the car, the only light was the luminous glow of the dashboard. Mrs. Z—— stared straight ahead, and her daughter—an enemy of mine, but a fine-looking girl of great height and chestnut brown hair—would inevitably be asleep in the backseat, her skull rapping on the glass of her window every time the vehicle struck a bump, though it never woke her. Next to her, the other girls would be staring into the middle distance, or also resting their eyes. Outside, the car's headlights cut through the night, illuminating a constantly rotating filmstrip of pavement, fallen branches and blowing leaves, and the occasional slurry of red and flesh where a stag had met its end since the last rainfall.

Occasionally, Mrs. Z—— would look over at me, take a breath through her nose, and then murmur something generic. ("How is school?" was a favorite.) I knew that she was keeping her voice low so as not to wake her daughter, or let her daughter know that she was talking to me, and so I did the same and said something generic in return. ("Good. I like English class.") There was no way to explain to this particular woman that school was adequate for learning and terrible for everything else, and that her own sweet-mouthed daughter (whom she had birthed, held, fed, and loved for many years) was a distinct percentage of this misery. And then we'd fall silent again, and the forest stretched on and on.

On either side of the road, the white trunks of the trees were illuminated to a degree, the kind of brief visibility provided by a camera's flash at midnight. I saw a layer or two of trees, and beyond that an opaque blackness that was disturbing to me. Autumn was the worst time to go into the mountains, I thought to myself. To drive into the wilderness when it writhed and gasped for air seemed foolish.

I turned off the air conditioner. If only those girls could see me now: an adult, married, magnificent in my accomplishments.

The radio was tuned to a classical station, which was playing a grand, jaunty song that moved along irregularly, dipping and swelling as I drove through the curves. It was like the beginning of an old film, a vehicle weaving along roads to reach its destination behind white-lettered credits. As the credits ended, the car would pull up to an old farmhouse, where I would get out, untying a white scarf from my hair and calling the name of my old friend. She'd emerge with a wave, and the laughter and rapport we'd share carrying my suitcases into the house would in no way foreshadow the gruesome plot whose wheels were already turning.

"That was Isaac Albéniz," the announcer intoned, "and his *Spanish Rhapsody.*" After a while, the peaks began to chew up the music, eventually reducing it all to static. I flipped the radio off and rolled the window down, resting my elbow on the rubber lip and feeling very satisfied.

Then I noticed the car behind me: a low, white behemoth that hovered too close. I felt a strange spiral behind my navel, the downward swirl that might precede fear or arousal. Then there was a change, which I perceived before I understood it. Red and blue light spilled into my car.

The police officer sat behind me for a full two minutes before opening his door and crunching in my direction.

"Good afternoon," he said. His eyes were small but oddly kind. He had a reddish patch at the corner of his lip: a fever sore, ready to bloom.

"Good afternoon," I responded.

"Do you know why I pulled you over?" he asked.

"I certainly have no idea," I said.

"You were speeding," he said. "You were going fifty-seven in a forty-five zone."

"Ah," I said.

"Where are you heading?" he asked.

As we spoke, the reddish patch seemed to sense me and expand outward, like an amoeba preparing for reproduction. He had a wedding ring, and so, barring any recent tragedies, there was a spouse who had seen this mark as recently as this morning. I imagined her (you may think me presumptuous to assume that his spouse was a woman, given my own particular circumstances, but there was something in his demeanor that suggested to me that he had never touched a man without anger or force or anxiety, and even now he touched the ring unconsciously with his thumb, suggesting affection, maybe even an erotic memory) being a woman entirely unlike me; that is, she was a woman unafraid of contagion. I imagined her kissing his mouth, perhaps even procuring a tiny tube of cream from a basket of many kinds of creams and dabbing it on, saying something soothing to him ("No one will notice, I'm sure") and squeezing his shoulder. Perhaps they had a single fever sore that they traded back and forth, like an infant exchanged between them.

When I emerged from my musings, his car had already driven out of sight. I looked at the paper he'd given me: a warning. "Drive slowly, arrive safe. Officer M———," it said in sad, blocky handwriting at the top.

I soon reached a T junction, where, the sign indicated, I was to turn left to go to Devil's Throat. The other direction would take me back to the past, that dilapidated campground where so many things had gone wrong, and right.

This last stretch was the most beautiful part of the drive. The trees bent over the road like footmen, acquiescing to the early heat. The glossy leaves were dense and blocked out the sky. I could hear the scream of cicadas, but I found it comforting. I felt renewed as I drove this lane—to paradise! To a completed novel! I had spent my life imagining a time when, instead of relying on the generosity of others, I would be able to stand on my own as an artist—refer to my published novel (released to modest but positive reviews—I was not so arrogant as to assume it would light up the world), teach where I wanted to, give small but respectable lectures for small but respectable sums of money. All of this now seemed within reach.

A creature darted beneath my car.

I swerved and braked so hard I could feel the car grinding in protest and the thunk of metal on body. Had it been icy or raining I would have surely died, swung into the nearest tree. As it was, I came to an abrupt halt in the middle of the lane.

I looked in my rearview mirror, terrified to see what lay in the road.

There was nothing.

I got out of the car and looked beneath the chassis. There, the black, lifeless eyes of a rabbit met mine. The lower half of her body was missing, as neatly as if she were a sheet of paper that had been ripped in two. I stood and walked around the car, looking for the other half. I even knelt down again and peered up into the labyrinth of the car's undercarriage. Nothing.

"I'm sorry," I said to her blank eyes. "You deserved better than that. Better than me."

I sat down heavily in the driver's seat, twin spots of dirt on my jeans for my trouble. Distress came over me like a wave of nausea. I hoped this was not some sort of omen.

Ahead of me there was a blue sign with an arrow, pointing right. DEVIL'S THROAT, it said. No pleasantries here.

As my car wound around the edge of the property, I understood that I would only be seeing a small fraction of it during my stay. It was hundreds of acres, much of it undeveloped. Devil's Throat had once been a lakeside resort for New York millionaires, but the owners overextended their finances and the entire endeavor collapsed during the Great Depression. The current owner was an organization that funded fellowships providing time and space to writers and artists to do their work. The residency, I discerned from the map that had arrived in the mail soon after my acceptance letter, occupied the southernmost corner of the resort: a cluster of studios and a main building that had once been the sumptuous hotel. The studios themselves rimmed the periphery of a lake, where the wealthiest of the residents had stayed for entire summers, lazing around in the muggy heat.

I followed the road until the trees finally parted. The former hotel swelled out of the ground like an infection, a disturbance in the woods. It had clearly once been a grand structure, radical in design, the kind of work done by ambitious young architects not yet crushed by years of anonymity and unfinished blueprints.

Two cars—one ancient and dirty blue, the other red and glinting in the sunlight—were parked haphazardly next to the hotel. I pulled in beside the red car, and then, nervous, pulled out again and parked next to the blue car instead. I suddenly felt self-conscious about the number of possessions in my trunk and backseat. I would have to unload, and it would take half a dozen trips.

I got out of the car, and left everything behind.

The hotel's first story was ordinary but elegant, with dark gray stone and black mortar, slender windows that revealed choice cuts of interior: red velvet, wood-paneled walls, an abandoned coffee mug leaking steam on a side table. But the second story made the building more closely resemble a large piece of saltwater taffy stretched and pulled to wild dimensions. The windows and their walls turned at odd angles from their first-floor cousins, tipping to and fro. You might, from one window, be able to see more of the ground than the sky;

from another more of the sky than the ground. One of the rooms bent so close to the surrounding trees that a branch was arched toward the window; surely a stiff breeze would instigate its advances. At the top, the roof sloped up and up until it came to a whorl of a point, like the tip of a dollop of cream. Resting there was a large glass orb.

The steps leading to the front door were wide, so wide that if one stood in the middle, the banisters would be inaccessible. I walked up the right side, sliding my hand along the banister, until a splinter bit into my palm. I lifted my hand and examined the shard between my heart line and head line. I pinched the exposed wood and pulled; my hand contracted around the wound, which did not bleed. I mounted the last few steps to the porch.

I hesitated before the opulent entrance, disliking how the wood curled in organic tendrils from where the doors met, like an octopus emerging arm-and-suckers-first from a hiding place. My wife had always teased me for my feelings and sensations, the things that I immediately loved or hated for reasons that took months of thought to articulate. I dithered there on the stoop for a full ten minutes before the door was opened by a handsome man in penny loafers. He looked startled to see me.

"Hello," he said. He sounded like a drinker, and possibly a homosexual. I took an immediate liking to him. "Are you—coming in?" He stepped to the side and nearly vanished behind the door.

"I—yes," I said, stepping over the threshold. I told him my name.

"Oh, yeah! I think—" He turned to the empty space behind him. "I think we thought you were going to come tomorrow? Perhaps there was a miscommunication."

The doorway to the adjacent room ejaculated a flurry of activity, and I realized that he had been speaking to a trio of women just beyond my line of vision: a slender, pale waif in a shapeless frock whose fractal pattern spiraled dozens of holes into her torso and created in me immediate anxiety; a tall woman with dreadlocks coiled on top of her head and a generous smile; and a third woman whom I recognized, though I was also positive I'd never seen her before.

The woman in the anxiety-provoking dress introduced herself as Lydia, a "poet-composer." Her feet were bare and filthy, as if she were trying to prove to everyone she was an incorrigible bohemian. The tall woman said that she was Anele, and a photographer. The woman I did and did not recognize called herself by a name that I immediately forgot. I do not mean that I wasn't paying attention; rather, she said her name and as my mind closed around it, it slipped away like mercury from probing fingers.

The man who had opened the door said, "She's a painter." He called himself Benjamin, and was, he said, a sculptor.

"Why are you not at your studios?" I asked, regretting the imprudent question as soon as it left my mouth.

"Midday boredom," said Anele.

"Midresidency boredom," clarified Lydia. "The more social among us," she gestured to the people around her, "sometimes eat lunch here in the main hall, to stop ourselves from going crazy."

"We just finished," said Benjamin. "I was heading back. But I bet if you stick your head in the kitchen you can catch Edna and she can fix you something to eat."

"I'll take you there," said Anele. She hooked her arm in mine and walked me away from the others.

As we crossed the foyer, I felt a fresh burst of fear regarding the woman whose name I could not seem to retain. "The painter—" I said, hoping that Anele would provide the relevant information.

"Yes?" she said.

"She is—lovely."

"She is lovely," Anele agreed. She pushed on a set of double doors. "Edna!"

A wiry woman was hunched over the sink, where she appeared to have been gazing into its soapy depths. She straightened and looked at me. Her hair was flame red, and was tied behind her head with a black velvet ribbon.

"Oh!" she said, upon seeing me. "You're here!"

"I—I am," I confirmed.

"My name is Edna," she said. "I'm the residency director." She pulled off her yellow rubber gloves and proffered a hand, which I took. It was cool and damp, like a freshly wrung-out sponge. "You're early," she continued. "A full day."

"I must have read my letter incorrectly," I whispered. I flushed scarlet, and I could hear my wife's gentle laughter, my mortification on full display.

"It's fine," she said. "No harm done. I'll take you to your room. Your bed might not have sheets—"

Back in the foyer, Benjamin was standing among all of my things—my suitcases, the hamper, even my car's emergency-supply backpack, which was not supposed to leave my trunk.

"Did I leave my car unlocked?" I said.

"Why would you lock it here?" he asked cheerfully. "Here you go." He bent down and lifted my suitcases. I picked up the hamper. Edna bent toward the backpack, but I said, "No need," and she straightened back up. We mounted the stairs.

I woke up after the sun had set, as the last dregs of light were pulling away from the sky. I felt disoriented, like a child who has fallen asleep at a party and woken up clothed in a spare bedroom. I reached out, instinctively, for my wife, and met only high-thread-count sheets and a perfectly fluffed pillow.

I sat up. The wallpaper was dark, and dappled with hydrangeas. I could hear sounds coming from the first floor—murmuring chatter, the kiss of silverware and porcelain. My mouth tasted terrible, and my bladder was full. If I could sit up, I could use the toilet. If I used the toilet, I could then turn on the light. If I turned on the light, I could locate the mouthwash in my suitcase and get rid of this musty feel. If I could get rid of the musty feel, I could go downstairs and have supper with the others.

As I swung one leg from the bed, I had a monstrous vision of a hand darting from beneath the bed's skirt, grasping my ankle, and dragging me beneath while the sound of delighted banter in the dining room drowned out my horrified screams, but it passed. I swung my other leg down, stood, and stumbled to the bathroom in the dark.

As I voided my bladder, I considered my novel, such as it was— that is, piles of notes and papers wedged into a notebook. I thought about Lucille and her predicaments. They were so many.

I came downstairs, the residue of mouthwash burning between my teeth. A long table of dark wood—cherry, perhaps, or chestnut; either way, it was stained a rich crimson—was set for seven people. My fellow residents clustered in the corners of the room, chatting and holding glasses of wine.

Benjamin called out my name and gestured to me with his glass. Anele looked up and smiled. Lydia remained deep in conversation with a slender, pretty man whose fingers were smudged with something dark—ink, I imagined. He smiled shyly at me but said nothing.

Benjamin handed me a glass of red wine before I could tell him that I do not drink.

"Thank you," I said, instead of "No, thank you." I heard my wife's warm voice as if she were next to me, whispering into my ear. *Be a sport.* I believed that my wife loved me as I was, but I had also become certain that she'd love a more relaxed version of me even better.

"Are you set up?" he asked. "Or were you resting?"

"Resting," I said, and took a sip of the wine. It soured against the spearmint, and I swallowed quickly. "I suppose I was tired from the drive."

"That drive is horrible, no matter where you come from," Anele agreed.

The kitchen door swung open, and Edna emerged, carrying a platter of sliced ham. She set the plate down on the table, and on cue, everyone left their conversations and began to gather around their chairs.

"Are you settled?" she asked me.

I nodded. We all sat. The man with smudged fingers reached across the table and shook my hand limply. "I'm Diego."

"How is everyone's work going?" asked Lydia.

Every head dipped down as if to avoid answering. I took a piece of ham, a scoop of potatoes.

"I'm heading out tomorrow morning," Edna said, "and I'll be back at the end of the week. Groceries are in the fridge, of course. Does anyone need anything from civilization?"

A smattering of *no*s rose from the table. I reached into my back pocket and produced a prestamped, preaddressed, prewritten letter to be sent to my wife, confirming that I had arrived safely. "Can you mail this for me?" I asked. Edna nodded and took it to her handbag in the hall.

Lydia chewed with her mouth open. She dug something out from between her molars—gristle—then ran her tongue over her teeth and took another sip of wine.

Benjamin refilled my glass. I didn't remember finishing but I had, somehow. My teeth felt soft in my gums, as if they were lined with velvet.

Everyone began talking in that loose, floppy way wine encourages. Diego was a professional illustrator of children's books, I learned, and was currently working on a graphic novel. He was from Spain, he said, though he had lived in South Africa and the United States for much of his adult life. He then flirted a little with Lydia, which lowered my estimation of them both. Anele told a funny story about an awkward encounter with an award-winning novelist whose name I did not recognize. Benjamin described his most recent sculpture: Icarus with wings made of broken glass. Lydia said that she'd spent all day "banging on the piano." "I didn't bother any of you, did I?" she said in a voice that suggested that she didn't give a whit one way or the other. She went on to explain that she was composing a "poem-song," and was currently in the "song" part of the process.

The walls were soundproof, Edna assured her. You could be murdered in there, and no one would ever know.

Lydia leaned toward me with an expression of deep satisfaction. "Do you know what the richie riches used to call this place, before they lost it?"

"Angel's Mouth," I said. "I was in scouting, as a girl, and we came here every year. I always remember seeing the sign."

"*Angel's Mouth*," she half-shouted, as if I hadn't spoken. She slapped the table and laughed uproariously. Her teeth looked rotten—stained

plum. I hated her, I realized with a start. I'd never hated anyone before. Certainly people had given me discomfort, made me wish I
could blink and disappear, but hate felt new and acidic. It rankled.
Also, I was drunk.

"What do they do at Girl Scout camp?" Benjamin asked. "Swim,
hike?"

"Fuck each other?" suggested Diego. Lydia slapped him playfully on the arm.

I took a sip of wine, which I could no longer taste. "We made
crafts and earned badges. Cooked over the fire. Told stories." That
had been my favorite part. "We usually were there in autumn, so it
was too cold to swim," I said. "But we did walk along the shoreline
and play chicken on the pier, sometimes."

"Is that why you're at this particular residency?" Anele asked.
"Because you know the area?"

"No," I said. "Just a coincidence." I set my glass down and almost missed the table.

Then there was Lydia's hideous barking laugh. Diego's face was
buried in her long hair, dropping some secret observation into her
ear. She looked at me and laughed again. I blushed and busied myself with my meal.

Anele finished her wine and placed a hand over the glass when
Diego lifted the bottle. She turned to me. "While I'm here I'm working on a project that I'm calling 'The Artists,'" she said. "Would you
be willing to spend an afternoon doing a portrait session with me?
No pressure, of course."

The pressure felt real, but I was drowsy and also I already liked
Anele in the way that I liked some people—she seemed overwhelmingly well intentioned and was, it could not be denied, strikingly

beautiful. I saw she was watching me expectantly, and I realized I was smiling for no apparent reason. I rubbed my numb face with my palms.

"Happily," I said, biting the inside of my cheek. My mouth went to metal.

By the next morning, a chill had descended upon the P——— Mountains, and the grounds outside the window of the kitchen were shrouded in mist.

"Do you drink coffee?" Anele said behind me. I had barely nodded when she placed into my hand a warm and heavy mug, which I sipped from without examining it.

"I can walk you down to the studios," she said. "I'd be happy to. It's hard to get there if you don't know the way, even when everything isn't obscured in fog. Did you sleep well?"

I nodded again. A small animal in my brain stirred with intent—to vocalize and thank Anele for her many kindnesses—but I could not remove my eyes from the whiteness beyond the window, how easily it obliterated everything.

When the front doors shut behind us, I jumped. From the steps, I could just see the outline of trees, which we had to pass through to reach the lakeside. Anele set off through them, finding the path. She hopped effortlessly over a fallen log and swerved around a patch of fat, glistening mushrooms. At some point, we passed a narrow white bench, whose design and dimensions suggested it was not meant for resting. Without turning, she gestured toward it. "The bench is about halfway between the lake and the hotel, just for reference."

When the trees were behind us, I saw the faintest impressions of buildings. One loomed directly in front of me. For the first time, I broke from Anele's wake and stepped toward it, hoping for clarity with proximity.

"Jesus!" Anele grabbed the strap of my bag and pulled me back. "Be careful. You almost just walked into the lake." In front of me, the air was like milk—no building in sight.

She gestured to her right, where a series of steps ascended toward shadow. "This is you. Mourning Dove, right?"

"Yes," I said forcefully. "Thank you for showing me the way."

"Be careful," she said. "And if you need to get back—" She pointed to where we'd come from. A ball of light glinted, even through the mist. "That's the hotel. That light is illuminated at night and during bad weather. So you can always find your way home. Happy writing!"

Anele vanished into the mist, though I heard her feet displacing pebbles long after she had gone.

My cabin was a generously sized building with an office that overlooked the rim of the lake—or would, when the fog abated. There was even a small deck, for work on the days without too much sun or rain, or for relaxation or observation. Despite its age, the building was reassuringly sturdy. I walked around, taking hold of various joints and railings, shaking them to see if anything was rotting or came off in my hand like a leprous limb. All seemed solid.

Inside, a series of wooden boards sat on a shelf above my desk. At first glance they resembled Moses's tablets, but when I stood on a chair and examined them I saw they were lists and lists of names— some clear, some illegible—of previous residents. The names and dates and jokes ran together like a Dadaist poem.

Solomon Sayer—Fiction Writer. Undine Le Forge, Painter, June 19—. Ella Smythe "Summer of Love!" C——

I frowned. Someone with my name—another resident—had

occupied this cabin, many years ago. I ran my finger over my name—over her name—and then rubbed it on my jeans.

A curious term, *resident*. It seemed at first glance incidental, like a stone, but then if you turned it over, it teemed with life. A resident lived somewhere. You were a resident of a town or a house. Here, you were a resident of this space, yes—not really, of course; you were a visitor, but whereas *visitor* suggests leaving at the end of the night and driving out in the darkness, *resident* means that you set up your electric kettle, and will be staying for a while—but also that you are a resident of your own thoughts. You had to find them, be aware of them, but once you located your thoughts you never had to drive away.

A letter on my desk welcomed me to Mourning Dove Cabin, and encouraged me to add my name to the newest tablet. From my desk I could see half of my porch, and then the opacity of the fog consumed the railing and all beyond it.

I unpacked my bag, and then placed my notebook next to the computer, where it fairly hummed with portent. The novel. *My* novel.

I began to work. I decided to outline my novel on index cards, so that they would be easy to move around. The entire wall was made of corkboard, and so I thumbtacked the cards in a grid, pinning up Lucille's trials and triumphs in a way that could be easily manipulated.

A centipede crawled along the wall, and I killed it with the card that said *Lucille realizes her entire childhood has been a terrible lie, from the first sentence to the last*. Its legs still twitched after I painted the plaster with its innards. I made a new card and threw that one away. The one that said *Lucille discovers her sexuality at the edge of an autumn lake* was pinned in the middle, which is where my plot abruptly stopped. My eyes scanned the cards. *Baxter escapes and*

is struck by a car. Lucille's girlfriend breaks up with her because she is
"difficult at parties." Lucille enters the art festival. I felt pleased with
my progress, though a little concerned that I wasn't entirely positive how I was going to maximize Lucille's suffering. Losing the
art festival's grand prize wasn't enough, probably. I made a cup
of tea and sat down, where I remained staring at the cards until
dinnertime.

Just before dawn, I woke up with a soapy taste gathering around
my molars. My body lurched from the bed. I fell to my knees before the toilet, still shoving away wisps of dreams as a hot burp sig-
naled what was to come.

I had been sick before, but never like this. I vomited so hard that
I wrenched the toilet seat from its hinges with a terrible *crack*, and
rested my head on the cool tile until it seemed clean, and the best
of things. I sat up again, and still more, impossibly more, emerged
from my body. To cool down, I crawled into the bathtub. When I
looked up at the showerhead in the seconds before it belched icy
relief, it was dark and ringed with calcified lime, like the para-
sitic mouth of a lamprey. I vomited again. When I was certain that
nothing remained inside me, I crawled back to the bed, where I
pulled the heavy duvet over my body and receded inside myself.

My illness persisted for some time. My fever spiked and the air
around me shimmered like heat over blacktop. I thought to myself
that I should get to a hospital, that my mind was, like the rest of my
body, baking, but the thought was a twig bobbing along through
Noah's deluge. I was freezing and buried myself in my blankets; I
was roasting alive and stripped naked, the sweat crystallizing on
my skin. At the very worst of it, I reached to the other side of the
bed to feel for the contours of my own face. I believe that I cried out

for my wife many times, though how loudly (or if I did so at all) is something I will never know. I believe it rained, because outside the window something wet smacked the glass in waves. In the height of my fever, I believed that this was the sound of the tide, and I was sinking beneath the ocean's surface, dropping out of sight of heat and light and air. I was thirsty, but when I tried to sip water from my trembling palm, I vomited again, my muscles aching from the heaving. I am dying, I thought to myself, and that is that.

I woke up in the thin strains of morning, with a person gently rapping on my door, calling my name. Anele.

"Are you all right?" she asked through the wood. "We're all really worried about you. You've missed dinner for two nights."

I could not move. "Come in," I said.

The door swung open, and I heard Anele suck in a sharp breath. I appreciated later what caused this: the room was hot and sour. It smelled of fever and stale sweat, of vomit and weeping.

"I have," I said, "been ill."

She came over to the bed, which I thought was kind considering the nuances of contagion. "Do you—should I call Edna?" she said.

"If you could bring me a glass of water," I said, "it would be much appreciated."

It felt as if she had dissolved, but then she was back with a glass. I took a sip, but for the first time in days my stomach did not move, except to growl with hunger. I downed the entire glass, and though it did not slake my thirst, I felt my humanity climb back into me.

"Another, please," I said, and she refilled the glass.

I finished it, and felt renewed.

"There's no need to call Edna," I said.

"If you're sure," she said. "Let me know if you need anything?"

"Has any mail come for me?" I asked. A letter from my wife would be comforting.

"No, nothing," she said.

I began to write that afternoon. My legs felt shaky and there was a strange rasping sensation in my chest, but I wrote in short bursts and felt mostly fine. The Painter came by my cabin and knocked on my door. I started at the intrusion, but she said something and offered me a small box of medicine. I did not reach for it. What was it that my mind kept from me, when forgetting her words?

She said something else, and shook the box at me, again. I took it. Then she reached up and touched my face; I flinched, but her fingers were cool and dry. She walked down the stairs and went to the lake's edge, where she reached down, picked up something from the grass, and flung it into the water.

I pushed one of the pills through the blister pack's foil and examined it. It was oblong, with no numbers or letters, and it was a reddish-orange, except also a little purple and blue, and greenish if you turned it, and if I held it in the light it went white as an aspirin. I tossed the box into the trash and the pills into the toilet; they drifted around the bowl like tadpoles before zooming out of sight when I flushed.

As I felt stronger, I began to take walks around the lake. It was bigger than it appeared, and even when I walked for an hour I covered only a fraction of its perimeter. On the third day of these journeys, I walked for two hours and discovered a beach with a partially submerged canoe lounging in the tide. The gentle motion of the water caused the canoe to rock ever so slightly and reminded me of the way the canopies of the trees had undulated in the wind during camp. *Thum-thum-thum-thum.*

The Girl Scout camp of my youth had been on a lake as well.

Could it be on the other side of this same lake? If I hiked long and far enough, would I come upon that dock where my own predilections were solidified and mocked on that crisp autumn evening? Would I locate that romantic, terrible idyll? The idea had not occurred to me before—I'd always assumed it was some other lake, up here in the mountains—but the rhythm of the water and the memory of the trees seemed to confirm that I had returned to a place from my past.

It was then I remembered that I had once been sick at camp. How had I forgotten? This was the unspoken pleasure of the residency: the sudden permission of memory to come upon you. I remembered one of the leaders taking my temperature and clucking her tongue at the number. I remembered a sense of despair. Here on the beach, the despair felt clear, as if I'd been seeking its signal for decades and had just now come in range of a cell tower.

I walked a little farther, and noticed something red in the beach's stones. I knelt and picked up a small glass bead. It looked like it had come from a camper's bracelet. Perhaps it had been in the water for quite a long time, and had washed up on this shore just for me.

I put it in my pocket and walked back to my cabin.

That evening, when I undressed for bed, I noticed a small, raised bump on the inside of my thigh. I pressed it. A shock of pain bisected my leg, and when it passed I observed that the bump was soft, as though filled with liquid or jelly. I felt my fingers twitch with the desire to squeeze it, but I resisted. The next day, however, there was another, and then another. They clustered on my thighs, erupted underneath my breasts. I was alarmed. Perhaps there was some kind of insect here that I hadn't known about—not ticks or mosquitos. Some kind of poisonous spider? But I thought about how I slept and in which kind of garment, and could not fathom how I'd been bitten. They did not itch, but they felt full, and I felt full, as if I needed release.

I sat on the edge of the bathtub, burning a safety pin over a lighter. The metal blackened slightly, and I blew on the shaft and tested it for heat with the pad of my finger. Satisfied that it was cool and sterile, I inserted the pin into the original abjection. It resisted only briefly—a split second of thrashing fists before yielding— and then discharged. A limb of pus and blood climbed the stalk of the needle before collapsing under its own weight and trailing down my leg like an untended menstrual cycle. I soaked half a roll of toilet paper—cheap toilet paper, but still—with my own blood, taking out one after another. I felt pleasantly sore afterward, but cleansed. I covered each one with a blob of ointment and a slick bandage.

Anele came to my cabin one early evening to collect her promised portrait session. She looked sweaty and triumphant, and straps of large camera bags crisscrossed her torso. I glanced behind her and saw dark clouds in the distance. A storm?

"It's a while off," she said, as if reading my mind. "A few hours at least. This won't take very long, I promise." We walked back toward the hotel, and then veered off into a meadow about a half mile away. The grasses became taller and taller and eventually came up to our waists, and more than once I leaned over to brush my thighs and calves with my palms, to discourage ticks and their bites. The third time I did this, I stood and noticed Anele had stopped and was watching me. She smiled, then kept walking.

"Did you enjoy scouting?" she asked. "How long did you do it?"

"From Brownies until Seniors. Almost my whole girlhood." The word *Brownies* broke off into my mouth like something cloying, stale, and I spit onto the ground.

"You don't seem like a Girl Scout," she said.

"What does that mean?" I asked.

"You just seem very—ethereal. I guess I think of Girl Scouts as hearty and outdoorsy."

"It is possible to be both." I stopped and looked down at my legs, where the thumb of a Band-Aid poked out from beneath my shorts. Anele had not stopped walking, and I rushed to catch up. The grass ended suddenly and we were at a large elm. In front of the trunk was a wrought iron chair, painted white.

"Oh, perfect timing," said Anele. "The light." I was not a photographer—I had never professionalized my visual observations, only my theories and perspective problems and narrative impulses—but she didn't need to explain further. The sun was low and everything was awash in honey light, including my skin. Behind the tree, the impending storm darkened the sky. Were we driving toward the storm, a photograph of the side mirror would reveal light in the past, and darkness in the future.

Anele handed me a white sheet.

"Can you wear this?" she asked. "Only this. Just wrap it around your body, however you feel comfortable." She turned around and began setting up her camera. "Tell me about the Brownies," she said.

"Oh," I said. "Brownies were little girls. Kindergarten age. The name came from these little house elves who supposedly lived in people's homes and did work in exchange for gifts. There's this whole story about a naughty brother and sister who always wanted to play and never wanted to help their father clean the house." I unbuttoned my blouse and unhooked my bra. "Then the grandmother tells them to consult this old owl nearby about these little imps. And while she technically tells both of the children, the little girl goes to find the owl—"

I wrapped the sheet tightly around my chest, like a modest lover in a television show aired before late night. "I'm ready," I said.

Anele turned. She came over and began to fiddle with my hair. "Does she find the owl?"

I tried to frown slightly, but Anele was brushing some lipstick over my mouth, blunt as a thumb. "Yes," I said. "She does. It gives her a riddle, to find the Brownie."

"Goddamnit," she muttered. She pushed around the outline of my mouth, her finger slipping against the cosmetic wax. "Sorry, I overshot the edge of your lip." She began to apply it again. "What's the Brownie riddle?"

The bottom went out beneath me, and for a very brief second I was certain that the distant lightning had reached out and flicked me, like the finger of a god.

"I don't remember," I whispered. Anele's eyes left my mouth and she looked at me for a long, hard second before twirling the tube shut.

"You're very beautiful," she said, though whether her voice was admiring or merely reassuring was difficult to tell. She pushed me down into the chair and returned to her camera. My skin was glazed with heat, and a mosquito screamed past my ear and bit me before I could flick it away. For the first time, I noticed the camera, which she must have set up while I was changing. It looked like an old-fashioned thing; it seemed that Anele would lean over and cover her head with a heavy cloth, and take the photo by depressing a button at the end of a cord. I did not know such cameras still existed.

She saw me looking. "It's called a large-format camera. The negative is about the size of your hand." She tilted my chin upward.

"Now," she said, "what I need you to do is to fall over."

"Pardon?" I asked. I felt a ripple of thunder through the bones of the chair. This detail had not been in her original request, I was certain.

"I need you to fall out of the chair," she said. "However you land, stay that way. Keep your eyes open and your body still."

"I—"

"The faster we do this, the less likely we are to get rained on," she said, her voice firm and friendly. She smiled widely and then disappeared beneath the camera's hood.

I hesitated. I looked down at the earth. The grasses were glowing with the light from the sunset, but I could see dirt and rocks. I did not want to injure myself. Truth be told, I didn't even want to dirty myself.

Anele came out from under the hood. "Is everything okay?" she asked.

I looked at her face, and then back at the earth. I tipped over.

The surprises came all at once: First, the earth was not as hard as I had imagined it; it yielded as if it were loam. The sun, which had been hidden behind Anele's body, was now uncovered and glowed between her legs like some mythical entreaty. I heard the dry click of the shutter, the sound of some insect biting down. There was lightning then, distinct, forking across the sky and over the distant hotel. So many omens. I felt strangely content there, on the ground, as if I could stay there for hours, listening to the cicadas and watching the light change and then vanish.

And then Anele was kneeling down in front of me, helping me sit back up. "We have to run, we have to run!" she said, and if I felt any anger or strangeness, it was crushed beneath this girlish appeal. She tossed my clothes to me and folded down the camera. At that moment, the last of the day's heat vanished, as if sucked down a drain, replaced with the chill of oncoming rain. Anele began to run, and I followed her, my clothes clutched to my bosom, the sheet flapping behind me. I felt light, airy. I laughed. I did not turn around to look at the sky but I could visualize it as clearly as if I had: clouds roiling upon us like men at a bar, suffocating, and us laughing, together, away. I heard the rain then, the sound of something tearing, and we were up on the porch in seconds. When I turned back, the distant trees and sky and even our cars were visually obliterated by the downfall. I was soaked through. The sheet was filthy, now, dirty and half-translucent and clinging to me like a condom. I felt elated, happier than I'd been in months. Perhaps even years.

Was this friendship? Was this how things were supposed to be? It felt that way, that I had ecstatically stumbled into happiness, and everything seemed right and correct. Anele looked beautiful, barely winded. She smiled at me. "Thank you for your help," she said, and disappeared into the hotel.

I made progress on my novel. I found that the index cards hindered my process, so I simply buckled down over my keyboard and wrote until I emerged from my trance. Sometimes, I sat on the porch and gave imaginary interviews to NPR personalities.

"When I write, I feel like I'm being hypnotized," I told Terry Gross.

"It was at that moment I knew everything was going to change," I told Ira Glass.

"Pickled things, and shrimp," I told Lynne Rossetto Kasper.

I crossed paths with the others at breakfast, sometimes. One morning, Diego told me about the previous day's social engagements—which I had ignored in favor of Lucille's social engagements near my novel's climax—and in doing so he said a curious word: *colonist*.

"Colonist?" I said.

"We're at an artist colony," he said. "So we're colonists, right? Like Columbus." He drained his orange juice and stood up from the table.

I suppose he meant it to be funny, but I was horrified. *Resident* had seemed such a rich and appropriate term, an umbrella I would have been content to carry all of my days. But now the word *colonist* settled down next to me, with teeth. What were we colonizing? Each other's space? The wilderness? Our own minds? This last thought was a troubling one, even though it was not very different from my conception of being allowed to be a resident in your own mind. *Resident* suggests a door hatch in the front of your brain, propped open to allow for introspection, and when you enter, you are faced with objects that you'd previously forgotten about. "I remember this!" you might say, holding up a small wooden frog, or a floppy rag doll with no face, or a picture book whose sensory impressions flood back to you as you turn the pages—a toadstool with a wedge missing from its cap; a flurry of luminous autumn leaves; a summer breeze dancing with milkweed. In contrast, *colonist* sounds monstrous, as if you have kicked down the door hatch of your mind and inside you find a strange family eating supper.

Now when I worked, I felt strange around the entrance to my own interiority. Was I actually just an invader, bearing smallpox-ridden blankets and lies? What secrets and mysteries lay undiscovered in there?

I still felt weak. I considered that I had died in that room with its drapes and pulls, and that the me who bent over my keyboard day after day was a ghost who was tethered to her work regardless of the fiddling details of her mortal coil.

I woke up to moaning. I was standing at the base of the stairs, barefoot and in my pajamas. My loosened bun hung limply against my neck. I registered the wooden panels of the hallway, the moonlight streaming through the windows that surrounded the door. I had not sleepwalked in years, yet here I was, upright and elsewhere.

I heard it again. I'd heard sounds like this before, when I was a child and our cat had eaten an entire loaf of bread. It was a sound of gluttony regretted, of wallowing in one's own excess. My feet made no sound as I padded across the hardwood floor.

The hallway was cast in shadow. Moonlight slanted through a window, cutting three silver bars across the paneled walls. At the end of the hall, I descended the stairs and followed the sound toward the dining room. From the doorway, I could see Diego on his back on the table. Straddling his pelvis was Lydia, in her seafoam nightgown, which was hitched up around her hips. The bottoms of her feet were facing me, dark with dirt.

As Lydia undulated, I noticed patches of moonlight appearing and disappearing beneath her, bisected by darkness. My mind sleepily turned over once, twice, like a struggling engine, and then surged to life. He gripped her hips to pull her into him and then push her away. The rhythm was organic, like wind rippling over the water.

They did not seem to notice me. Lydia was facing away, and Diego's eyes were screwed shut, as if to open them would be to release some of his pleasure.

The moonlight was overbearing, illuminating details that seemed impossible: the slickness of him, the sheer fabric that surrounded her flesh like an aura. I knew I should move—I should go back to my bedroom, perhaps rub out this mounting wave of pleasure and horror and then sleep—but I could not. Their lovemaking seemed to go on and on, but neither appeared to climax, just rut with impossibly consistent tempo.

After some time, I left them there. Back in my own room, I touched myself—how long it had been!—and my mind was a jumble of static. I thought of my wife, the dark stain of her nipples, her mouth open and ribbons of sound coiling out.

The next day, the mist returned. When I woke it was hovering in my open window, like a solicitous spirit with something to tell me. I slammed it shut so hard the frame rattled. I felt disoriented from the previous evening. Should I say something to them? Ask them to be more discreet, perhaps? Or perhaps my inadvertent observation was only my problem, and not theirs? In the kitchen, Lydia was making coffee but I did not meet her eyes.

In my cabin, I tried hard to focus. I stood out on my balcony and strained to see the lake, but I could not. Exhausted by the weather, I lay down on the floor. From there, the room changed, utterly. I felt stuck to the ceiling by a force equivalent to, though the opposite of, gravity, and from here I could see the hidden spaces beneath the furniture: a mouse's nest, a stranger's index card, a lone, bone-white button tilted on an axis.

I was reminded, for the umpteenth time, of Viktor Shklovsky's idea of defamiliarization; of zooming in so close to something, and observing it so slowly, that it begins to warp, and change, and acquire new meaning. When I'd first begun to experience this phenomenon, I'd been too young to understand what it was; certainly too young to consult a reference book. The first time, I lay down on the floor examining the metal-and-rubber foot of our family refrigerator, wreathed in dust and human hair, and from this reference point all other objects began to change. The foot, instead of being insignificant, one of four, et cetera, suddenly became everything: a stoic little home at the base of a large mountain, from which one could see a tiny curl of smoke and glinting, illuminated windows, a home from which a hero would emerge, eventually. Every nick on the foot was a balcony or a door. The detritus beneath the fridge became a wrecked, ravaged landscape, the expanse of kitchen tile a rambling kingdom waiting for salvation. This was how my mother found me: staring at the foot of the refrigerator so intensely my eyes were slightly crossed, my body curled up, my lips moving almost imperceptibly. The second time is not worth explaining in detail, though it was the reason Mrs. Z——'s daughter transferred out of our shared high school English class, and by the third time—I was an adult, then—I'd come to understand what it was that I was doing, and began to do it more consciously. This process has been useful for my writing—in fact, I believe that what talent I have comes not from some sort of muse or creative spirit but from my ability to manipulate proportions, and time—but it has put a strain on my relationships. How I married my wife is still a mystery to me.

I finished the day's work long after dark. The fog had burned away by midday, and now everything was clear and sharp. The moon was nearing fullness and glinted off the lake's waves, agitated by the wind. I set off through the trees, my feet crunching on rock. Everything shone with a thin, silvery light. I imagined myself a cat, night vision illuminating what was otherwise secret. The hotel glowed in the distance: a lighthouse beckoning me home.

But then, before me, liquid shadow spilled across my path, darker than the darkness. I tried to look past it. If I could reach the bench, I could reach the other side of the trees. But the flatness of the dark in the intervening woods was a horror. I pulled my bag tightly to my side.

You are a fool, I thought to myself. *You have been reading too much and your mind is wound too tightly. You have been drowning in memory. Your wife, she would be embarrassed for you if she knew that you had drifted this far.*

But I could not take my eyes from the bench. The whiteness seemed transformed, as if it were no longer painted wood but bone. As if a thousand years ago, some creature had climbed out of the lake and died in this exact spot in anticipation of my arrival. Around me, black bushes roiled in the wind, and I did not see thorns before touching one. It sank into my index finger, and I sucked the wound as I walked. Perhaps this blood offering kept whatever was nearby at bay. I sucked and sucked and then, at the other side of the shadows, the moonlight was restored. I did not look behind me.

Anele suggested one evening at dinner that we get together to share the work we'd been doing. I balked, but the others seemed enthusiastic. "After supper?" Lydia suggested. I pushed my chicken around my plate, hoping that someone would register my displeasure, but no one seemed to notice.

And so as we digested, we looked at Diego's drawings, several panels of a dystopian world ruled by zombies thirsty for knowledge. Then, the Painter let us into her studio but said nothing about her work. The walls were covered from floor to ceiling in tiny square canvases with the same unsettling red design delicately painted on each one. They resembled handprints, but had an extra finger and

were entirely too small to be human hands. I was too afraid to examine them closely, to see if they were as identical as they appeared.

When we got into Benjamin's studio, he was sweeping a space for
us to stand in. "Careful," he said, "there's a lot of glass on the floor."
I stayed near the wall. His sculptures were massive, assembled from
clay and broken ceramic and windowpanes. Mostly they were mythical figures, but also there was a beautiful one of a naked man with
a jagged slice of glass between his legs. "I call that one 'William,'"
Benjamin said when he saw me looking.

In Anele's studio, there were the photographs. "This is my newest series, 'The Artists,'" she said. Everyone moved to their respective images, drinking them in before looking at their neighbor's.
Lydia laughed, as if she were remembering some cheerful childhood dream. "I love it," she purred. "They're posed but not posed."

Each print was set in a different place around the property.
Benjamin was lying next to the lake, muddied and bound in filthy
strips of linen, limbless as a silk-wrapped fly. His eyes were open,
fixed on the sky, but glassy, reflecting a single bird. Diego was
crumpled at the base of the hotel steps, body awkwardly jutting
this way and that, his dark irises swollen with his dilated pupils. In
Lydia's, she stood with her neck in a noose on the top of a stump,
and tipped forward, her arms outstretched, a serene smile on her
face. And mine, well.

Anele stepped next to me. "What do you think?" she asked.

I did not remember that afternoon very clearly—all the ac-
tion that passed before our breathless dart across the meadow was
hazy, like a watercolor painting—but here I looked completely,
irrevocably dead. My body was crumpled like Diego's, as if I'd been
sitting demurely on the chair and then shot through the heart.
Several of my many bandages were visible. My breast had slid out

from underneath the sheet—this I did not remember—and there was nothing in my eyes. Or even worse—there was *nothingness*. Not the absence of a thing but the presence of a non-thing. I felt as if I was seeing a premonition of my own death, or a terrible memory I'd long forgotten.

Like the others, the composition was beautiful. The colors were perfectly saturated.

I did not know what to say to her. That she knew perfectly well that she had betrayed my trust, that our beautiful afternoon was ruined? That I had been exposed in a way I had not intended, and that she should feel guilty about this exposure even though it was clear she did not? I could not look at her. I trailed the group as they went to Lydia's studio, where she played something for us. It was infuriatingly beautiful, a song in several movements that conjured an image of a terrified girl being chased from a manor, and then stumbling into the forest and nearly dying upon the banks of a surging river, and then transforming into a hawk. She then narrated the "poem" part, in which a young woman floated through space and meditated on the planets and her own life before the accident that had launched her from orbit.

When it was my turn, I primly read a brief passage from the scene where Lucille rejects the gift from her old piano teacher and then breaks into her house to retrieve it.

"Standing before the blazing inferno," I concluded, "Lucille realized two terrible facts: that her childhood had been tremendously lonely, and that her old age would be, if possible, even worse."

Everyone clapped politely and stood. We retired to the table, where we opened several bottles of wine.

Lydia filled my glass to the brim. "Do you ever worry," she asked me, "that you're the madwoman in the attic?"

"What?" I said.

"Do you ever worry about writing the madwoman-in-the-attic story?"

"I'm afraid I don't know what you mean."

"You know. That old trope. Writing a story where the female protagonist is utterly batty. It's sort of tiresome and regressive and, well, *done*"—here she gesticulated so forcefully that a few drops of red spattered the tablecloth—"don't you think? And the mad lesbian, isn't that a stereotype as well? Do you ever wonder about that? I mean, I'm not a lesbian, I'm just saying."

There was a beat of silence. Everyone was studying his or her glass closely; Diego reached his finger into his wine and removed some invisible detritus from the surface.

"She isn't batty or mad," I said, finally. "She's just—she's just a nervous character."

"I've never known anyone like that," Lydia said.

"She's me," I clarified. "More or less. She's just in her head a lot."

Lydia shrugged. "So don't write about yourself."

"Men are permitted to write concealed autobiography, but I cannot do the same? It's ego if I do it?"

"To be an artist," Diego interjected, derailing the subject, "you must be willing to have an ego and stake everything on it."

Anele shook her head. "You have to work hard. Ego only creates problems."

"But without ego," Diego said, "your writing is just scribbles in a journal. Your art is just doodles. Ego demands that what you do is important enough that you be given money to work on it." He gestured to the hotel around us. "It demands that what you say is important enough that it be published or shown to the world."

The Painter frowned and said something but I could not hear it, naturally. Everyone took deep sips of their wine.

That night, I heard Lydia walk past my room. Through my door's crack I could see her feet shuffling along the hardwood. She discarded her nightgown in the hallway, and as she turned into Diego's room her nudity was like a blade unsheathed.

I felt something strange move through my body. Once, when I was visiting my grandfather as a girl, I'd startled a garter snake out of the grass, and it had dived for the safety of the neatly assembled woodpile so fast that its muscular body snapped rigid before being slurped into the darkness. I felt this way now, as if I was plummeting somewhere so quickly my body was out of control. I crawled back into bed, and had a dream.

In it, I was sitting across from my wife, who was nude but wrapped in a gauzy fabric. She had a clipboard in her hand, and was moving a pencil down it as if ticking off entries on a list.

"Where are you?" she asked.

"Devil's Throat," I said.

"What are you doing?"

"Carrying a basket through the forest."

"What's in the basket?"

I looked down, and there they were: four beautiful spheres.

"Two eggs," I counted. "Two figs."

"Are you sure?"

I did not look down again, afraid that the answer would change. "Yes."

"And what is through the forest?"

"I do not know."

"And what is through the forest?"

"I am not certain."

"And what is through the forest?"

"I cannot tell."

"And what is through the forest?"

"I don't remember."

"And what is through the forest?"

I woke up before I could answer.

The abjections returned. They were more plentiful. They spread to my stomach, my armpits. They grew large and had segments within, so when I lanced them they crumpled chamber by chamber, like a temple from which an adventurer is feverishly tearing. I could hear their insides. They crackled, like Pop Rocks. I could *hear them*. I remembered from science class years ago that aging stars bloat and swell in their final days, before collapsing and then exploding in a hypernova. *Hypernova.* This is what it felt like. As if my solar system were dying. I soaked in the tub for a while.

On this same day, I opened up my mind and remembered several scenes from my Girl Scout days. I remembered dropping a roasted marshmallow into the dirt of the fire pit and eating it anyway, the carbonized sugar and stones crunching in equal measure. I remembered sharing with my peers a list of interesting facts I'd memorized: most white dogs are deaf; you should never wake sleepwalkers, but you may be able to gently guide their sleeping forms to bed; cashews are related to poison ivy. I remembered eating all the graham crackers that our counselor had hidden in the bottom of the plastic food tub. When she asked us who had taken them, I did not answer. I remembered, in greater detail, my illness there, sleeping through the day on my cot, listening to the birds and the distant shouts of my comrades. The thought of events passing without my being there—of shared events and shared pleasure from which I was situationally excluded—

caused me suffering beyond measure. I became very convinced that I was fine, and when I stood I became so dizzy that I swooned back onto the taut fabric. It were as if I were a minor character in someone else's play, and the plot required me to stay there at that moment, no matter how I resisted. Perhaps that is what caused my grief.

Here, at Devil's Throat, everything felt wrong. I became disgusted by my own dramatizations and tried to imagine the opposite of what I felt, that my significant pain in that moment was of no significance whatsoever. That I was dwarfed by the smallest minutiae: The complex comedies and tragedies of insects. Atoms, dancing. A neutrino, tunneling through the earth.

To distract myself from my troubles, I decided to continue exploring the lake. I left my cabin and struck off toward where I'd seen the canoe, which was no longer there. I recognized the pulse of the water, however, and beyond that the shore curved farther. I followed it for another half an hour or so, examining the pebbles and sand at the shore, breaking off tree limbs when they disrupted the outline of the woods. Eventually, I came to a small pier—no boats there, either, but I could practically feel the rough wood grain on the backs of my thighs—and there was a gap in the trees, marked by a slender red ribbon tied to the trunk. A path.

I started down it. I felt certain this was the way. Indeed, before I reached each turn I remembered the turn, but as though I was coming from the opposite direction. Had I taken the boat onto the lake? Or just sat on the pier? And next to me—who had been next to me?

An animal cried out, and I stopped. It was the sound of suffering, of fear or mating, and was objectively terrible. A fisher cat? A bear?

But then: a young girl—no older than five or six—was standing next to a tree. Her eyes were wide and wet, as if she'd been crying but had stopped when she'd heard my footsteps galumphing on the forest floor. She was wearing shorts with knee socks and sneakers, and her neon green sweatshirt said "YES I CAN / BE A TOP COOKIE SELLER" in bubble font.

"Hello," I said. "Are you all right?"

She shook her head.

"Are you lost?"

She nodded.

I went over to her and showed her my palm. "If you'd like, you may take my hand, and we can walk to the camp. You're with the Girl Scouts, right?"

She nodded again, and placed her soft little hand into mine. I did not expect it to be so precise. We started walking. I remembered the Brownies story I'd told Anele and it felt fortuitous that I'd come across a soul who could answer the inquiry I could not.

"May I ask you a question?" I said.

She nodded gravely and did not meet my eyes. Finally—a kindred spirit.

"In Brownies, there's a rhyme. Do you know it?"

I felt the shudder pass through her body and, via her warm, sticky hand, into my own.

"I'm sorry," I said. "You don't have to say it."

We walked a little farther. The path seemed more overgrown here than would be appropriate for a camp for young people.

"Twist me, and turn me—" the girl began. Her voice was reedy but strong, like a steel wire. She faltered. I did not press. We continued to walk, breaking rhythm only when it was necessary to avoid a patch of poison ivy, where a beam of sunlight struck the oily leaves and they glistened.

"Twist me, and turn me, and show me the elf," she finished. "I looked in the water and saw—"

She stopped, and I remembered.

"Myself," I whispered.

Horrifying. It was grotesque in the extreme—no wonder the rhyme had removed itself from my memory. Sending a child after an enslaved mythical brownie, and then providing a rhyme that— assuming the child did not fall into the pond and drown, or get lost in the night—would only serve to tell the child that she *herself* was the enslaved mythical brownie? And not her brother, mind you, but her? Every adult and speaking animal in that story was suspect— having either not taken proper care of the protagonist or actively sent her into harm's blundering path.

"I understand," I said to her.

The path widened, and then there we were, at the edge of a campsite. A ways off, large military-style platform tents circled a blackened fire pit. A fresh stack of wood was nearby, draped in a blue tarp. To our left there was a low, wide building, and in front of it, teenage girls were clustered around picnic tables. Sound gathered over them like smoke: conversation, clattering mess kits, the clank of ladle against pot, creaking benches, howls of laughter. One of them—lean and tan and wearing a baggy T-shirt with a bear on it—leaped up when we cleared the trees.

"Emily!" she said. "How did you—?"

"She was wandering in the woods," I said. I waited for her to ask me who I was, or where I was from, but she didn't. She tilted her head a little, and there was something older in her features, something wry and correct. Perhaps she was waiting for me to ask where the adults were, but even though there were none in sight, I didn't. The question was hardly necessary. If the civilized world ended, these girls would go on forever with their mess kits and bonfires and first aid and stories, and it wouldn't matter either way where the adults were.

"Thanks for bringing her back," she said. She took Emily's hand.

"You all look very happy," I said. "Very content."

The girl smiled wanly, and her eyes glinted with an unspent joke.

"Thank you for our conversation," I said to Emily, who blinked and then ran toward the picnic benches, where the voices of the older girls greeted her in smatters. "Good-bye," I said to the teenager, and then walked back into the trees.

When I emerged on the other side, the light had changed. I took off my shoes and walked to the edge of the water, and then in. It lapped up and slapped my legs.

"Twist me, and turn me," I mumbled, circling slowly over the stones. They dug up into the soft arches of my heels. "And show me the elf. I looked in the water and saw—"

When I tipped over and searched for my face, I saw nothing but the sky.

On the first day of August, I opened my studio door to discover the lower half of a rabbit lying across my porch steps. Behind me, the cursor blinked in the middle of an unfinished sentence: "Lucille did not know what was on the other side of that door, but whatever it was, she knew it would reveal—"

I knelt down before the unfortunate creature. The wind ruffled its fur; the back legs were loose, as if it were sleeping. Its visible organs glistened like caramels, and it smelled like copper.

"I'm sorry," I whispered. "You deserved better than that."

When I had collected myself, I gathered it up in a tea towel. I took the rabbit to the dining room of the hotel, where Lydia, Diego, and Benjamin were laughing over mugs. I laid the bundle down on the table. "What is it?" Lydia breathed playfully, lifting the edge of the hem. She gasped and jumped out of her chair, her chest heaving with the force of a retch.

"What's—" Diego began. He leaned a little closer. "Jesus."

"She's fucking crazy!" Lydia howled.

"I found it," I said. "In front of my studio."

"It was probably an owl or something," Benjamin said. "I've seen a bunch of them around."

Lydia spat. "Oh god. I'm so done. You're crazy. *You're crazy.* You just walk around mumbling and staring all of the time. What is *wrong* with you? You should be ashamed of yourself."

I took a step toward her. "It is my right to reside in my own mind. *It is my right,*" I said. "It is my right to be unsociable and it is my right to be unpleasant to be around. Do you ever listen to yourself? This is crazy, that is crazy, everything is crazy to you. By whose measure? Well, it is my right to be *crazy,* as you love to say so much. I have no shame. I have felt many things in my life, but shame is not among them." The volume of my voice caused me to stand on my tiptoes. I could not remember yelling like this, ever. "You may think that I have an obligation to you but I assure you that us being thrown together in this arbitrary arrangement does not cohesion make. I have never had less of an obligation to anyone in my life, you aggressively ordinary woman."

Lydia began to cry. Benjamin grabbed my shoulders and steered me forcefully into the foyer.

"Are you okay?" he asked. I tried to answer, but my head weighed a thousand pounds. I bent toward him, pressing my scalp into his shirt.

"I feel so sick," I said.

"Maybe you need to just go work in your studio for a while. Or take a nap. Or something."

I felt a plug of mucus release itself from my nose. I wiped it on my hand.

"You look terrible," he said. I must have looked stricken at this, because he corrected himself. "You look troubled. Are you troubled?"

"I suppose I must be," I said.

"When was the last time you heard from your wife?"

I closed my eyes. So many letters, sent off into oblivion. Never a letter for me.

"You're the kindest one," I said to him.

As I sat on my studio's deck that night, I considered the rabbit. I thought about the wind-strewn puffs of fur that had blown across the wood, the dark entrance to its torso. I swirled water in a wineglass.

Many years ago—the night after I kissed Mrs. Z——'s tall daughter on the mouth on the dock and felt something unfold inside me like a morning glory—I woke up in the darkness.

How could I have known she'd shared none of my ecstasy? How could I have known that she was merely curious, and then afraid?

It was not very different from waking up in my grandmother's spare bedroom, or on some finished basement floor, surrounded by slumbering classmates. But unlike those moments, where confusion was followed by drowsy recognition of vacation or a sleepover, this disorientation did not resolve itself. For I had gone to sleep drunk on pleasure and warm in a cocoon of nylon, listening to the dry, tinny whispers of the girls around me in the cabin, a sound as soothing as the tide. But I awakened upright, freezing, and surrounded by the kind of darkness insomniacs long for: matte, consuming oblivion.

How could I have known that they'd seen?

Around me was not the absence of sound, but the sound of absence: a voluptuous silence that pressed against my eardrums. Then, a pulse of wind goaded the tree branches, and there was a groan, a whispery shimmer of leaves. I trembled. I wanted to look up—for a moon, or stars, or something to tell me where I was—but I was rigid with terror.

How could I have known that they had guided my trusting, sleepwalking body out of the cabin and through the forest? That they crouched mere feet away, watching my form suspended in the clearing, circling slowly in the blackness like an errant satellite?

My body was so cold it felt like it was disappearing at the edges, like my shoreline was evaporating. It was the opposite of pleasure, which had pumped blood through me and warmed my body like the mammal I was. But here, I was just skin, then just muscle, and then merely bone. I felt like my spine was pulling up into my skull, each vertebra *click-click-click*ing like a car slowly ascending a roller coaster's first hill. And then I was just a hovering brain, and then a consciousness, floating and fragile as a bubble. And then I was nothing.

Only then did I understand. Only then did I see the crystal outline of my past and future, conceive of what was above me (innumerable stars, incalculable space) and what was below me (miles of mindless dirt and stone). I understood that knowledge was a dwarfing, obliterating, all-consuming thing, and to have it was to both be grateful and suffer greatly. I was a creature so small, trapped in some crevice of an indifferent universe. But now, I knew.

I heard a light crescendo of laughter, running footsteps. I wanted to call out to them—"I see you, friends; I know you're there. This hilarious prank will make me stronger, in the end, and for that I should certainly thank you, friends—friends?"—but I only managed a half-moaned exhalation.

Something pushed through the underbrush, coming toward me. Not a girl, not an animal, but something in between. I came back into myself and began to scream.

I screamed and screamed and when the leaders got there—the beams of their flashlights bobbing in the dark like demented fireflies—one of them tried to keep me from frightening the others by sealing the fissure of my mouth with her palm. I fought her like a wild thing, an explosion of limbs and kicking. Then I went limp. They carried me back to the cabin, and though my numb limbs barely perceived their touch, I was grateful for the assistance.

The next morning, the leaders told me I'd sleepwalked deep into the woods. They let me rest, and when I woke again a fever had taken me. My awakening had been so severe it provoked in my body an immune reaction, a summoning of antibodies that clashed with this new information like armies on a medieval battlefield. I lay there, imagining the script of the conversation they'd all shared as I'd shuffled deeper and deeper into the trees. I slept and dreamt of a roomful of owls regurgitating onto the floor pellets that when opened revealed the skulls of rabbits. I woke up with long scratches down my arms. The tree branches? My own fingernails? No one would tell me.

Once, I awoke to see a body in the doorway, backlit by soft autumn light.

"I'm sorry," she said. "You deserved better than that. Better than—"

From behind her, there was a murmur, and the door swung

shut. Later, the adults conferred with each other in the next room about my situation, and agreed that I was not ready for camping, at least not that year.

The next day, Mrs. Z—— drove me down the mountain early, back to my parents' house. I slept on and off for many days, insisting on doing so on my bedroom floor in my sleeping bag. And when my fever broke, I pulled my shaking body up to the vanity, glanced into the mirror, and for the first time, saw who I'd been looking for.

When I came to the table for dinner, I realized Lydia was not among us. There was not even a place setting for her.

"Where is Lydia?" I asked

Anele frowned. "She left," she said.

"She left?"

Anele was trying not to be unkind, I could tell. "I think she was exhausted and sick, so she left early. Drove back to Brooklyn."

"And upset," said Diego. "She was upset. About the rabbit."

The Painter sliced into her beef, which was rarer than I would have thought safe to eat. "Oh well," she said, her voice throaty and clear. "Not everybody's cut out for this, I guess."

My wineglass had tipped over, though I didn't remember it tipping over. The stain spread away from me like blood, predictably.

"What did you say?" I said to the Painter.

She looked up from her fork, where a cube of red beef was leaking onto her plate. "I said, not everybody's cut out for this, I guess." It was the first sentence of hers that stayed in my mind the way speech should. She pushed the meat between her lips and began to chew. I could hear the crushing, tearing force of her mastication as clearly as if she were gnawing on my throat. A chill rippled underneath my shoulder blades, as if I were under the grip of a new fever.

"Is that—from something?" I asked her. "That sentiment? A show, or—"

She put her fork down on her plate, and swallowed. "No. Are you accusing me of something?"

"No, I just—" The faces of the group were knitted in confusion, glossed with concern. I stood up and backed away from the table. When I pushed the chair back into its place, the screech caused everyone to flinch.

"Don't be afraid," I said to them. "I'm not. Not anymore."

I hurried out of the room and out the front door, down the steps, tumbling onto the lawn and scrambling to my feet. Behind me, Benjamin began to jog down the steps.

"Stop," he shouted. "Come back. Just let me—"

I turned and ran for the trees.

In the realm of sense and reason it seemed logical for something to make sense for no reason (natural order) or not make sense for some reason (the deliberate design of deception) but it seemed perverse to have things make no sense for no reason. What if you colonize your own mind and when you get inside, the furniture is attached to the ceiling? What if you step inside and when you touch the furniture, you realize it's all just cardboard cutouts and it all collapses beneath the pressure of your finger? What if you get inside and there's no furniture? What if you get inside and it's just you in there, sitting in a chair, rolling figs and eggs around in the basket of your lap and humming a little tune? What if you get inside and there's nothing there, and then the door hatch closes and locks?

What is worse: being locked outside of your own mind, or being locked inside of it?

What is worse: writing a trope or being one? What about being more than one?

I walked to my cabin for the last time. I finally added my name to the tablet above my desk. *C——M——*, I scrawled. *Resident colonist & colonizing resident & madwoman in her own attic.*

I threw my novel notes and laptop into the lake. After the plush splash subsided, I heard the sound of girls, laughing. Or maybe it was just the birds.

I drove away from Devil's Throat in the early-morning darkness. The car barreled down the road that had once seemed so lush and inviting, and as I descended the mountain I felt as if I was being rewound back to the beginning—not just the beginning of the summer, but of my life. The trees whipped past, the same trees that I had observed from a middle-aged woman's car. Now I was that woman, but I was speeding wildly and the trees flashed by so fast I felt nauseated. No limpid daughter slept in the backseat; no strange teenage girl sat next to me, stewing in her own nightmarish consciousness. (And isn't that how you become tender, vulnerable? The tissue-softening marination of your own mind, the quicksand of mental indulgence?)

I needed to be home. I needed to be home with my wife, in our home in civilization and away from other artists—at least, the sort of artists who cloister themselves from the rest of the world. Dying profession, dead hotels. I had been foolish.

After I passed through Y——, an orange-limbed sign sat on the side of the road. SPEED LIMIT 45 it read. Beneath, a dark-paneled digital screen was waiting for drivers to approach, to admonish (by blinking) or praise (by not blinking). As I approached, I waited for my own car—now pushing sixty—to register. But the panel remained dark. As I zipped past, I felt a strange sensation, as if some-one were pressing a thin membrane to my throat and I was inhaling no air. The thought came so suddenly upon me that my car almost veered off the side of the road. I pressed my fingers to my throat, where my pulse hummed beneath my skin. Fast, but there. I was alive, surely.

How much time had passed since I departed our little house, since I'd seen my wife's face? What if I'd misstepped and overshot her lifetime, Rip Van Winkled myself away from her in an irre-versible act?

I pressed on my brake once, twice, and the dark road behind me flooded red. The light revealed a herd of deer moving liquidly over the pavement, eyes glinting with each tap.

Two hours later, I pulled the car up next to the curb. People drifted along the street, stood on their lawns, watching me. I could not remember if these were the neighbors from before. It seemed like a lifetime since I had last seen their front doors and fences. I stepped out of the car and approached our home, where a woman in a blue dress was kneeling in the dirt, a sun hat concealing her face. My wife was always a morning planter, finding the cool, thin dawn air to be bracing and healthful. She had a dress like that, and a hat. Was that her? Did her shoulders bend and crook with advanced age, or merely with the exhaustion of being married to someone like me?

I walked up to the sidewalk and called her name.

The woman stiffened, and as her head rose up, her sun hat tilted, too. I waited for the outline of her face to emerge from beneath the brim: to assure me I was still needed, to assure me I was still here.

I know what you're thinking, reader. You're thinking: Does this woman have the temperament to come to *our* residency, having failed so thoroughly at this one? Surely she is too fragile, too sick, too mad to eat and sleep and work among other artists. Or, if you're being a little less generous, perhaps you're thinking that I'm a cliché—a weak, trembling thing with a silly root of adolescent trauma, straight out of a gothic novel.

But I ask you, readers: Thus far in your jury deliberations, have you encountered any others who have truly met themselves? Some, I'm sure, but not many. I have known many people in my lifetime, and rarely do I find any who have been taken down to the quick, pruned so that their branches might grow back healthier than before.

I can tell you with perfect honesty that the night in the forest was a gift. Many people live and die without ever confronting themselves in the darkness. Pray that one day, you will spin around at the water's edge, lean over, and be able to count yourself among the lucky.

DIFFICULT AT PARTIES

Afterward, there is no kind of quiet like the one that is in my head.

Paul brings me home from the hospital in his ancient Volvo. The heater is busted and it's January, so there's a fleece blanket wedged at the foot of the passenger seat. My body radiates pain, is dense with it. He buckles my seat belt. His hands are shaking. He lifts the blanket and spreads it on my lap. He's done this before, wrapping it snug around my thighs while I make jokes about being a kid getting tucked into bed. He is cautious and fearful, now.

Stop, I say, and I do it myself.

It is Tuesday. I think it's Tuesday. The condensation on the inside of the car has frozen. The snow outside is sullied, a dark yellow line carved into its depths. The wind rattles the broken door handle. Across the way, a teenage girl shouts to her friend three unintelligible syllables. Tuesday is speaking to me, in Tuesday's voice. Open up, it says. Open up.

Paul reaches for the ignition. Around the hole there are scratches in the plastic where I imagine that in his rush to get me, the key had missed its destination over and over again.

The engine struggles a little, as if it doesn't want to wake up.

. . .

The first night back in my house, he stands in the doorway of the bedroom with his wide shoulders hunched inward and asks me where I want him to sleep.

With me, I say, as if it's a ridiculous question. Lock the door, I tell him, and get into bed.

The door is locked.

Lock it again.

He leaves, and I can hear the stifled jerks of a doorknob being tested. He comes back into the bedroom, flips back the covers, buries himself next to me.

I dream of Tuesday. I dream of it from start to finish.

When the thin light of morning stretches across the bed, Paul is sleeping in the recliner in the corner of the room. What are you doing? I ask, pushing the quilt off my body. Why are you there?

He tilts his head up. Around his eye, a smoky-dark bruise is forming.

You were screaming, he says. You were screaming, and I tried to hold you, and you elbowed me in the face.

This is the first time I actually cry.

I am ready, I tell my black-and-blue reflection. Friday.

I draw a bath. The water gushes too hot from the spotted faucet. I peel my pajamas away from my body and they fall like sloughed skin to the tiled floor. I half-expect to look down and see the cage of my ribs, the wet balloons of my lungs.

Steam rises from the bath. I remember a small version of myself, sitting in a hotel hot tub and holding my arms rigid against my torso, rolling around in the churning water. I'm a carrot! I shriek at a woman, who might be my mother. Add some salt! Add some peas! And from her lounge chair she reaches toward me with her hand contorted as if around a handle, the very caricature of a chef with a slotted spoon.

I add a fat dollop of bubble bath.

I slip my foot into the water. There is a second of brilliant heat that slides straight through me, like steel wire through a block of wet clay. I gasp but do not pause. A second foot, less pain. Hands on the sides of the bathtub, I lower myself down. The water hurts, and it is good. The chemicals in the bubble bath burn, and that is better.

I run my toes along the faucet, whispering things to myself, lifting up my breasts with both hands to see how high they can sit; I catch my reflection in the sweaty curve of the stainless steel, tilt my head. On the far side of the tub, I can see the tiny slivers of red polish that have receded from the edges of my toenails. I feel buoyant, bodiless. The water gets too high and threatens the lip of the tub. I turn the faucet off. The bathroom echoes unpleasantly.

I hear the front door open. I tense until I hear the rattle of keys on the hallway table. Paul comes into the bathroom.

Hey, he says.

Hey, I say. You had a meeting.

What?

You had a meeting. You're wearing a dress shirt.

He looks down at himself. Yes, he says, slowly, as if he didn't believe his shirt had existed until now. Actually, he says, I went and looked at a few apartments.

I don't want to move, I tell him.

You should find another place. He says this firmly, as if he had spent his entire day building up to this sentence.

I shouldn't do anything, I say. I don't want to move.

I think it's a bad idea to stay. I can help you find a new apartment.

I wind a hand into my hair and pull it away from my skull in a wet sheet. A bad idea for whom?

We stare at each other. My other arm is crossed over my chest; I let it drop.

Unplug the tub for me? I ask.

He kneels in the cold puddle on the tile next to the tub. He unbuttons the sleeve at his wrist and begins to roll it up in a neat, tight coil. He reaches past my legs, into the water still thick with bubbles, down to the bottom. Suds catch on the roll of fabric around his upper arm. I can feel the syncopated drumming of his fingers as he fumbles for the beaded chain, weaves it around them, pulls.

There is a low *pop*. A lazy bubble of air breaks the water's surface. He withdraws, and his hand brushes my skin. I jump, and then he jumps.

My face is level with his shins when he stands; there are wet circles on the knees of his dress pants.

You're spending a lot of time away from your place, I say. I don't want you to feel like you have to spend every night here.

He frowns. It doesn't bother me, he says. I want to help. He vanishes into the hallway.

I sit there until all of the water drains, until the last milky swirl disappears down the silver mouth and I feel a strange shiver that starts deep within me. A spine should not be so afraid. The receding bubbles leave strange white striations on my skin, like the tide-scarred sand at the beach's edge. I feel heavy.

Weeks pass. The officer who'd taken my statement in the hospital calls to say she might have me come in to identify someone. Her voice is generous, too loud. Later, she leaves a clipped message on the answering machine, telling me it's not necessary. The wrong person, not the right one.

Maybe he left the state, Paul says.

I stay away from myself. Paul stays away, too. I don't know who is more afraid, he or I.

We should try something, I say one morning. About this. I gesture to the space in front of me.

He looks up from an egg. Yes, he says.

We lay out suggestions on a hot-pink Post-it note that is too small for many solutions.

I place an order for a DVD from a company that advertises adult films for loving couples. It arrives in a plain brown box, neatly placed on the corner of the cement stoop in front of my apartment. When I pick it up, the box is lighter than I expect. I tuck it under my arm and fiddle with the doorknob for a minute. The new deadbolt sticks.

I put the box on the kitchen table. Paul calls. I'm coming over soon, he says. His voice always sounds immediate, present, even when he's speaking over the phone. Did you get the—

Yeah, I say. It's here.

It will take him at least fifteen minutes to get to this side of town. I go to the box and open it. The number of limbs tangled on the front cover doesn't appear to match the number of faces. I count, twice, and confirm that there is one extra elbow and one extra leg. I open the case. The disc smells brand-new and doesn't snap easily from its plastic knob. The shiny side gleams like an oil slick, and reflects my face strangely, as if someone had reached out and smeared it. I set it down in the DVD player's open tray.

There's no menu; the movie plays automatically. I kneel down on the carpet in front of the television, lean my chin into my hand,

and watch. The camera is steady. The woman on the video looks a little like me—the same mouth, anyway. She is talking shyly to a man on her left, a built man who has probably not always been so—he seems to be straining out of his shirt, which is too small for his new muscles. They are having a conversation, a conversation about—I cannot make out any of the individual pieces of the conversation. He touches her leg. She takes the tab of her zipper and slides it down. There is nothing underneath.

Past the obligatory blow jobs, past the mouth-that-looks-like-mine straining, past perfunctory cunnilingus, they are talking again.

the last time, I told him, I told, fuck, they can see my—
I can't hold this down, I can't hold this down, I can't—

I sit up. Their mouths are not moving. Well, their mouths are moving, but the words dropping from those mouths are expected. *Baby. Fuck. Yeah, yeah, yeah. God.* Underneath, something else is moving. A stream running beneath the ice. A voiceover. Or, I guess, a voiceunder.

if he tells me again, if he says to me that it's not okay, I should just—
two more years, maybe, only two, maybe just one if I keep going—

The voices—no, not voices, the sounds, soft and muted and rising and falling in volume—blend together, weave around each other, disparate syllables ringing out. I don't know where the voices are coming from—a commentary track? Without taking my eyes off the screen, I reach for the remote control and press the pause button.

They freeze. She is staring at him. He is looking somewhere out of the frame. Her hand is pressed down on her abdomen, hard. The swelling knoll of her stomach is vanishing beneath her palm.

I unpause it.

okay, so I had a baby, this isn't the first time that's—

and if it's only a year, then maybe I can follow—

I pause it again. The woman is now frozen on her back. Her partner stands between her legs, casually, like he's about to ask her a question, his cock curved to the left against his abdomen. Her hand is still pushed into her stomach.

I stare at the screen for a long time.

When Paul knocks, I jump.

I let him in and hug him. He is panting and his shirt is damp with sweat. I can taste the salt in my mouth as I press my face against his chest. He kisses me, and I can sense his eyes flicking to the screen.

I feel sick, I tell him.

He asks me if I am soup-sick or Sprite-sick. I tell him soup-sick. He goes into the kitchen and I lie down on the couch.

Jane and Jill have invited us to their housewarming party, he calls from the kitchen. I hear the *thunk* of the cupboard door striking the cabinet next to it, the dry sliding of cans being sorted through, the sloshing of liquid, the tap of a pot on a burner, the metallic clink of him using the wrong spoon to stir.

They moved? I ask.

To a big house in the country, he says.

I don't want to go, I tell him, the pale blue light from the television casting shadows on my face as three men intertwine with each other, each mouth full. When he brings the soup out to me, chicken broth brimming precariously at the top of the bowl, napkin resting beneath it, he warns me that it's hot. I sip the burning soup too quickly and drop a mouthful back into the bowl.

I'm worried that you're spending too much time in the house, he says. It'll be mostly women.

What? I say.

At the party. It'll be mostly women. All people that I know. Good people.

I don't answer. I touch my numb tongue with my finger.

I wear my turquoise dress with black stockings underneath and take a small aloe plant as a gift. In my car, we speed out of the dim lights of our small town and onto a country road. Paul uses one hand to steer, and rests the other on my leg. The moon is full and illuminates the glittering snow that stretches for miles in every direction, the sloped barn roofs and narrow silos with icicles as thick as my arm hanging from their outcroppings, the herd of rectangular and unmoving cows huddled near the entrance to a hayloft. I hold the plant protectively against my body, and when the car makes a sudden left, some of the sandy soil spills out onto my dress. I pinch it from the fabric and drop it back into the pot, brushing a few crumbs of dirt off the fleshy leaves. When I look up again, I see that we are approaching a large illuminated building.

So this is a new house? I ask, my head pressed against the window.

Yeah, he says. They just bought it, oh, I don't know, about a month ago. I haven't been there yet, but I hear it's really nice.

We pull up next to a row of parked cars, in front of a renovated turn-of-the-century farmhouse.

It looks so homey, says Paul, stepping out and rubbing his gloveless hands together.

The windows are draped with gauzy curtains, and a creamy honey color throbs from within. The house looks like it's on fire.

The hosts open the door; they are beautiful and have gleaming teeth. I have seen this before. I have not seen them before.

Jane, says the dark-haired one. Jill, says the redheaded one. And that's not a joke! They laugh. Paul laughs. It's so nice to meet you, Jane says to me. I hold the small aloe plant toward her. She smiles again and takes it, her dimples so deep I feel the urge to push my fingers into them. Paul looks pleased, and then leans over and scratches the ears of a large white cat with a smooshed face that is rubbing against his legs.

We've made a coatroom out of the bedroom, Jill says. Paul reaches for my coat. I slip it off and hand it to him, and he vanishes up the stairs.

A man in the hallway with buzzed hair and pale skin is holding an ancient camcorder on his shoulder. It is gigantic and the color of tar. He swings it toward me, an eye.

Tell me your name, he says.

I try to pull away, out of its view, but I cannot shrink tightly enough against the wall.

Why is that here? I ask, trying to keep panic out of my voice.

Your name, he repeats, tipping the camera toward me.

Oh Jesus, Gabe, leave her alone, says Jill, pushing him away. She takes my arm and pulls me along. Sorry about that. There's always some retro-loving jackass at parties, and he's ours.

Jane comes up on the other side of me and laughs down a scale. Paul, she says, where'd you go?

He reappears. Onward, he says, sounding giddy.

They ask us if we want the tour. We wander from the living room to a wide-open kitchen, shiny with brass and steel. They tap each shiny appliance in turn: Dishwasher. Refrigerator. Gas stove. Separate oven. *Second* oven. There is a door toward the back with an ornate, bronze-colored handle. I reach for it, but Jane grabs my shoulder. Stop, she says. Careful.

That room is being renovated, says Jill. There's no floor. You could go in there, but you'd go straight down to the cellar. She opens the door with her manicured hand and, yes, the no-floor yawns at me.

That would be terrible, says Jane.

The camera follows me around. I stand near Paul for a while, awkwardly smoothing my dress. He seems anxious, so I move, a satellite released from orbit. Away from him, I feel strange, purposeless. I do not know these people, and they do not know me. I stand near the hors d'oeuvres table, and eat one shrimp—meaty, swimming in cocktail sauce—tucking the stiff tail into my palm. Another one, then a third, the tails filling up my hand. I swallow a glass of red wine without tasting it. I refill it, and drain another. I swirl a cracker in something dark green. I look up. In the corner of the room, the single eye of the camera is fixed on me. I turn toward the table.

The cat saunters over and paws playfully at a hunk of pita bread in my hands. When I pull it away, she swipes at me and takes a chunk out of my finger. I swear and suck at the wound. In my mouth, I can taste hummus and copper. I'm so sorry, says Jill, who swans up as if she had been waiting offstage for the cue of my blood. He does that to strangers sometimes; he really needs anxiety medication or something. Bad pussycat! Jane touches Jill's arm lightly and asks her to come and help clean up a spill, and they both vanish.

Friendly people I have never met ask me about my job, about my life. They reach across me for wineglasses, touch my arm. Each time, I move away, not directly back but a half step to the right, and they match my movements, and in this way we move in a small circle as we speak.

The last book I read, I repeat slowly, was—

But I can't remember. I remember the satiny cover beneath the pads of my fingertips, but not the title, or the author, or any of the words inside. I think I am talking funny, with my burned mouth, my numb tongue fat and useless inside my mouth. I want to say, Don't bother asking me anything. I want to say, There is nothing underneath.

And what do you do?

The questions come at me like doors thrown open. I begin to explain, but as soon as the words leave my mouth I find myself searching for Paul. He is in the far corner of the room, talking to a woman with short hair and a strand of pearls that wraps around her neck like the coils of a noose. She touches his arm familiarly; he bats her away with his hand. His muscles look taut enough to snap. I look back at the woman who asked me about my profession. She is curvy and taller than most and has on the brightest shade of red lipstick that I have ever seen. Her eyes flicker over to Paul. She takes another long swig of her martini, the olives rolling around in the glass like eyes. How are things with the two of you? she asks. A pimento iris lolls in my direction. The woman with the pearls touches Paul's arm again. He shakes his head, almost imperceptibly. Who is she? Why is she—

I excuse myself and walk into the dim hallway. I press my palm into the iron sphere at the base of the railing, and swing myself up onto the staircase.

The coatroom, I think. The bedroom full of coats. The repurposed—

The stairs move away from me, and I rush to catch them. I search for the door, a darker patch among darkness. The coatroom is cool. I press my hand on the wooden panel. The coats will not question me.

In the shadows, two figures are struggling on the bed. My heart surges with fear, a fish with a steel hook through the ridge of its lip. As my eyes adjust to the darkness, I realize that it's just the hosts, writhing on the heaps of shiny down jackets. The dark-haired one—Jane? or is it Jill?—is on her back, her dress gathered around her hips, and her wife is over her, grinding her knee between her legs. Jane—maybe Jill—is biting her own wrist to keep from crying out. The coats rustle, slide. Jane kisses Jill or Jill kisses Jane and then one leans down and rolls down the top of the other's stockings, a rolled line of underwear, her face disappearing into her.

A pleasurable twinge curls inside of me. Jill or Jane writhes, pulls up fistfuls of down coat with her hands, makes a soft noise, a single syllable stretched in two directions. A long red scarf slides to the floor.

I don't wonder if they can see me. I could stand here for a thousand years and between coats and syllables and mouths they would never see me.

I close the door.

I get drunk. I have four flutes of champagne and a strong gin and tonic. I even suck the gin out of the lime wedge, the citrus stinging the scratch on my finger. Gabe finally puts the camera down on a chair in deference to its extraordinary weight. It sits there, quietly, but it holds me inside, somewhere, for precious seconds that I cannot take back. A face that I have yet to really look at, resting deep in the coils of its mechanical innards.

I walk past the camera and take it, my fingers tightening around the handle. I control it now. As I walk nonchalantly toward the front door, taking care to point the lens away from my body, I see the white cat with the smooshed face, watching me from the landing. His pink comma tongue slides out and makes a leisurely trip over his upper lip, and his blue eyes narrow accusingly. I stumble. I do not bother to get my coat before I walk through the front door.

Outside, my boots crunch loudly through the glittering ice and mean snow. Near the end of the path that leads to the drive-way, someone has emptied a half-full coffee cup, and dark brown is splattered grotesquely across the white lawn. Narrow tracks in the snow suggest a deer has seen this sight, too. My skin is stippled with goose bumps. I realize I don't have the keys, but I reach for the trunk handle anyway.

It's unlocked. The trunk opens to me, and I thump the camera down into its shadows.

I go back inside and have a glass of wine. Then a shot of some-thing green. The world begins to slide.

Instead of passing out like a dignified person, I stagger out to the car again, sit in the cold passenger seat, recline it, and stare out the sunroof at a sky crowded with delicate points of light.

Paul gets into the driver's seat.

Are you all right? he asks.

I nod, and then throw open the door and vomit cocktail shrimp and spinach dip onto the gravel driveway. Pink chunks and long dark strands like hair settle among the stones and snow; the puddle gleams and reflects the moon.

We drive. I recline and watch the sky.

Did you have fun? he asks.

I giggle, laugh. No, I guffaw. I snort. Fuck no. Fuck—

I feel something cold on my face and I pick it off. Spinach. I roll down the window. Icy air hits my face. I throw it out of the car.

If that were a cigarette, I say, it would spark. It should be a ciga-rette. I could use one of those.

The cold stings.

Can you roll the window up? Paul asks loudly over the rushing wind. I roll it back up and lean my heavy head against the glass.

I thought it would be good for us to get out of the house, he says. Jane and Jill really like you.

Like me for what? I pull my head away, and there is a circle of grease obscuring the sky. I see a black stain flash briefly under the headlights, then a huddled mass on the side of the road—a deer, blasted apart by the tires of an SUV.

I can almost hear the line between Paul's eyebrows deepening. What do you mean, like you for what? What does that even mean?

I don't know.

They just like you, that's all.

I laugh again, and reach for the window crank. Who was that woman with that pearl necklace? I ask.

No one, he says, in a voice that doesn't fool either of us.

At my house, he carries me to bed. When he lies down next to me, I reach over and touch his stomach. He doesn't ask me what I am doing.

You're drunk, he says. You don't want this.

How do you know what I want? I ask. I inch closer. He takes my hand and lifts it away. He holds it aloft for a minute, seemingly not wanting to drop it, but not wanting to put it back either. He settles for resting it on my own stomach, and then rolls away from me.

I reach for myself. I don't even recognize my own topography.

Most mornings, Paul asks me what I dreamt about.

I don't remember, I say. Why?

You moved around. A lot. He says this carefully, with restraint that betrays itself.

I want to see. I set up the camera on the highest shelf of the bookcase next to my bed, to record my sleep. The DVD from the other day is obviously broken, so I put it into the garbage can, shoving it deep into the bag past potato peelings curling like question marks. Then, I order another DVD. It shows up on my cement stoop.

This one is in many parts, smaller parts, like film shorts. The first one is called *Fucking My Wife*. I start it. A man is holding the camera—I can't see his face. The woman is blond and older than the last woman and she has meticulously applied mascara.

How do I say, how do I say, how do I say—

I cannot hear him. I look at the video case again. *Fucking My Wife*. I don't understand the title. I can't hear him. Only her voice, tinged with desperation.

How do I say, how do I say, how do I—

I don't want to hear her anymore. I hit mute.

How do I say, how do I say, how do I—

I turn off the DVD player. The television blinks to the news network. A blond woman is staring gravely at her audience. Over her left shoulder, like an advising devil, there is a square graphic of a bomb, blasting apart the pixels that make it. I unmute the sound.

—a bombing in Turkey, she is saying. Viewers should be advised that the following images are—

I turn off the TV. I yank the plug out by the cord.

Paul comes over. How are you feeling? he asks.

A little better, I say. Tired. I lean into him. He smells like detergent. I lean into him and I want him. He is solid. He reminds me of a tree—roots that run deep.

The DVD player is broken, I say, heading off the question before it can be asked.

Do you want me to look at it? he asks.

Yes, I say. I plug in the TV again. As the DVD begins to play, and the bodies begin to unfold, I can hear it again. That voice, that sad, desperate sound, the questions repeated over and over again like a mantra, even as she smiles. Even as she moans and her mind flits between her question and the pattern of the carpet. Paul watches with determined courtesy, absently stroking my hand as it plays. The next one begins, a different scenario. Something about a massage.

Can't you hear it? I feel the nails of my free hand digging into my jeans.

He tilts his head to the side and listens again.

Hear what? he says, his voice tinged with exasperation.

The voices.

It's not like it's on mute.

No, the voices underneath.

He moves away from me so quickly I lose my balance. His right hand hovers next to him, flexing and unflexing as if he's holding the disembodied heart of an enemy. What is *wrong* with you? he snaps. When I don't respond, he slams his hands against the wall. God*damnit*, he says.

I turn back to the screen. A man looks down at a woman going down on him. Let me look at those pretty baby blues, he says, and her amber eyes flick upward, and different names run through their respective minds like a chant for the dead. I turn the TV off.

Don't be angry with me, please, I say. I stand in front of him, my hands dangling heavily at my sides. He puts his arms around me, rests his chin on my head. We rock back and forth slowly, dancing to the sound of the heating vent struggling to keep us warm.

I think I found you an apartment, he says into my hair. It's on the third floor of a building on the other side of the river.

I don't want to leave, I say into his chest.

His muscles tense, and he pulls me away from his body by the length of his impossible arms.

It's like you're not even in there. He grabs the sides of his arms. You're responding to all of the wrong things.

Please stop, I say. He reaches for me, but I knock his hand away. I need you to be simple and good, I say. Can't you just be simple and good?

He looks straight through me, as if I already know the answer.

The next morning, I slide the cassette out of the camera, rewind it, and put it in the VCR. I fast-forward through the stillness, though there is not much of it. Camera-me flails. She grabs for the air as if she is trying to pull party streamers down from the ceiling. She knocks her limbs against the wall, the oak headboard, the nightstand, and does not recoil in pain but goes back to them, over and over. The slender lamp crashes to the floor. Paul gets up, tries to help, holds her arms, holds my arms, trying to pin them to her sides, then looks guilty and releases them. She comes down. She struggles against the blankets. She slides down onto the floor, rolling half under the edge of the bed, partially hidden by the pulled sheets. Paul tries to get her back up onto the bed and she takes a wild swing at his head, and I can hear her steady *no, no, no, no, no, no, no* even as he tugs her back up onto the mattress, getting close enough to talk into her ear, something too low for the camera to catch, and then getting her down, down onto the mattress, down into his arms in a grip that looks both threatening and comforting. This lasts for a moment before she is—before I am—up again, and Paul pulls me into him, even as I hit his chest, even as I slide again to the floor. A whole night of this.

When I am done, I rewind it to the beginning and replace it in the camera.

I stop ordering DVDs by mail. There are no voice tricks in Internet porn, no weird commentary tracks. I begin free trials at four different websites.

I can still hear them. A man with slender wrists wonders endlessly about someone named Sam. Two women are surprised about each other's bodies, the infinite softness. *No one said, no one said,* a tanned woman thinks. It echoes around her mind, around mine. I lean in so close to the screen that I cannot even see the picture anymore. Just blotches of color, moving. Beiges, browns, the black of the tanned woman's hair, a shock of red of which, when I pull back, I can't see the origins.

A woman mentally corrects a man who keeps referring to her *pussy*. *Cunt*, she thinks, and the word is dense and sits in the air like a wedge of underripe fruit. I love your pussy, he says. *Cunt*, she repeats over and over again, a meditation.

Some are silent. Some have no words, just colors.

A woman with a black harness around her fleshy hips prays as she fucks a thin man who idolizes her. Each thrust punctuates. At the end, she kisses his back, a benediction.

A man with two women on his cock wants to be home.

Do they know what they are thinking, I wonder, clicking through videos, letting them load like a slingshot being pulled back. Do they hear it? Do they know? Did I know?

I cannot remember.

At two in the morning, I am watching a man make a delivery. A woman with breasts that float wrongly against gravity opens the door. Not the right house, of course. I think that I have watched this before, maybe. He sets the empty cardboard box on the table. She takes off her shirt. I listen.

Her mind is all darkness. It is full, afraid. Fear rushes through it, white-hot and terrified. Fear weighs on her chest, crushing her. She is thinking about a door opening. She is thinking about a stranger coming in. I am thinking about a door opening. I can hear him clutching the doorknob. I cannot hear him clutching the doorknob, but I can hear it turning. I cannot hear it turning, but I hear the footfalls. I cannot hear the footfalls, I cannot hear them. There is only a shadow. There is only darkness blotting out light.

He, the delivery man, the no-delivery man, thinks about her breasts. He worries about his body. He wants to please her, really.

She smiles. There is a smear of lipstick on her teeth. She likes him. Below this, there is a screaming, rushing tunnel. No radio signal. It fills my head, it presses against the bone of my skull. Pounding, pushing it apart. I am an infant, my head is not solid, these tectonic plates, they cannot be expected to hold.

I grab my laptop and hurl it across the room at the wall. I expect it to shatter, but it doesn't—it strikes the drywall and hits the ground with a terrific crash.

I scream. I scream so loudly the note splits in two.

Paul comes running out of the basement. He cannot get close to me.

Don't touch me, I howl. Don't touch me, don't touch me.

He stays near the door. I slump down onto the floor. My tears run hot and then cool on my face. Please go back downstairs, I say. I cannot see Paul, but I hear him open the basement door. I flinch. I do not get up until my heart slows.

When I finally stand and walk over to the wall, I tip the computer right side up. There is a massive crack down the center of the screen, a ruptured fault line.

In the bedroom, Paul sits across from me, his fingers tapping idly on the denim of his pants.

Do you remember, he says, what it was like before?

I look down at my legs, then up at the blank wall, then back to him. I do not even struggle to speak; the spark of words dies so deep in my chest there is not even space to mount them on an exhale.

You wanted, he says. You wanted and wanted. You were like this endless thing. A well that never emptied.

I wish I could say that I remember, but I do not remember. I can imagine pumping limbs and mouths on mouths but I cannot remember them. I cannot remember ever being thirsty.

I sleep, long and hot, the windows open despite the winter. Paul sleeps against the wall and does not stir.

The voices aren't happening, not now, but I still perceive them. They drift over my head like milkweed. I am Samuel, I think. That's it. I'm Samuel. God called to him in the night. They call to me. Samuel answered, Yes, Lord? I have no way of answering my voices. I have no way of telling them that I can hear.

I hear the door open and then close but I don't turn my head. I am staring at the screen. An orgy, now. The fifth. Dozens of voices, too many to count, overlapping, tangling, making the air tight, crowding it. They worry, they lust, they laugh, they say stupid things. Sweat glitters. Badly placed tungsten lights cast shadows, slicing up a few bodies for a few moments into slick skin and canyons of darkness. Whole again. Pieces.

He sits down next to me, his weight sinking the cushion so far that I fall into him. I do not take my eyes off the screen.

Hey, he says. You okay?

Yes. I curl my fingers tightly against one another, my knuckles locking in a line. This is the church. This is the steeple.

He sits back and watches. He looks at me. He settles his fingers lightly on my shoulder blade, catching the strap of my bra and running his finger on the curve of my skin beneath the elastic. Gently, over and over.

A woman at the center of a male orbit reaches up, up over her head, so far up. She is thinking about one of them in particular, the one filling her, making her whole. She thinks about the lighting for a bit, then her thoughts drift back to him. Her leg is falling asleep.

Paul talks very close to my skin. What are you doing? he asks.

Watching, I say.

What?

Watching. Isn't this what I should be doing? Watching this?

The way he is still, I can tell that he is thinking. Then he reaches and puts his hand over mine—covering the church.

Hey, he says. Hey, hey.

One of the men is sick. He thinks he is going to die. He wants to die.

Bodies linking, unlinking, muscles twitching, hands.

Through the woman's mind, a ribbon of light tightens and slackens and tightens again. She laughs. She is actually coming. The first time we kissed, Paul and I, on my bed, in the dark, he was almost frantic, humming with energy, a screen door banging in the wind. Later he told me that it had just been so long, *so long*, that he felt like he was coming out of his skin. *Skin*. I can still hear them thinking, echoing around my head, slipping into the crevices of my memory. I cannot keep them away. This dam will not hold.

I do not realize that I am crying until he stands and brings me with him, pulling me from the couch. On the screen, pearly arcs of come crisscross the laughing woman's torso. I lift easily. He holds me and touches my face and his fingers are wet for the effort.

Shhhh, he says. Shhhh. I'm so sorry, he says. We don't have to watch it, we don't have to.

He weaves his fingers through my hair and supports the small of my back. Shhhh, he says. I don't want any of them. I want only you.

I stiffen.

Only you, he says again. He holds me tightly. A good man. He repeats, Only you.

You don't want to be here, I say.

The floor rumbles; a large truck darkens the front window. He doesn't respond.

He sits there quietly, radiating guilt. The house is dark. I kiss him on the mouth.

I'm sorry, he says. I'm so—

Now it is my time to *shhhh*. He stammers into silence. I kiss him, harder. I take his hand from my side and rest it on my thigh. He is hurting, and I want it to stop. I kiss him again. I trace two fingers along his erection.

Let's go, I say.

I always wake before him. Paul sleeps on his stomach. I sit up and stretch. I trace the rips in the comforter. Sunlight streams through my curtains. I can hardly sleep through such daylight. I get up. He does not stir.

I cross the room and pull the camera from its spot. I carry it into the living room. I rewind the tape, and it whines as it whirs back over itself.

I insert the cassette into the VCR. I run my finger down the buttons on the machine like a pianist choosing her first key. As I press it down, the screen goes snowy, and then black. Then, the static diorama of my room. The wrinkled sheets with the spray of blue-china pattern, unmade. I fast-forward. I fast-forward, spinning through minutes of nothing, unsurprised by how easy it is for them to slip away.

Two people stumble in, my finger lifts, the rush-to-now slows. Two strangers fumble with each other's clothes, each other's bodies. His body, slender and tall and pale, leans; his pants hit the floor with a *thunk*, the pockets full of keys and change. Her body—my body, mine—is still striped with the yellowish stains of fading bruises. It is a body overflowing out of itself; it unwinds from too many layers. The shirt looks bulky in my hand, and I release it onto the floor. It drops like a shot bird. We are pressing into the side of the mattress.

I look down at my hands. They are dry and not shaking. I look back up at the screen, and I begin to listen.

ACKNOWLEDGMENTS

It turns out that when you publish a debut book, you have an impossible task: not just thanking the people who directly influenced this particular title, but thanking everyone who has ever had a hand in your becoming a writer. And, as it turns out, when you sit down and think about it, that list can be dauntingly long.

Throughout my career, there have been so many people willing to take a chance on me, even when I wouldn't have taken a chance on me. And so here is my attempt to rise to the monumental task of doing justice to their astonishing generosity and faith.

This book—and this life—would have been impossible without:

My parents, Reinaldo and Martha, who read to me long before I could read, siblings Mario and Stefanie, who listened to all my stories, and my grandfather, who taught me how to tell them.

Laurie and Rick Machado, who have always been a stable and loving presence.

The women who gifted me books and stoked my nascent imagination: Eleanor Jacobs, Sue Thompson, Stefanie "Omama" Hoffman, Karen Maurer, Winnifred Younkin.

Marilyn Stinebaugh, who let me rail against Hemingway in her classroom and handed me texts from her personal library and showed me what literature could be.

Adam Malantonio, who made me a soundtrack.

Mindy McKonly, who took me seriously.

Marnanel Thurman, who has given me fifteen years of friendship and brilliance.

Amanda Myre, Amy Weishampel, Anne Paschke, Sam Aguirre, Jon Lipe, Katie Molski, Kelli Dunlap, Sam Hicks, Neal Fersko, and Rebekah Moan, who grew with me and helped me become myself.

Jim, James, and Josh, who listened and helped me arrive at my answers.

Harvey Grossinger, who provided the gift of his time and his wisdom.

Allan Gurganus, who encouraged me to make the right choice.

John Witte and Laura Hampton, whose love and friendship kept me together when nothing else could.

The Iowa Writers' Workshop, and the magnificent people who keep it running: Connie Brothers, Deb West, Jan Zenisek, and, of course, Lan Samantha Chang.

My Iowa classmates and dear friends, who made me a smarter person and a better writer: Amy Parker, Ben Mauk, Bennett Sims, Daniel Castro, E. J. Fischer, Evan James, Mark Mayer, Rebecca Rukeyser, Tony Tulathimutte, and Zac Gall.

My many writing teachers—Alexander Chee, Cassandra Clare, Delia Sherman, Harvey Grossinger, Holly Black, Jeffery Ford, Kevin Brockmeier, Lan Samantha Chang, Michelle Huneven, Randon Noble, Ted Chiang, and Wells Tower—who were hard on me when they needed to be, encouraging when they needed to be, and always kind.

The Clarion Science Fiction & Fantasy Writers' Workshop class of 2012: Chris Kammerud, Dan McMinn, Deborah Bailey, E. G. Cosh, Eliza Blair, Eric Esser, Jonathan Fortin, Lara Donnelly, Lisa

Bolekaja, Luke R. Pebler, Pierre Liebenberg, Ruby Katigbak, Sadie Bruce, Sam J. Miller, and Sarah Mack. (You will always be my Awkward Robots.)

The thoughtful and inspired writers of Sycamore Hill 2014 and 2015: Andy Duncan, Anil Menon, Chris Brown, Christopher Rowe, Dale Bailey, Gavin Grant, Jen Volant, Karen Joy Fowler, Kelly Link, Kiini Ibura Salaam, L. Timmel Duchamp, Matt Kressel, Maureen McHugh, Meghan McCarron, Michael Blumlein, Molly Gloss, Nathan Ballingrud, Rachel Swirsky, Richard Butner, Sarah Pinsker, and Ted Chiang.

The gift of time and financial support of Beth's Cabin, the CINTAS Foundation, the Clarion Foundation, the Copernicus Society of America, the Elizabeth George Foundation, Hedgebrook, the Millay Colony for the Arts, my Patreon patrons, Playa, the Speculative Literature Foundation, the Spruceton Inn, the Susan C. Petrey Scholarship Fund, the University of Iowa, the Wallace Foundation, the Whiting Foundation, and Yaddo.

Yuka Igarashi, who gets me.

Kent Wolf, who believed in me from the beginning and is a patient and tireless advocate.

The dedication and hard work of Caroline Nitz, Fiona McCrae, Katie Dublinski, Marisa Atkinson, Steve Woodward, Yana Makuwa, Casey O'Neil, Karen Gu, and the entire Graywolf team.

Ethan Nosowsky, whose guidance and trust made this book better than I thought possible.

Every woman artist who has come before me. I am speechless in the face of their courage.

And my wife, Val Howlett, who is my first and best reader and my favorite writer. I wouldn't be able to do any of this without her.